Murder in Postscript

Murder
in
Postscript

MARY WINTERS

BERKLEY PRIME CRIME

NEW YORK

BERKLEY PRIME CRIME
Published by Berkley
An imprint of Penguin Random House LLC
penguinrandomhouse.com

Library of Congress Cataloging-in-Publication Data

Names: Winters, Mary, author.
Title: Murder in postscript / Mary Winters.
Description: First edition. | New York: Berkley Prime Crime, 2023.
Identifiers: LCCN 2022033478 (print) | LCCN 2022033479 (ebook) |
ISBN 9780593548769 (trade paperback) | ISBN 9780593548776 (ebook)
Subjects: LCGFT: Detective and mystery fiction. | Regency fiction.
Classification: LCC PS3601.N5535 M87 2023 (print) | LCC PS3601.N5535 (ebook) |
DDC 813/.6—dc23/eng/20220808
LC record available at https://lccn.loc.gov/2022033478
LC ebook record available at https://lccn.loc.gov/2022033479

First Edition: March 2023

Printed in the United States of America
1st Printing

Book design by George Towne
Interior art: quill © veronchick_84/Shutterstock Images

For my mom, who always gave the best advice

Murder in Postscript

Chapter 1

London, England
1860

Amelia Amesbury hated to admit it, but she was bored. Mind-numbingly bored. She supposed this was what contentment felt like: a beautiful young charge, bless her heart, playing the pianoforte; a governess, prim and proper, turning pages; and three tiers of cakes to choose from in a tastefully papered drawing room. But if she was so content, why was she itching for the afternoon's post?

She glanced at the portrait of her dead husband above the fireplace mantel. She could put the brunt of the blame on him, bless his heart, too. When they met, she had no idea who he was. He presented himself like any young man in Somerset, looking for a room at her family's respected inn, the Feathered Nest. Well, not exactly *any* young man. His manners were a little too refined, as were his features: smooth skin, straight nose, good teeth. When he revealed he was an earl, after she'd accepted his proposal, she was surprised, yes, but assumed that's how it was done. Wealthy aristocrats had to protect themselves and their fortunes. Like Lancelot, Edgar Amesbury had come in disguise, and the subterfuge hadn't bothered her in the least. In fact, it added to the excitement.

Amelia set down her flowered teacup with a plunk, earning her a glance from the governess. Despite her last name, Amelia was no Amesbury. Yet here she was, now the widow of one of the wealthiest families in London, responsible for the upbringing of Edgar's niece, Winifred. She was the reason he'd chosen a wife so quickly—that and his degenerative illness, which took him just two months after their marriage. He had wanted Winifred cared for when he was gone, and Amelia was doing a good job, if she did say so herself. Smart, well behaved, and kind, Winifred was, in every aspect except blood, her daughter. As Winifred tinkled her way through Mozart's Piano Concerto No. 21, Amelia was so proud. And yet, there was the afternoon post at the door!

"I'll get it, Jones," Amelia called to the butler. Winifred paused at the instrument. "Please continue, dear. You're doing wonderfully."

The letters she'd been waiting for all afternoon were here, the letters addressed to Lady Agony, her secret pseudonym and life-giving alter ego. Amelia's black dress rustled noisily as she alighted for the door. She opened it before the deliverer could knock.

"Good afternoon," greeted Amelia. "A lovely day to poke your head out for a breath, isn't it?"

The man blinked. "My lady."

Amelia inhaled the thick London air—and choked. It was no matter to her whether it was smoke filled, smelly, or rank, however. It was the thrum of the city that had enticed her to leave Somerset without protest. Mells, the small village where she grew up, delivered newspapers directly to the Feathered Nest—and into her small hands. She spent many afternoons poring over news from the city, young dreams arising in her heart even then, and when Edgar asked her if she would move to London, she answered with a resounding *yes*. "I'll take that, thank you."

The deliverer bowed wordlessly, and Amelia shut the door, returning to the drawing room as she opened the parcel and thumbed the correspondence: one, two, three letters. They requested advice on love, labor, and life. Well, mostly love, but letters all the same. Correspondents needed help traversing the murky waters of life's greatest unsolved mystery, and who better to guide them than a member of the social elite? Her title was the reason her responses were so popular—that and her honest advice. Times had changed, and readers were desperate to change with them, reaching for the next rung of the social pecking order. Plus, they and the *ton* wanted to know who Lady Agony really was and how she had become involved in writing in the first place.

It was her childhood friend and fellow newspaper fiend, Grady Armstrong, now an editor at one of the most popular penny weeklies in London, who put her in touch with the task. No one but he and Amelia knew the true story. A year ago, his office was flooded with letters addressed to the magazine's agony column, called such because of the angst in the letters. When the writer became discouraged with young people's outrageous behavior and quit, Grady had neither the time nor the talent to respond. That's when he asked Amelia—who needed something to occupy her hours after her husband's death—if she would be interested in the chore. He knew she enjoyed reading and writing. Would she enjoy a secret job at the weekly magazine? *Did the queen enjoy tea?* She agreed in a heartbeat. Now Grady's office was busier than ever before, but in a good way. Her unconventional wisdom and mysterious identity kept readers hooked—and buying more magazines.

"Letters!" exclaimed Winifred, leaving the pianoforte. "Are any for me?"

Amelia slipped them into the crevice of the chair. "I'm afraid not. But your performance was top-notch. I've hardly enjoyed Mozart more."

"Really?" Winifred pushed a fair lock of hair from her face.

"Really." The Amesburys were known for their handsome hair, and Winifred's was no exception. Winifred would grow into a beauty before long, but for now Amelia was enjoying the plumpness of her cheeks, the crookedness of her smile, and her enthusiasm for life. At ten years old, Winifred was at that precious age between child and young woman, and Amelia was going to savor every moment.

Unlike Winifred, Amelia had long auburn locks with honey highlights that hung to her waist when it wasn't swept up, which was only at bedtime. Her hair, streaming behind her as she rode into the inn's stable, was the first thing Edgar had noticed about her. The second was that she wasn't riding sidesaddle.

The governess tsked from the corner. "Lady Winifred, you've not been excused from the pianoforte. The last page went dreadfully fast."

"That's all for now, Miss Walters," said Amelia. "I'd like to have a cup of tea with Winifred before I reply to my correspondence."

Miss Walters bowed deeply, her light brown bun a perfect swirl. "As you wish, Lady Amesbury. Please send her up to the music room when you're finished."

Winifred jumped into the patterned chair next to Amelia, her feet not touching the floor. She reached for a strawberry tart, then drew back her hand, waiting for permission.

When Miss Walters was gone, Amelia turned to Winifred. "Would you like a sweet?"

"Yes, please, and tea also."

Amelia poured out the tea. "Do you like playing the piano-forte?"

"Very much," answered Winifred. "Three sugars, please."

Amelia raised her eyebrows but dropped in the sugars. "I can tell. I can feel it when you play."

"Governess Walters said I played it too fast." Winifred took a bite of the strawberry tart, closing her blue eyes as she savored the sweetness. Only a child could enjoy the full pleasure of tartlets.

"She knows best." Amelia placed the girl's tea next to her. "She's been classically trained." It was one of the reasons Amelia had hired her; also, she was terribly good at French. Winifred had a talent for music, and Amelia wanted to make sure her musical instruction was taken seriously. Much to Amelia's delight, Winifred performed for her every afternoon in the drawing room. Most of the practice went on in the music room, so the performances were a treat. They also helped Amelia keep an eye on her lessons.

"Amelia, may I ask you something?" asked Winifred. When no one was around, she called Amelia by her Christian name.

"Anything, dear." Amelia took a sip of her tea.

Winifred leaned in. "What's *really* in those letters?"

Amelia paused, her cup at her lip. Children were smart, and she and Winifred had spent a lot of time together since Edgar's passing. In some ways, they'd weathered the tragedy together. There was no lying to the girl. First, she would know it, and second, Amelia respected her too much to deceive her. "The most wonderful things. Secret things that I cannot discuss with you today."

"But someday?" Winifred gulped her tea.

"Yes, someday I will tell you. I will *show* you." Amelia set down her empty cup. "For now, it must be enough to know they bring me pleasure, as your pianoforte brings you pleasure. And for that reason alone you must keep quiet. Can I trust you?"

Winifred popped the rest of the tart in her mouth and nodded.

"I know I can," said Amelia. "Now you had better be off to see Miss Walters. She'll be wanting you to rework those last measures."

Winifred gave Amelia an impulsive hug, and Amelia breathed in the beautiful strawberry scent of the child. Edgar hadn't given her love—he wouldn't risk passing on his degenerative condition— but he had given her his dear niece, and for that, Amelia would always be grateful.

When the girl was gone, Amelia took the letters into the library, her favorite room in the house. It was something else Edgar had given her that she'd enjoyed very much—a home with books. While the Feathered Nest had plenty of room for dining and entertaining, it did not afford much room for books, just the special theatricals the family loved and performed. One of her favorite performances was *Romeo and Juliet*, probably because she and Grady were central characters. Most times her eldest sister, Penelope, took the lead roles. Indeed, Penelope was better at memorizing lines, but Amelia was better at improvising.

She stopped and inhaled a breath. The room smelled of cloves and paper and past cigars. Hundreds of leather-bound tomes filled the wooden bookshelves that lined the two-story room. She bypassed the books and made for the large rosewood desk, situated in a bright alcove of windows. It faced a dark green couch, striped chairs, and an ornate oval table. In a nearby corner was a smaller table, with heavy crystal glasses and fine liquor. And on the far wall was a grand stone fireplace, surrounded by two soft damask chairs, comfortable enough for reading and dozing. She'd spent many nights there doing just that.

Slice went the letter opener, revealing the contents for her eyes only. She scanned the penmanship: hurried, sloppy, and slightly smudged from tears. Definitely a relationship problem. Settling into her chair, she began to read the letter.

Dear Lady Agony,

You are a lady of repute. Please tell me what to do. I love the boy next door, but he's unaware of my feelings. I am certain we possess a special bond, for he smiles at me so. But he's going to ask another girl to marry him. He told me his plan on the way to the well. I stumbled away, confused, but how I longed to tell him the truth of my feelings. Am I too late?

Devotedly,
Too Late for Love

Amelia dunked her quill in the ink. This one was easy, a drop in the bucket of love letters. She began her response, which would be printed in the magazine. Readers' letters weren't included, and a good thing, too. Amelia had a feeling many writers would be embarrassed later by the emotion they'd poured into their requests.

Dear Too Late for Love,

It's never too late for love. In fact, I prefer the old, and perhaps wiser, adage, Better Late than Never. In your case, it cannot be truer. You love the boy and are late to admit it. Yes.

However, there is still time. He hasn't asked anyone to marry—yet. Best he knows your true feelings before he proceeds. Even if he does not reciprocate them, you will feel secure in the knowledge that you told him. And that is a feeling you can live with. The other is not.

Yours in Secret,
Lady Agony

The next letter was just as clear-cut. It was from a reader who was jealous of her friend's hair, though she didn't say so outright. The letter accused the friend of spending too much time dressing her long, blonde, thick locks, but it was obvious to Amelia that the letter writer wished for the hair herself.

Another dunk into the inkwell, and Amelia was poised to respond.

Dear Hair, There, and Everywhere,

Some women are born with great hair. Others are born with great wit, vivacity, or kindness. Cultivate one of the latter. Or purchase a wig. The choice is just that simple.

Yours in Secret,
Lady Agony

She waited a moment before opening the last letter, savoring the unknown contents. It would be tomorrow afternoon before she received more letters, the mysteries that made up her day. Because of the popularity of the column, Grady made certain the letters arrived daily so that she wouldn't fall behind.

She turned the envelope over in her hands, positioning it in front of the light. A few drops of spring sunshine shone through the windows, making burgundy flecks on the wall as it bounced off the nearby decanter of brandy. Soon a housemaid would be in to start a fire, to warm the chill brought on by the late afternoon. Then Amelia would enjoy a glass of sherry before dressing for dinner, a complicated affair that she had never quite mastered.

She noted the seal of the envelope had been hastily done. Dashed out at the last minute, perhaps, the letter might contain time-sensitive information. Amelia unfolded the paper. The handwriting, no better than chicken scratch, was hard to decipher. Written at a slant, possibly in this morning's rain burst, it was wrinkled and marked. Yet the writer's desperation was clear from the first sentence. Amelia scanned the letter twice before dropping her quill, splattering ink on the desk. She grabbed her spectacles and read it a third time. Her eyes must be deceiving her. It was indeed dated this morning.

Dear Lady Agony,

You are my last hope, for I have nowhere else to turn. Could you meet me at St. James's Park at nine o'clock this evening? Make sure no one follows you. I believe someone is following me. I'll be at the bench by the pond. You will know me by my red hat. Please make every effort. I've witnessed something dreadful, and I fear the worst.

Devotedly,
Charlotte

Postscript: I think my mistress was murdered.

Chapter 2

Amelia set down the letter. Her eyes had not tricked her. A woman named Charlotte had penned the missive, but why and to what end? Amelia gave advice. She did not solve murders. Not that she couldn't. Working at the Feathered Nest, she'd witnessed her share of sordid scenes. But why had the author turned to her for help? Amelia pushed back her chair.

Two possibilities came to mind. Charlotte had seen something she shouldn't have and was too afraid to report it to Scotland Yard. Or Charlotte was a clever girl who wanted to unmask the identity of Lady Agony. The last theory was cynical but quite possible. In the past six weeks, Amelia had received dozens of letters requesting everything from her marital status to her favorite color. Readers were increasingly interested in knowing who she was and why a Lady with a capital *L* would work for a penny paper.

She poured herself a hefty glass of sherry. Because she was no *Lady*, that's why. At least not in her own mind. Before marrying Edgar Amesbury, she helped manage her family's small but respectable inn. Amelia was used to working, and—contrary to popular belief—dressing for dinner did not constitute work.

She checked her frock in the window's reflection. Layers of black dress over a crinoline, a corset, and stockings stared back at her. Perhaps it was work, but not the kind of work she desired. The letters were exciting, and writing was addictive. It was the one activity she did for herself, not for Winifred or the Amesburys, though she took her duties as head of the household seriously. Edgar counted on her to bring up Winifred, which was why her secret identity had to remain hidden. If anyone found out she was Lady Agony, the gossip would be too much for the family to bear.

But what choice did she have? A woman's life might be in peril. Of course Edgar had wanted her to bring up Winifred properly, but he would never have left a lady in the lurch. He'd plucked her from the countryside because she was honest and forthright. He hid his title because he didn't want his fortune to have influence, and it hadn't. When he told her, she announced her uncle was a baron. She'd hobnobbed with the country gentry, for goodness' sake. He needn't have concealed it from her.

Edgar had laughed at that and said her attitude was *refreshing*. She supposed it was, compared to the mothers of the *ton*, who would stop at nothing to find their daughters good matches. After attending their soirées for two years, Amelia understood his need to branch out to find a suitable mother for his niece. They had their best interests at heart; he had Winifred's.

Amelia set down her cordial. Whatever might come, she would go to St. James's Park that night. It would be dark, and she would have to disguise herself to cloak her identity. If it was a ruse, she would know it and flee. *Flee.* Glancing around at her posh surroundings, she decided a word never sounded so delightful. Indeed, she hadn't felt this much excitement since taking a duke's Thoroughbred for a ride through Somerset before stashing it in the stables of the Feathered Nest for the evening.

Three taps on the floor turned her blood to ice. Her eyes flew to the doorway to find Edgar's aunt, Tabitha, and her jewel-handled walking stick. Neither age nor injury had trimmed her height. Nearly six feet tall, she was shoulders above most ladies, including Amelia.

Amelia shoved the letters in the drawer.

Tabitha pointed her stick at Amelia—or at Amelia's glass, as it were. "Drinking alone is no occupation for a lady."

A smile bubbled to Amelia's lips. "Then join me, Aunt."

A brief nod. "I suppose I must."

"Always one to do your duty." Amelia reached for the sherry.

"None of that sweet stuff," said Tabitha.

Amelia changed direction, grasping the decanter of amber liquid. "How are you feeling this afternoon?"

"Everything hurts." Tabitha situated herself on the green leather sofa.

That certainly covered it. "Are you taking the new tonic—"

"Yes," Tabitha snapped.

Amelia handed her the drink and selected the paisley chair across from her. Nothing helped Tabitha's arthritis more than a strong glass of liquor.

Her clear blue eyes watched Amelia as she took a drink. They were always watching for a mistake, a faux pas, a gaffe. As the eldest Amesbury, Tabitha felt it her duty to ensure Amelia did hers. And Tabitha, a spinster who'd learned from the sidelines, knew every single obligation.

"When I came in, you were up to something," said Tabitha. "What was it?"

The woman could sense fun and quell it with the tap of her stick. "Up to something? I'm not sure what you mean."

"Your face was pink, and it is never pink. What caused it?"

Amelia's skin tone was warm, like her auburn hair, and the opposite of every fair-haired Amesbury she'd ever seen in person or portrait. Tabitha was right. It rarely turned pink. "Maybe the sherry. I drank it rather quickly."

Tabitha took another drink. "Suffice it to say, you're not going to tell me."

"It could be hunger. What's Cook preparing this evening?" The quickest way off any subject was food. Aunt Tabitha relished menu planning and was excellent with details. Amelia enjoyed the best meals in London, thanks to Tabitha and the cook. Her teas, also, were coveted by neighbors, who happened by at the perfect time to enjoy a baked good. Indeed, Tabitha ran the household like a well-oiled carriage.

Tabitha's eyes grew excited as she divulged the menu, a lengthy list of courses. Amelia listened halfheartedly until she heard the words *curried lobster*. She sat up at them and repeated, "Curried lobster? Winifred hates fish. Are we expecting company?"

Tabitha stiffened, the pleasant look leaving her face. "You know we are. I told you last week we would be receiving the Marquis of Bainbridge. He's a special friend of the family."

Amelia internally groaned. How could she forget? Simon Bainbridge had recently returned from his time in America because his sister, Lady Marielle, was coming out this season. He'd been away when Edgar passed. Of course he wanted to pay his respects, but tonight, two years after Edgar's death? Amelia had an appointment at St. James's Park, and not duke nor dandy would stop her from meeting Charlotte.

A determined Aunt Tabitha, however, was another matter. She *was* someone who could put a halt to her plans. Amelia must be careful not to draw suspicion to herself.

"Of course." Amelia recovered smoothly. "Lord Bainbridge. I didn't forget. I've been anticipating his arrival."

"Obviously." Tabitha glanced at her untidy desk. "I can see you've been preparing." Her naturally high cheekbones sharpened. "His father is a duke, mind you. He'll have certain expectations."

Amelia had heard it before. It was Tabitha's way of saying, *Behave. Act like a lady, a countess.* It was a role that didn't always come naturally, but she'd met her fair share of the *ton*. They didn't rattle her as they once had done. "Don't worry, Aunt. I'll be on my very best behavior."

"Which means no untoward banter about child labor." Tabitha set down her empty glass and reached for her walking stick.

Amelia rushed to help her stand. "That was over a year ago, and Lord Grey was absolutely in the wrong. I could never agree with his stance on children working in the coal mines."

"Nor I," said Tabitha, waving away the assistance. "But it's hardly appropriate dinner conversation, especially when it leads to *someone* leaving early."

That someone was Lord Grey when Amelia told him he could ditch his opinions at the doorstep, which was where he immediately went following dinner. Amelia admitted it was awkward, but she stood by her convictions, especially concerning children. Winifred was like her own daughter, and all Amelia had to do was imagine her in the deplorable working conditions at the mines and her blood boiled hot. "I doubt it will come up, Aunt, and if it does, you can rest assured I will give the marquis the quickest reproach before passing the soup."

"Dear God, Amelia," Tabitha warned. "Don't pass the soup. Let the help do it."

Amelia waved away the remark. "You know what I meant."

Shaking her head, Tabitha stumped up the steps, her shoulders bent over the cane.

Amelia watched her from the entryway, making sure she made it up the stairs. Tabitha was like a mountain goat, stubborn, determined, and a bit ornery. Once she disappeared, Amelia noticed a fragrant bouquet of roses on the front table. The display alone should have reminded her company was coming. It was fit for a king, let alone a marquis. But like so many domestic details, she'd missed it. They just weren't her forte.

Dreaming was her forte. She removed a pink rose and inhaled deeply. She loved this time of year, the end of spring and the promise of summer. In Somerset, it was the season that allowed her the most freedom of movement. The weather was good, and the speed of travelers had not yet reached its full flurry. Anticipation hung in the air like heady apple blossoms awaiting fruit. Like a letter writer, awaiting an answer.

She walked to the third floor. A marquis was a marquis, and she would need to put on her finery—and then change out of it before going to St. James's Park. She would also need to talk to Winifred about dinner, curried lobster. Since Simon Bainbridge was a friend of the family, Amelia wanted Winifred to attend, no matter what convention said about children at the dinner table. It was silly, if you asked Amelia, not that anybody did. Winifred was a pleasant young girl, almost eleven, and capable of keeping still. She was a perfect dinner companion.

Amelia knocked on the door. When Winifred answered, Amelia curtsied. "A rose for my rose." She straightened and blinked at Winifred's gown. "You're already dressed."

"Thank you, Amelia." Winifred twirled in a circle, rose in hand. The light yellow chiffon dress was the same color as her hair. "Isn't it beautiful? Lord Bainbridge is coming to dinner, and I'm invited."

"Yes, I know." Amelia sat on the edge of Winifred's bed while Winifred's maid fussed with the ribbon.

"Auntie said you'd forget." She quit sashaying. "Did you?"

"Of course not, I've been—" Seeing the girl's quirked eyebrow, Amelia stopped. "Yes, I did forget, but mum's the word." She lowered her voice. "I wonder if Auntie has a pretty yellow gown for me."

"Your dress is in your room, my lady," answered Winifred's maid, Clara. "It arrived yesterday."

"Lovely," said Amelia. "Thank you." She returned to Winifred. "Did Auntie tell you what Cook is making?"

Winifred stuck out her tongue. "Curried lobster."

"You must make a special effort," Amelia insisted. "Promise me . . . and I will sneak you an extra dessert."

Clara pretended to retie the ribbon, ignoring the conditions of their bargain.

Winifred stuck out her hand. "You have my word."

They shook on it, and Amelia left to see her gown. She hoped the marquis's visit meant a colored frock. Her eyes landed on a dark splotch on the bed. It was an improvement from black, and that was about it. Gray and primly cut, it was suitable for a woman in mourning—deep mourning, no less. But it wasn't suitable for a woman of five and twenty who was still very much in love with life. "Is this mine?" Amelia asked her maid, Lettie.

"It is, my lady." Lettie walked from the oversized wardrobe to the dress. Her almond-shaped eyes landed on the fabric. "I hope you're not disappointed."

It was clear from the wistfulness in Lettie's voice that *she* was disappointed. No need to add to the dismay of the young woman, who was only a few years older than Amelia. Their friendship allowed for silent commiseration. "Not at all. It's very nice . . . cloth," lied Amelia, touching the stiff lace trim. For two years, Amelia's wardrobe had been a menagerie of black and gray. It was tiresome, but what could one do? She wasn't particularly interested in fashion, and if it made Tabitha feel better, who was Amelia to argue? She would rather save her breath for important disputes, like child labor.

"Lord Bainbridge is a special friend of the family, you understand," Lettie explained. "Everything must be done right and proper." She lowered her voice. "Mum said she's dressing you herself."

Amelia laughed. As if she'd go rogue and throw on a red dress . . . although some days she was tempted. Lettie's mother was the respectable Patty Addington, Tabitha's maid, who was fastidious to a fault. Amelia wondered at the change, then left it be. She didn't want Lettie censured, and Tabitha had her reasons. As long as those reasons didn't impact Amelia's meeting tonight at St. James's Park, she didn't care. She picked up the gown and squared her shoulders. There was nothing to be done but don the ugly dress and get on with it.

Chapter 3

Dear Lady Agony,

What do you make of corsets? My friend says they are God's gift to women. I say they are Satan's spawn. What do you say?

Devotedly,
Too Tight for My Taste

. . . .

Dear Too Tight for My Taste,

I say you are right. There's nothing natural about a thirteen-inch waist, except on a young child. Indigestion, headache, fainting—these are a few of the problems women suffer from corsets. Are they encouraged by the devil himself? I think you know what This Author believes.

Yours in Secret,
Lady Agony

Two hours and many hairpins later, Amelia cared very much about the change in dressing maids. She could barely breathe, her corset was so tight. Mrs. Addington was a stickler for details, painful details. Amelia would be glad when the marquis left and she could get out of the drab gown. It was too tight, too prim, too much of everything.

Stiffly, she walked down one flight of stairs to the drawing room, where the Marquis of Bainbridge was waiting to receive her. She hoped his visit was worth the effort, though she doubted it would be. He probably wanted to recite what a good friend he'd been to Edgar. *Rubbish, to be sure.* She'd heard it all before, and all with the same distaste in her mouth. Edgar had understood his friendships were false, which is why he'd come looking for her. He needed someone he could trust with Winifred, not just his inheritance.

Simon Bainbridge was eyeing the sheet music on the pianoforte when she entered. Tall, straight shoulders, good clothes. Confirmed. He looked like most of the nobles she'd met in London. Then he faced her, and she tweaked her assessment. Besides all those things, he had a clever smile and dangerous green eyes. She'd have to watch out for this one.

"Lady Amesbury, it's nice to finally meet you." He took her hand and kissed it, his lips lingering a moment longer than necessary. "My condolences on your gown."

"Thank you, Lord Bainbridge," said Amelia. *"Excuse me?"* She jerked back her hand. Had she heard right? "What did you just say?"

Simon cleared his throat. "I was sorry to hear of Edgar's passing. You have my deepest sympathy."

Amelia was pretty sure she'd heard something else. She perched on a chair by the fireplace, barely able to sit down.

Blasted Patty Addington! She invited Simon to join her. "I understand you were friends with my late husband."

"Very good friends when we were young." Simon smiled, perhaps recalling a private memory. "Then later we were business partners of sorts."

Amelia frowned. Edgar wasn't in business.

"The business of keeping people alive in Her Majesty's Royal Navy."

Ah. Edgar had been in the navy. Simon Bainbridge had been, too. According to Aunt Tabitha, the family's naval lineage went back five generations. "Thank you for your service to the Crown, my lord."

Simon's black eyebrows lifted, giving him a crafty look. "Certainly. It came with an unlimited supply of rum."

Amelia smiled despite herself. She liked his easy manners and sense of humor. They were uncommon among the aristocracy and inevitably came from his time in the navy, serving with a diverse group of men. It made sense that Edgar was in the navy: he was a younger son. But Simon was the only son of a duke. The family must have been committed indeed. "Aunt Tabitha tells me you have been to America. What was it like?"

"Interesting, although I was sorry to miss Edgar's funeral." Simon laced his fingers. "I mean that sincerely. I knew he was ill, but I didn't realize how ill until his passing."

Amelia was surprised he had known about Edgar's condition. Few people had, for Edgar kept its severity a secret, even from her at first. But soon there was no hiding it. After they were married, he started bumping into things, then tripping, and before he passed he couldn't walk at all. Nobody but those in the household understood how he'd suffered.

"He had his first symptoms in the navy," explained Simon.

"He started forgetting things. After his family died at sea, it became worse. Entire days were lost. He wouldn't hear of leaving, stubborn man that he was. Until Winifred came to live with him. Then he knew he had to retire. But at least he listened to me about one thing."

"What was that?"

"*You*," said Simon.

Aunt Tabitha entered the room just in time to see Amelia's stupefied stare. "Lord Bainbridge, I hope this evening finds you well and in favor of child labor laws," quipped Tabitha.

"Absolutely in favor." He grasped her hands in a kind embrace. "Good evening, Lady Tabitha. It's so good to see you again. I've missed you."

"If you must stare, Amelia, do us all a favor and pair it with a smile, won't you?" Tabitha turned her attention to Simon. "It's good to see you as well."

Amelia shook off her befuddlement at Simon's statement. She would ask him what it meant later, when Tabitha wasn't in the room. "Aunt Tabitha," she gritted through a tight-lipped smile. "Your dress is lovely."

Tabitha wore a gray gown with a high neck that made her seem even taller, if that was possible. The cobalt lace collar framed her face like a flower petal, her eyes crystal blue. She scanned Amelia's dress for fit. Satisfied, she continued. "We're so pleased you could come. It's been a long time, and Edgar always spoke so highly of you."

Amelia had never heard Edgar mention Simon's name, but that didn't mean they weren't friends. Edgar thought to distance her from as much angst as possible, including personal conversations, when his condition quickly worsened. He knew he didn't have much time. Growing closer would make his death only harder on her. But it was a lonely way to live, and she missed the life they might have had, the life she *thought* they would have when she married him.

When they first met, he was so kind and generous. He complimented the inn as if it were the finest establishment in all of England and even sang a duet with her sister. His voice had a beautiful tenor, and the way he spoke of his niece, Winifred, turned her heart to butter. He loved her so. And his laugh! When Amelia said something he thought was funny, which was always, he would let out a laugh that belied his impeccable manners and expensive wardrobe. It was a laugh, she imagined, he indulged on the deck of a ship. In the drawing rooms of London, it would have been out of place. How she cherished that laughter now. Whenever she felt lonely, she only had to imagine it, and the memory would bring a smile to her face.

Simon squeezed Tabitha's hand. The kind gesture didn't escape Amelia's observation. "The family has been through a lot. I just wish I'd been able to pay my respects sooner."

"You're here now," said Tabitha. "That's what matters." The butler called them for dinner, and Tabitha motioned toward the door. "Shall we?"

Amelia eagerly agreed. It was seven o'clock, and every second counted. As it were, she'd have to rush through dinner and claim a headache just to get to St. James's on time.

Winifred met them at the bottom of the stairs in her yellow dress. *At least one of us is wearing a pretty gown.* She gave Winifred a hug.

Winifred drew back. "Careful for my curls! You'll flatten them."

Simon chuckled and stuck out his hand. "You must be Lady Winifred. I'm Simon."

"Oh, I know who you are, my lord." Winifred took his hand briefly. "You're a marquis, and that means I'm allowed to wear a new dress." She twirled herself around, her petticoat showing.

"Winifred!" exclaimed Tabitha.

"Glad to be of service." Simon bowed, hiding a smile.

Amelia and Winifred walked hand in hand into the dining room. Amelia paused to admire the wainscoting and warm tapestries before taking her chair. Although the long mahogany table was gleaming with expensive crystal and china, the room was inviting. Most nights, she enjoyed delicious, languid dinners and long conversations here. Aunt Tabitha was surprisingly bookish and well-informed on several subjects.

Tonight, however, was not most nights.

Amelia scooted into her chair, waiting impatiently for the first course. She would have been happy to retrieve her own soup, especially with the minutes ticking away. But Edgar would disapprove—as would Aunt Tabitha. While he appreciated her fresh perspective, he wanted Winifred to be a lady in every way. So Amelia waited for her cream of asparagus, tapping her toe beneath the table.

For the most part, Tabitha and Simon's conversation monopolized the dinner hour with talk of holidays and house parties from days long past. Amelia nodded politely, enjoying the history she hadn't been privy to until now. It warmed her heart to hear about Edgar's childhood in Cornwall, which had been pleasant, with no signs of the suffering that would take hold of him later. He had been a strong man and an admired leader in the Royal Navy. It was obvious Simon Bainbridge revered him a good deal.

By the time the curried lobster was served, Amelia decided the marquis wasn't as bad as his polished boots had led her to believe. He was different from the nobility she'd met, more re-laxed, with a sense of adventure. Maybe it was his travels to India that turned her head with talk of adventure. They certainly sounded interesting—and dangerous. She had no difficulty imagining him in a seafaring hat, sipping a pillaged bottle of rum. And just like that, he'd gone from navy captain to pirate and she from countess to sailor.

She returned to her plate, stopping her imagination from running amuck, and slyly handed a pastry to Winifred, who gave her an appreciative grin. Amelia winked, and Tabitha cleared her throat. *Drat.* Amelia had been caught. She hadn't been so sly after all.

"The child must learn to eat the food we eat," Tabitha in-structed. "No exceptions."

"Which is why she's dining with us this evening," said Amelia.

Simon changed the subject. "What I enjoyed at her age was a heaping dish of plum pudding. Nothing better."

Just then, a footman entered with dessert. "Perfect timing, my lord. Here comes the blancmange!" exclaimed Winifred.

Amelia had no time—or room—for a round of sweets. She was bulging out of her dress from the previous courses, which were not meant to be eaten in a tight corset. However, she wasn't going to neglect the need of a decent dinner for tonight's business. But now she must make her exit. "I apologize, but I seem to have acquired a sudden headache. The heat, perhaps . . ." She looked out the window. It was not hot. It was early June. She cleared her throat and continued. "I think I need to rest for a spell. It was good to meet you, Lord Bainbridge. Thank you for coming."

Simon stood. "May I assist you? A glass of wine, perhaps, or another pastry?"

She waved away the concern. "Not at all. I'm fine, really. Enjoy the rest of your meal." She touched Winifred's soft blonde hair. "You especially."

Tabitha bid her good evening, but her face was pinched with disappointment. Tabitha could be angry; Amelia had done her duty. Now Charlotte needed assistance, and she was going to get it. Lady Agony wasn't going to desert a woman in need, especially when it meant a cloaked walk through the London fog. Life allowed her little real excitement or danger these days. She couldn't even race her bay horse Marmalade down a hill. A walk in the dark, in disguise, was perhaps the next best thing.

Amelia took the stairs two at a time, then remembered she was supposed to have a headache. She checked her pace until she reached her bedroom on the third floor. There she dismissed Lettie so that she wouldn't be privy to her next steps. *No sense getting her involved if something goes amiss.*

Amelia wriggled out of the tight corset and into a shirt and riding breeches, taking a breath of relief before tying her hair into a knot. Her long auburn locks would be a dead giveaway if someone was looking to unmask her identity, so they were the first thing to go.

After donning a low hat and tweed jacket, she poked her head out of her room, her trusty parasol traded for a plain umbrella. The tinkling of dishes, conversation, and the occasional burst of laughter from Winifred. It sounded as if they were enjoying dessert immensely. *Perfect.* Their preoccupation gave her the opportunity to leave via the servants' staircase. Tiptoeing down the hallway and around the corner, she made quick work of the steep stairs at the rear of the house, not nearly as beautiful as the grand staircase at the main entrance.

She contemplated calling her coachman for about two seconds and then decided her plain attire would get her nowhere if she rode up in a carriage with the Amesbury crest. She would walk the mile to St. James's Park. It wasn't that she didn't trust her servants. They were discreet and knew how to keep a secret. Whom she didn't trust was the letter writer herself—*or himself*, she added as she stepped into the dank spring air. For all she knew it was a man. Grady had plenty of complaints from men who were put off by her independent and sometimes cheeky advice. They preferred advice to come directly from themselves. No surprise there.

The fog was thick, making it hard to determine if it was the fog or the mist giving Amelia a chill. She quickened her pace, warming her blood and leaving her home in Mayfair behind. Not taking a carriage or cab meant she could cut across the area quickly, turning at Berkeley Square toward Piccadilly. With her umbrella shielding her face and her androgynous attire cloaking her curves, she might have been a man leaving the office, a boy on his way home, or a seamstress leaving her shop. No one would guess it was Amelia Amesbury, a countess and successor of the Amesbury fortune—and a jolly good agony answerer, if she did say so herself.

St. James's Park was one of her favorite places in all of London. Although she'd fled rural England, green open spaces still tugged at her heart (as long as they were surrounded by busy thoroughfares). Shaped like a kite, the park had beautiful trees, a glossy lake, and plenty of flower beds. She enjoyed spending afternoons reading on a bench, letting the moments slip past, until Winifred called out for Amelia to join her in a boat race or some other game. Then time would go by even more quickly, until they'd walked so far that Amelia would insist on stopping for an ice or snack. Winifred never minded. Winifred's governess, however, was another matter.

The grass was soft and wet, making no sound as Amelia scanned the area for a woman with a red hat. The park was large, around ninety acres, and Amelia wished Charlotte had been more specific. A bench by the pond could mean anywhere.

Amelia surveyed the tranquil evening, the flutter of pelican feathers still fresh on the water. It was hard to imagine a desperate woman lingered at the edge of such a place, seeking help. And she was desperate. The smeared ink of the letter testified to her distress. A thought came to Amelia. She wondered if the smudge read *bridge*, not *bench*.

That would make more sense and narrow down the location. Amelia changed direction, heading toward the popular footbridge. Even from a distance, however, she could see no one on it. As the moon broke free from a cloud, the white light shining like a lamp on a watercolor, she had a clear glimpse. Plodding forward, she checked random trees and shrubs for red hats. Nothing. Had she been sent on a wild-goose chase?

A twig snapped, and she froze in place. Slowly she turned, checking the silvery tree behind her. "Hello? Is anybody there?" When she didn't receive a response, she kept walking toward the bridge. She'd come this far. She might as well go all the way.

As she drew near the body of water, she saw something floating on the surface. Worry pierced her heart, and she rushed toward the bridge. *It's nothing. It's a plaything or a newspaper, thoughtlessly discarded. Vagrants are always leaving trash behind.*

She stopped at the water's edge. It was neither of those things. It was a large red hat. Amelia's stomach sank with the knowledge. She spun around. Where was the girl?

There, in the tall ornamental grass, was a crumpled black frock, and Amelia knew at once it was Charlotte. Her hands flew to her mouth, covering her gasp. Her hands were shaking. Amelia willed herself to move, but her feet wouldn't follow her command. For a long moment, she was paralyzed, questions flooding her brain. What had happened? Why wasn't Charlotte moving? Was she dead? Did someone kill her? Moments earlier, Amelia had heard a twig snap. Was that someone still here?

It was the last question that propelled her on. In her letter, Charlotte mentioned someone following her. Was that someone now following Amelia? Cautiously, she inched toward the shoreline, her spine prickling with fear. Before she reached it, she understood Charlotte was gone. Amelia was familiar with death. She'd held Edgar's hand as he passed. But this wasn't the same. Charlotte had not died peacefully.

Her stomach lurched at the knowledge. The hurried handwriting, the smudged ink, the postscript of the letter. The person who had written those words was gone, her life taken, and Amelia felt the closeness of their connection. The letters to Lady Agony were always intimate, personal. It was the nature of the business. But never had she felt a deeper link between herself and a reader. Her heart hurt with the discovery.

She brushed the hair from Charlotte's face and revealed a gash over one eye. It was just as she had thought. Her death was not natural. She turned her ear toward Charlotte's mouth. No breath passed her lips. Her skin was notably cool as Amelia held her wrist, feeling for a pulse. Nothing. Amelia leaned back on her haunches, scanning the surrounding area. The person who had done this could still be out there. She could be next. Fear and guilt washed over her in alternating waves.

She felt the dread of the situation at her core. Charlotte had thought her mistress had been murdered, perhaps even witnessed it, and now she was dead, too. She had come to Amelia for help, and Amelia had failed her. She should have left the dinner sooner. She should have walked faster. She should have—what did it matter now? A moan escaped her throat. It was too late for Charlotte, but it wasn't too late to catch the criminal and bring him to justice.

Tamping down her own fear, she sat up straighter. Yes, that's what she would do. She would catch the cold-blooded killer who was responsible for both murders, for Charlotte's murderer must be the same as her mistress's. But how to do this without revealing her own identity . . . ? Nobody even knew she was here.

At least that's what she thought until she heard a deep voice behind her. "Good evening, Lady Amesbury. I see your headache's cleared, but another problem has befallen you."

Amelia spun around and let out a startled squeak. Beneath her, her foot slipped, and she landed on her rump. "Lord Bainbridge! What are you doing here?"

"I could ask the same of you." His dark eyebrows were a shade thicker than most, like his hair, and along with the moonlight concealed the brightness of his eyes. They lent him an air of wickedness, and for a moment, she considered his arrival at the park. Was it possible *he* had done this to Charlotte? Could he be the person who had been following her?

Impossible. Fear was clouding her thinking. He'd been dining with her all evening. His whereabouts were indisputable. She swallowed hard. "This woman is not breathing."

Simon stepped forward, bending close enough for Amelia to see the start of whiskers beginning at his jawline. His eyes no longer looked wicked but concerned. "This woman is dead."

He held out his hands, and Amelia welcomed the assistance.

A tremble had settled in her bones, from the shock or the cold or the guilt of not getting to the girl soon enough. His limbs were warm, like life itself. After being in the company of death, she appreciated the small comfort.

"How do you know her?" he asked.

The answer came instantly. "I do not."

"So you weren't meeting her." He still held her hands.

Amelia shook her head.

"And you weren't looking for her on the bridge."

Another shake.

His eyes roved over her, stopping on her breeches. "And you're not in disguise."

Amelia cleared her throat. "I thought it would be more comfortable walking in trousers than the beast of a dress I had on earlier, if that's what you mean."

He let go of her hands. "Then I must call the constable at once. A woman is dead, and you will give your testimony."

"No!" she gasped. "You cannot."

His head tilted in mock surprise. "And why is that?"

She looked at the dead woman, then back at him. This was no time for selfishness. She'd been brought up to put others first. Charlotte had come to her for help, and instead of assistance she had received a death blow. Charlotte deserved justice, as did her mistress, and Amelia wasn't going to allow her own problems to prevent that. She would find a way around her secret identity. The women's deaths wouldn't be in vain. "They cannot find out who I am."

Simon's brow wrinkled in consternation. Now the shadow on his face was from real confusion. "Because you are the Countess of Amesbury?"

"No, because I'm Lady Agony."

Chapter 4

Dear Lady Agony,

I understand I'm not supposed to ask, but does anyone know your real identity? My friends and I have taken up the question, and we have decided only your cat knows the answer, for all spinsters own cats. It's an unrefuted truth.

Devotedly,
No Name, No Place

. . . .

Dear No Name, No Place,

I'm happy to inform you that you are wrong, about me and the cat. I do not own a cat, but I like cats. They are smart, independent, and do not lick your face. I cannot think of a better companion.

Yours in Secret,
Lady Agony

"*The* Lady Agony? From the magazine?" Simon's voice was laced with shock.

"Shh." Amelia gave him a nudge with her umbrella. "Not so loud." Secretly, she was impressed he knew the name. She hadn't been sure if a man like Simon Bainbridge read popular magazines or would recognize her pseudonym.

"Careful with that thing," warned Simon. "Someone might be tempted to classify it as a weapon, and one woman is dead already."

"This is not the time for jokes." Amelia glanced at Charlotte, and a fresh bolt of sickness coursed through her veins. She refocused on Simon to steady her stomach. "What are we going to do?"

Simon slid his hands in his coat pockets, thinking. Amelia assumed he was forming a plan, and she was looking forward to hearing it when a smile broke out on his face. Considering the situation, she was aghast.

"I must admit I agree with most of the advice, except your opinions on relationships." His smile widened. "What you don't know about love might surprise you."

Amelia gripped her umbrella tighter, willing herself not to use it. "Don't tell *me* what I do and do not know about love. First of all, you just met me. Second, I have been engaged, married, and widowed—accounts you couldn't possibly speak to. I took care of a very sick man and watched him die in my arms and with it my dreams for a normal life. So do not talk down to me or *enlighten* me about love. Help me with this woman—now."

"My sincerest apologies. I didn't mean to impugn your sensibilities." Simon bowed, donning the look of a marquis like a cape.

No doubt it's an article he easily takes off and on. She scanned the park, vacant and murky. He'd been right about one thing: she would need to fetch a constable. But where? One was never around when you needed help. Furthermore, what would the constable say when he discovered that she was Lady Agony? Amelia would have to explain the letter, the reason for meeting Charlotte in the park. She shook her head. The revelation was unfathomable.

"I need to know details if I am to help," Simon prodded. The humor was gone from his voice now, and his eyes implored her to trust him. "Explain how you came to know the recently deceased."

Amelia weighed her options. If she told Simon, he would no doubt help her. What kind of help that entailed, she could not say. If she didn't tell him, she would be forced to report Charlotte's death herself and reveal her identity. Even if she stopped writing—never!—word would still get around about her alter ego, which might lead to repercussions for Winifred. The *ton* were notoriously judgmental. They might ostracize Winifred for Amelia's actions. And while Amelia didn't care in the least, Winifred might care a good deal. Plus, she'd made a promise to Edgar. If he trusted Simon, maybe Amelia should, too . . .

As if reading her mind, Simon added, "I won't divulge the information to anyone. You have my word."

In that moment, she believed him as a child believes a teacher. It was an instinctual feeling. She took a breath and recounted the letter. "So you see," she finished, "I must find out who did this to Charlotte. She came to me, and I let her down. I won't rest until her killer is caught."

The statement seemed to baffle him. It was as if he couldn't reconcile the person and the words. "How do you propose to do that?"

Amelia frowned. "It isn't as if we're empty-handed. We have her body, after all. It will reveal some clue to her identity and perhaps the person who was following her."

"Of course, a *clue*." Now he guessed at her train of thought. "Why didn't I think of that? Oh, I know. I put away my sensation novels years ago."

She fisted her hands on her hips. "Do you have a better idea, my lord?"

"In fact, I do. We let the dead body alone, you scamper back to Mayfair, I call the constable, and we pretend this conversation never happened."

Amelia could feel the blood travel to her face. Her skin flashed hot. Maybe he *was* a pirate, a very bad pirate. "I do not scamper anywhere. If you feel the need to scamper, by all means, go. Scamper. I'm perfectly capable of taking care of this on my own."

"What about Winifred?" asked Simon. "What will happen to her reputation if word gets out about your identity?"

Amelia dug her umbrella into the ground. "I'm not going anywhere."

"Then we find ourselves at an impasse, because neither am I."

The moon broke free from a cloud overhead, revealing the imposing size of said impasse. And the handsomeness. She swallowed. "Fine."

"Fine." His green eyes narrowed, testing her.

Fed up with the banter, she shook off the challenge. It was time to act. Determined not to waste one more second, she knelt near Charlotte. Unfortunately, determination wasn't enough to overcome her emotions. She fought back tremors as she bent closer to the body.

Simon must have sensed her reluctance and joined her. His

closeness steadied her, or perhaps forced her to steady herself. She wasn't going to look the weak woman in front of him.

She noted the sizable gash near Charlotte's hairline, but what weapon had made the mark? "It looks as if she was hit with some object." Amelia scanned the area for a weapon but found nothing. "The villain must have taken it with him."

Simon turned over Charlotte's white, swollen hand. Amelia had to force herself not to look away. "Not necessarily," he said. "From all appearances, she drowned to death. I've witnessed this many times before, at sea. Pale, wrinkled hands. I assume her feet look the same."

"The water's not deep enough here to drown."

"It doesn't have to be." Simon ticked off the bridge, water, and shoreline with his eyes. "If she hit her head on a rock, she would be unable to swim or stand. She would drown within minutes in the shallowest water."

Amelia focused on the footbridge. "Her killer could have pushed her from behind, making it appear as if she drowned. It would explain why there's no weapon."

"If she was murdered."

"Which she was." Amelia surveyed Charlotte's dress, recognizing the black garb she herself had worn for two years. If Amelia had to guess, Charlotte was a lady's maid, in mourning for the recent death of her mistress. But who was her mistress? That's what Amelia needed to find out, and the only way to do that was to search her pockets.

Her hand quivered above the body. She wasn't a skittish woman. Mells hadn't sheltered her from rural life or death. Was she going to let fear deter her from finding justice for her reader? *Never.* Taking a breath, she reached into Charlotte's pocket.

"What are you doing?" asked Simon.

"I need to know who she is, where she came from." Amelia pulled out a hankie, a ribbon, and a calling card. She studied the square of ivory paper. In a swirl of feathers she read the name Flora Edwards. A colorful hummingbird perched on the *s*. Amelia said the name out loud. It sounded familiar, but she couldn't place it.

"Edwards? Let me see that." Simon studied the card.

An owl hooted in the distance, signaling the lateness of the hour. The night was growing darker and the water murkier. Amelia wished the constable were there and the business were over. But she knew it would be a long time before justice was found. The secrets surrounding Charlotte's death assured it.

"Flora Edwards passed away recently." Seeing Amelia's perplexed look, Simon continued. "I know the family and planned to pay them a call tomorrow. Flora was Admiral James Edwards's daughter. She was betrothed to Henry Cosgrove."

That's where she'd seen the name, in the engagement announcements. Henry was a duke, and his title made him popular at parties.

"According to my staff, it was a tragic accident," said Simon. "Flora was a sleepwalker. The admiral once told me they would find her asleep in all sorts of places. When she was a child, they insisted a maid sleep with her. The night of her death, Flora sleepwalked to the balcony and fell off."

Amelia stood and dusted off her breeches. She couldn't bear being so close to death any longer. "*Fell* off? I think not. Unfortunately, only Charlotte saw what truly happened to her mistress that night, and now she cannot tell me." She paused, silently apologizing to Charlotte. "It's reasonable to assume the person who killed Flora also killed Charlotte. The murderer pushed them both to their deaths. Same modus operandi. Same despicable coward."

Simon lifted his eyes from the body. His thick, dark lashes concealed his thoughts, and she speculated on his retort. "I would agree with your supposition, my lady, except for one thing."

"What is that?"

"There are no signs of a struggle. No scratches, bruises, or rips in her dress."

"What of it?" Amelia questioned.

"She was waiting for you," said Simon. "Waiting and watching. She wouldn't have been caught unaware by an attacker. She wouldn't have gone down without a fight."

"I should hope not," Amelia agreed. "I'd think she would have fought to the bitter end."

His eyes returned to the body. "Yet I find no evidence to support that theory."

"Just the gash on her head," argued Amelia.

"From a rock."

"And her letter," Amelia pressed. "To me."

"Certainly."

A moment passed, a silent struggle of wills. Amelia swore that if Simon didn't report the crime, which *was* indeed a crime, she would. Identity be hanged. "Are you going to call the constable, or shall I?"

"I will call, if you promise to go home." He shook his head. "You should not be here. You *cannot* be here."

She wanted his help. She *needed* his help. But she wanted justice for Charlotte more. He had to understand that. "I'll go home, but on one condition: you must promise to help me investigate," Amelia bargained. "You know the family. You said so yourself. It will be easier to determine the circumstances with your connection."

He stood. She'd momentarily forgotten how tall he was—and how imposing. His face didn't give an inch. "Lady Amesbury, you test my patience."

The scent of sandalwood wafted from him, musky and dark like the night. Amelia held her breath. A woman had died. Her reader. That should be her focus, not the marquis or his cologne. But being this close to a man her age, matched in wit and spirit, was exciting. There was no denying the pulse of her heart. She tried anyway, holding out her hand. "Do we have an agreement?"

He grasped it. "I won't let you forget it."

Chapter 5

Dear Lady Agony,

My mother and I disagree about exercise. She says swimming will turn my cheeks ruddy. A lady should be wan and pale, but I like to swim. Must I stop if I am to avoid becoming a homely old maid?

Devotedly,
A Fish Out of Water

. . . .

Dear A Fish Out of Water,

When I spot a wan, pale-faced woman, I assume she is miserable, for misery brings that look upon a lady. Conversely, when I see a rosy-cheeked girl, I know she is healthy and happy. So get back into that water, dear fish, and keep swimming. Your mind—and cheeks—will thank you.

Yours in Secret,
Lady Agony

The next morning, Amelia was downstairs early despite her late night. She always took a brisk walk before breakfast. In her opinion, it was the best time to enjoy London. The drizzle, the burst of sunshine afterward, the streets coming to life with people. It was her time to think, and this morning she had a lot to consider.

In case the drizzle turned to rain, she fetched her parasol. Charlotte was dead, and she and Simon needed to find her killer. And her mistress's killer, too. Perhaps the constable found something valuable last night, maybe even a witness. The thought was encouraging, and Amelia picked up her pace. Her sensible congress boots clicked along to the sounds of the streets—and the story forming in her head.

Charlotte had jotted off what she thought was a secret letter but was found out, presumably, by her follower. She might have worried about this very thing, which was why she mentioned the person in the note. The easiest explanation came from Charlotte's house itself, the Edwardses' residence. Times devoted to correspondence were generally known among staff and family. She might have been easily observed. Still, she would have been extra cautious, so perhaps she was seen delivering the missive. Maybe her suspicious behavior gave her away. She was desperate, and in Amelia's experience desperation was often as noticeable as a blanket covering a babe.

A horse trotted closely past, jolting Amelia into the present, and she started back for Mayfair. The sooner she talked to Simon, the better. Would he pay her a call today? She winced at her dark gray walking dress, the hem dampened by a faint line of dew. She hadn't asked him before leaving the park, but fashion dictated that he wouldn't call until later. She doubted Simon was the kind of man who followed protocol, however. She had a feeling he did whatever he wanted, etiquette be hanged.

Ascending the steps of her large brick home, a warm contrast to the gray sky, she decided it didn't matter when he called, as long as he did. Paying him a visit would be awkward, not to mention inappropriate. Although she was a widow and mother, paying a personal call on a gentleman was not done in London. She didn't rule out the possibility, however, as she returned her parasol to the hall tree. He was a friend of the family, a good friend. It wasn't justification but an excuse all the same. She would use it to her advantage if it came to that.

Famished from her exercise, Amelia welcomed the sight of ham, eggs, porridge, fruit, kippers, and fresh bread on the sideboard in the breakfast room. She loaded her plate, poured her coffee, and took a seat at the oversized table. She inhaled deeply. Nothing was as good as the smell of hot coffee on a cool spring morning.

The peaceful moment disappeared with a commotion at the door. Panic hit her heart, and Amelia touched her hair. She felt a sparkle of perspiration on her forehead and dabbed it with her napkin. She was in no shape to receive callers.

"It's only me. No need to make a fuss."

The panic subsided. It was her good friend Kitty Hamsted admonishing Butler Jones. Amelia would recognize the sound of her voice anywhere. It was the voice that first welcomed her to Mayfair. Living two mere streets away, Kitty was the daughter-in-law of Viscountess Hamsted, a *ton* favorite. The viscountess's eldest son was the scholarly Oliver Hamsted, Kitty's husband. When she first met them, Amelia was struck by their differences: Kitty all flounces, and Oliver all books. But the old maxim "Opposites attract" held true. They went together as perfectly as scones and jam.

"Mrs. Hamsted," Jones announced as Kitty joined her in the breakfast room.

"Thank you, Jones." Amelia stood to give her friend's hand a squeeze. Turned out in an exquisite pink morning dress, Kitty was the most smartly dressed woman in London, and that was saying something. Her blush hat, dotted with silk flowers, sat just so on her head, tilted perfectly above one eyebrow. She had a *je ne sais quoi* that couldn't be replicated, no matter how hard other ladies tried. Indeed, if Amelia wore such a contraption on her head, she was certain it would look as if she'd robbed a bride's bouquet. But on Kitty, it looked pretty. With her blonde curls, button nose, and blue eyes, it was hard for her to look anything but exquisite.

Kitty walked to the sideboard. "If you don't mind, I'll help myself."

"Please do." Amelia returned to her chair. "I have an interesting letter to tell you about."

"Not a word about your letters until we talk about my costume ball." With a freshly baked pastry and fruit, Kitty joined her at the table. "Promise."

Amelia took a breath. There was no putting it off. Kitty loved her parties, and she was hosting one in less than a week. Not even murder could deter her from the subject. "Fine."

Kitty poked a fork in her direction. "First things first. You are not wearing *that*. You'll be dismissed by every eligible gentleman in the room."

"Of course I'm not wearing this," said Amelia. "It's hardly ball gown material." It was a jest. Amelia knew what Kitty meant. Kitty didn't want her wearing mourning garb to her party.

"Never fear. I will be in costume, like everyone else. I promise to figure something out."

"I mean that color—gray." Kitty leaned in closer. "I loathe it."

"You should be me," whispered Amelia. "But what's one to do? I don't want to offend Aunt Tabitha. It's not worth the argument."

Kitty glanced over her shoulder before continuing. "How long does she expect you to wear gray? Until your hair matches your dress? If you ask me, it's ridiculous. It's been two years since Edgar passed."

Amelia smiled. "Two years last week. However, let's move on. What remains undone?" It was best to let Kitty get to the details so that Amelia could return to the more immediate problem: Charlotte's murder.

Kitty swallowed a bite of her pastry before answering. "The flowers. I'm not happy with the limited selection. Oliver says I'm being finicky." She shook her head, and her yellow ringlets bounced about her face. "Pink roses for a spring gala? That's not finicky."

Amelia agreed with Oliver. Kitty could be fussy to a fault. But in this case, Amelia sided with Kitty. Pink roses in June were not out of line. "Aunt Tabitha knows a seller," Amelia suggested. "She procured the most beautiful arrangements for Winifred's recital. Should I give her your name?"

Kitty clasped her hands together. "Would you, Amelia?"

"Of course I will. Consider it done." Amelia was happy to help her best friend. She wasn't much into parties herself, so this was one small way to contribute to the event. And Amelia knew how much Kitty loved entertaining. She enjoyed it just as much as Amelia did her letters. Like writing, parties were outlets for her creativity.

"You're the best." Kitty dabbed her face with a napkin. "Go ahead, now. Get on with it."

Amelia tried for nonchalance. "What?"

"The letter," prodded Kitty. "What did it say?"

Amelia pushed away her plate. Kitty was the only person, besides Grady and now Simon, who knew her secret identity. In fact, she'd joined her on several escapades. From spying on workhouses to eavesdropping at dress shops, they'd gone on many adventures for the sake of a letter. But even Kitty, her collaborator in crime, wouldn't believe what had happened last night. Amelia was considering where to begin when the bell rang again. A deep voice echoed in the foyer, and in an instant, she knew it was Simon.

"Who on earth?" started Kitty.

Jones rushed into the breakfast room, out of breath. He took a moment to smooth back a piece of wispy brown hair over his balding scalp. "Lord Bainbridge is here. He requests—"

Simon appeared at his elbow. "Good morning, Lady Amesbury. Forgive the intrusion. I saw you walking this morning and knew you were available to take a call."

For a moment, Amelia was speechless. She quickly recovered her faculties. "Of course. Please join us. This is Mrs. Hamsted. Mrs. Hamsted, this is Lord Bainbridge. He's a good friend of the Amesburys."

"A pleasure," greeted Simon. He poured a cup of coffee at the sideboard as he continued. "I know your husband, Oliver, from Eton. A very good man and a notable scholar. I just finished his book on seventeenth-century naval history. It's quite fascinating."

"Thank you." Kitty beamed with pride. "There isn't a subject in history he's not acquainted with. If he's not reading a book, he's writing one."

"I hope you don't mind the intrusion." Simon settled in with his coffee at the table. "I know this house like the hull of a boat. I didn't mean to barge in."

"I'm glad you're here. Are you sure you won't have breakfast?"

"No, thank you," said Simon. "I've already eaten. I'm an early riser myself. Never could break the routine."

"I was worried I would have to call upon you if you didn't come," Amelia continued. "We have much to discuss."

Kitty glanced between them. "If this is a private conversation—"

"On the contrary," Amelia interjected. "I want you to hear this, too. It has to do with the letter." Briefly, she relayed yesterday's events. She made quick work of the story because she didn't want Tabitha or Winifred to drop in unannounced.

"So *murder* was mentioned in the letter?" asked Kitty.

"In the postscript." Amelia turned to Simon. "When I left, you were going to find the constable. What news do you have from him? Did he have any idea who might have done this?"

"He believed it to be an accident for the same reasons I mentioned last night. He could find no signs of a struggle."

"Dash it all!" Amelia clapped the table. "It was not an accident. No one reveals a murder, schedules a meeting, and then falls into the pond."

"Remember, the constable had only one of those three facts." Simon took a sip of his coffee. "It might have been a slip of the foot. The night was foggy, as you recall. Or she might have intentionally taken her life."

"I agree with Lady Amesbury," said Kitty. "Someone killed the woman, and the sooner you find him, the better."

"Thank you." *Good old Kitty!* Amelia felt closer to her best friend than ever before. She saw the truth of the situation in a heartbeat. If only she were the constable.

Simon set down his coffee cup. "As important as it is to weigh all considerations, I agree with you. Despite the lack of physical evidence of an altercation, I believe your reader was murdered. It's the only explanation that makes sense."

Amelia breathed a sigh of relief. No more time need be wasted on convincing him. "As long as we agree on that, we can start investigating."

"'We'?" repeated Kitty.

"When Lady Amesbury recalled the story, she forgot to tell you one small detail of our accord last night." Simon inclined his head toward Amelia. "Before your good friend would leave the scene of the crime, she made me promise we would investigate the misdeed—together."

Kitty held her napkin to her lips to hide a smile. "That sounds like her. I think it's a grand idea. She has more experience than you might expect."

"And our first stop should be the Edwardses' house," said Amelia. "We could go this afternoon."

"Why not now?" asked Simon.

Amelia checked Kitty's empty plate. "I see no reason. It's best to call while the event is fresh in our memories."

"You cannot do that!" Kitty exclaimed. "It's not even noon."

Simon dismissed the concern. "The admiral's an early riser. He won't mind, and he's expecting my call."

Kitty leaned closer to Amelia. "Your dress," she whispered.

Amelia glanced at the ugly drab gown, wet at the hem. Then she remembered her hair. She touched her head and realized several auburn tendrils had come loose from their hasty coiffure.

She must look quite different from the put-together marquis, who was dressed in a fashionable black jacket, a smart waistcoat, and neat trousers.

Since Edgar's death, her looks were the least of her concern. She'd been in mourning so long that she put clothes out of her mind altogether. But she couldn't pay a call on an admiral looking like this. She shouldn't have received a marquis, either, but he'd given her no choice. "Mrs. Hamsted is right," Amelia admitted. "I need to freshen up. Come back this afternoon. I'll be more . . . presentable."

Simon stood to leave. "As you wish. I'll see you this afternoon." He gave a slight bow, a black curl landing on his forehead. "Mrs. Hamsted."

Amelia watched him walk out of the room. If only all her wishes were granted so easily.

Chapter 6

Dear Lady Agony,

Musical performances are all the rage, but after listening to three this season already, I believe they should be limited by time and talent. Yesterday, a family trio went on for two hours, and not one of the daughters had an ounce of musical aptitude. I left with my ears ringing—only to be invited back next week! Must I go?

Devotedly,
Not Music to My Ears

. . . .

Dear Not Music to My Ears,

Indeed, family concerts are all the rage and perhaps for good reason. Nothing gives a mother more pleasure than watching her daughter pound away at the keys of the pianoforte or put a *bow to some strings. I've endured my fair share of concerts for the sake of the smile on a mother's face. If you focus on that, and not the music itself, I'm certain you can tolerate one more concert. Cotton in the ears might improve your chances.*

Yours in Secret,
Lady Agony

That afternoon, Amelia listened to the last measures of Mozart's Piano Concerto No. 21 with new unease. She feared Winifred was rushing the last page, as her governess had warned. The recital was next week, and Amelia wondered if Winifred was nervous. It was her first formal concert at the house, and although Amelia had done everything she could to ensure a relaxed atmosphere, she knew Winifred must be anxious, despite her denials. Governess Walters addressed the problem by repeating the measures, thinking the problem lay in the music itself. Although Amelia wasn't her natural mother, she had three sisters. She recognized a trepid child when she saw one. It wasn't the notes themselves that had the girl worried. It was something else.

"It's still dreadfully fast," said Miss Walters. "You must continue to count, until the very last measure."

"I *am* counting," insisted Winifred.

"You're counting too fast, then." Miss Walters pointed to the sheet music. "Again, please."

Amelia intervened. "You're right, Miss Walters. The ending feels a bit rushed. But I need to talk to Winifred for a moment, and I'm paying a call later in the hour. Have a cup of tea while you wait. We won't be long."

"Of course." Miss Walters ducked out of the room.

When she was gone, Amelia patted the chair next to her. "Come and sit, Winifred."

Winifred slouched toward the chair, fussing with the blue bow on her dress. "It was dreadful, wasn't it? It's getting worse."

"Not at all," said Amelia. "If I could play half as well as you, I would demand an audience with the queen."

Winifred gave her a small smile. The dimple above her apple-shaped cheeks showed.

"I mean it," continued Amelia. "Listening to you brings me such joy, and I know your guests will feel the same." She touched Winifred's dress. "But that doesn't mean you're not nervous. It's understandable and even normal."

Winifred looked into her lap. "It's not nerves, Amelia. It's my parents."

If Winifred said she wasn't nervous, Amelia believed it. "Do you want to talk about it?"

"No, but I suppose I must."

Amelia didn't insist. She waited patiently to see if the girl would continue.

After a few moments, Winifred met her eyes. "My mum loved hearing me play. But when a song was over, she would quickly leave to attend to her other duties. I always thought if I rushed, I would catch her before she left. We would have more time together." A tear fell, turning a spot on her blue frock navy. "It's silly, but I can't get it out of my mind. And once it enters, it will not leave."

"I understand," Amelia sympathized. Poor Winifred. She'd lost her grandparents, parents, and uncle. Of course they were on her mind when she played. The entire family had been musical. Amelia wished she could do something to help. What that would be, she couldn't say. But she knew what loss felt like, the emptiness that, no matter how hard one tried, was never completely filled. It became a part of one's skin, like a scar. Amelia couldn't change it. She couldn't make it disappear, and she wasn't sure she should. It was a strong memory. To ask Winifred to put it out of her head seemed wrong.

Amelia sat for a moment, thinking. "Your mother was a special woman. I bet there were other times you enjoyed each other's company, just the two of you." A thought came to her. "You mentioned reading once."

"Mum loved reading aloud. She put me to sleep every night." The dimple appeared again in Winifred's cheek. "*Gulliver's Travels* was never my favorite, but it was hers. I never told her."

Amelia tapped her chin. "I wonder. Maybe next time you play, you could imagine your mother reading. The slowness of the pace, the drone of the pages. I don't want to put you to sleep, mind you, but maybe it will slow you down."

Winifred shrugged. "It is worth a try."

Amelia stood, and they hugged. She inhaled the soft scent of strawberries that followed the girl everywhere. Although it must have been soap, it reminded Amelia of the quintessential scent of youth and promise. She gave her an extra squeeze before releasing her. "I wish I could take away the pain, Win. To make it disappear with the snap of my fingers."

"I know," said Winifred. "You feel the same about Uncle Edgar."

Amelia nodded, still holding Winifred's hands. They understood each other's past and didn't try to hide or change it. It was the best thing about their relationship.

Jones entered the room. "Lord Bainbridge is here, my lady."

"Thank you," said Amelia.

"*The marquis?*" whispered Winifred. "Where are you going?"

Amelia checked over her shoulder. "You promise not to tell?"

Winifred crossed her heart.

"We are conducting a . . . what shall I call it?" Amelia raised her brow suggestively. "An *inquiry*. Something has happened, and we must figure out why."

"Like an adventure?"

"Yes, like an adventure. But with a purpose."

Winifred smiled. "Oh, I do hope you have fun. You don't have much fun because of . . . well . . . me and Aunt Tabitha."

Amelia tweaked her chin. "Ha! That's how much you know. Being your guardian is the most fun of all. I get to see you grow and mature into a young lady. I feel very lucky."

"But still," added Winifred, "Simon Bainbridge is very handsome."

"Yes, he is," Amelia agreed. "Maybe a little too handsome for me."

"Nonsense!" exclaimed Winifred. "You're just as good-looking as he—or almost."

Amelia laughed and gave her a nudge toward the pianoforte. "Back to your practice, you rascal. I want to hear the piece again when I return. Slower this time."

As the first notes of Piano Concerto No. 21 began to tinkle from the instrument, Amelia left the drawing room. Simon stood near the window in the morning room, his broad shoulders a dark square in the bright window. It'd been a long time since she noticed a gentleman: his shape, his scent, his smile. Other good-looking men had crossed her path since Edgar's death, hadn't they? It couldn't be that. Maybe it was pure vitality, plain and simple. He emanated energy, excitement, and vigor. It made her feel alive being near him.

"Lord Bainbridge," greeted Amelia. "Thank you for coming back."

Simon turned from the window. "Good afternoon, Lady Amesbury." His eyes landed on her gown. "You're still wearing gray."

"I'm still in mourning," Amelia explained.

Simon lifted his brow. "It's been two years."

"I'm well aware of the passage of time," said Amelia. "Aunt Tabitha thinks three years is an appropriate period, and I would be remiss to disappoint her."

"Three years? That seems excessive." He adjusted the sleeve under his coat. "May I ask how long you were married?"

"Two months."

He forgot about the sleeve and, for a moment, seemed genuinely shocked and saddened by the information. Then he inhaled a breath and his face returned to its usual handsomeness. "Tabitha is waiting for you to take the initiative. Trust me."

Amelia blinked. "Are you sure we're speaking about the same person?"

"Tabitha likes nothing better than a good challenge," said Simon.

"Then *you* take up the task." She motioned to the foyer, where he helped her into a jacket. "I'm content to live in black the rest of my days if it means fewer reproaches."

"Indeed?" Simon handed her her parasol. "I didn't figure you as one for compromises."

"We've only just met." Amelia nodded a goodbye to Jones as they passed. "There's quite a lot you don't know about me."

Waving away his footman, Simon helped her into his carriage. "I have a feeling I'll enjoy finding out."

Admiral James Edwards lived in a fashionable townhome, a stately white walk-up with arched windows and navy blue shutters. If a house could look like a boat, it did, and the staff added to the idea. The butler, a man called Tibens, looked unlike any butler she'd ever met. The first thing one noticed about him was his sharp weathered face; it was all angles. The second was his tight-fitting jacket. He was not only younger than most butlers but more muscular, almost obtrusively so. He certainly didn't disappear into the background as most butlers did.

He was showing them to the drawing room when Admiral Edwards joined them in the entryway. "Bainbridge, I thought that was you!" A rotund man with white hair and a commanding voice, Admiral Edwards filled the small area. "I was expecting your call."

Simon clapped him on the back as they shook hands, greeting each other warmly.

"It's a surprise to see you with my own eyes." The admiral took in Simon's appearance. Despite heavily creased skin, his blue eyes were full of energy. "How are you?"

"Very good, sir, but I was sorry to hear of your loss. I wish I could've attended the ceremony."

"Thank you, Bainbridge. I know you would have." The admiral dipped his whiskered chin. "Flora admired your skills with a boat, and my girl knew her way around a ship. You know she did."

Simon gave a brief smile. "She was an excellent seawoman."

"And a dear daughter. But where are my manners." Admiral Edwards turned to Amelia. "Who'd you bring with you?"

"This is Lady Amesbury." Simon introduced her. "Edgar's widow."

"Of course," said the admiral. "Please excuse me, Countess. I haven't received a lady caller in a very long time. I leave that to my daughters."

"Not at all." Amelia took his outstretched hand. "I'm also sorry for your loss."

"Thank you." Admiral Edwards motioned up the stairs. "Cook has laid out some things for tea. Shall we?"

The drawing room was nicely papered and decorated with naval memorabilia. A large anchor was encased in a box on the wall, and Amelia guessed the admiral ruled his house as he did his ship. Simon had told her that the admiral's wife passed many years ago, and a woman's touch was absent. But the room was not without its comforts: soft chairs, bright lamps, books, and maps—lots of maps.

Amelia took a chair near the table. The "things" the admiral had described were cakes and sandwiches laid out on an ancient silver tray. Everything had an old-world feeling, and Amelia admired the sentiment. The admiral's travels had taken him to every corner of the world, and the nooks and crannies reflected that. She wished *she* could travel to every corner of the world. London had given her a thirst for adventure, a thirst that might be quenched only with more travel.

After tea was poured, they exchanged a few pleasantries before breaking into real conversation. It naturally gravitated to Flora, and that's when Simon mentioned Charlotte's death, describing it as a chance happening in the park. "I was the one to call the constable, as it were. I thought I recognized her from your house."

"Charlotte Woods's death came as a surprise. I heard of the business early this morning." He took another piece of cake. "As Flora's maid, Charlotte felt responsible for the accident, and I can't say as I blame her. She should've been watching my daughter that night. She promised me she would."

Amelia heard the edge in his voice. Could he have exacted revenge on Charlotte? Amelia brought the tea to her lips, inhaling the warm scent of bergamot. If he thought Charlotte was responsible for his daughter's death, it was possible. She wouldn't put vigilante justice past the old admiral. She could tell how much he loved his daughter. "What happened the night of the accident? May I ask?"

The admiral reached for his tea. "It was Flora's engagement, and I threw a party in honor of her and Cosgrove. He was her fiancé, a good man all around." He sipped. "Poor chap. The situation has wrecked him." After a moment, he shook off the idea and continued. "It was a perfect night with dancing and champagne, all of it, you understand. But Flora didn't feel well after dinner, said she felt dizzy from the champagne, and went to lie down upstairs. Charlotte followed her, knowing Flora's penchant for sleepwalking, and her state of mind."

The admiral leaned back in his chair, not talking for a few seconds. "I awoke many hours later to the sound of a scream. Charlotte rushed to see why, but she was too late. When we found Flora, she was in the courtyard. She'd fallen off the balcony."

Amelia folded her hands. It was a terrible tragedy to hear retold, especially from the lips of a grieving father. Her heart went out to him.

"And her maid Charlotte blamed herself?" asked Simon.

"Correct," he affirmed. "She'd fallen asleep. Everyone in the house knew of her dereliction, which is why I suspect she took her own life last evening." He lowered his voice. "The staff said she'd been acting strange. Fearful." He emphasized the last word.

Fearful for a good reason. Amelia set down her tea. "Is it possible one of the staff sought revenge for her failure to protect Flora? That they did something to her on purpose?"

The admiral opened his mouth in surprise. "I'm a lenient employer, Lady Amesbury, but that's taking it a wee bit far. My staff would never do such a thing. You're talking about murder now."

"Of course, but you wouldn't mind if we talk to them?" asked Simon. "It would comfort Lady Amesbury a great deal."

"Not at all." The admiral turned to Amelia with a sympathetic look. "But why, may I ask? Who was Miss Woods to you?"

Amelia came up with the most honest answer she could. The admiral was the kind of man to see right through a lie. "She was an . . . acquaintance of mine. We corresponded."

The admiral puffed out his chest, looking a bit like a stuffed parrot. He reached over and patted her hand. "Why didn't you say so in the first place, dear? Take all the time you need. Unfortunately, I cannot stay. I'm needed at the docks, and it wouldn't do to keep the men waiting."

Simon agreed. "You go ahead. I would like to pay my regards to your daughters as well. Are they in?"

The admiral stood. "Hyacinth is, and she'd like that very much. I'll send her down." He nodded to Amelia. "Lady Amesbury."

"Thank you, Admiral. Take care."

After he left, Amelia turned to Simon. "I knew she was murdered."

"Who?" Simon crossed a leg over his knee. "Flora or Charlotte?"

Amelia stood and inspected the anchor. She'd never been on a real ship. The admiral had been all over the world. Lucky him. "Both, but I was talking about Flora."

"Pray tell, how do you *know*?"

She heard the smile in his voice and glanced over her shoulder. "Have you been to many places?"

He *was* smiling. "Yes, several."

"I haven't been outside of England." Shaking off the dismal thought, she returned to the subject at hand. "Didn't you hear what the admiral said?"

"About Flora?" he asked.

"About her fall," Amelia clarified. "He said he woke up to Flora screaming."

"I'm not sure what you're getting at."

Amelia returned to the seating area. "Don't you see? If Flora were sleepwalking, she would not have screamed."

Simon's smile faded as he followed her train of thought. "She would have walked silently off the balcony."

"And *that's* how we know she was murdered."

Chapter 7

Dear Lady Agony,

Is there anything worse than black crepe? My mother says I must wear it a full six months for my grandmother's passing, but I hardly knew her. She lived many miles away. Shouldn't I be allowed an exception, especially since I'm young and the man next door is quite handsome? I will heed your advice. I read your responses and know you are fair and just.

Devotedly,
Black Is Not My Color

. . . .

Dear Black Is Not My Color,

There are far worse things than black crepe, trust me. Six months may seem like a long time, but it's a drop in the bucket of life. If the gentleman next door is worthy of your time, he will

understand your costume, for a foundation of love is not built on
the color of a dress but something much more indelible.

Yours in Secret,
Lady Agony

Hyacinth was a young woman with a petite figure disguised by her voluminous mourning dress. Though Amelia had worn her share of mourning garb, she'd never seen anything quite like it. The black crepe was trimmed in gold at the sleeves, neck, and waist, and the shawl she wore at her shoulders was accented with fringe. If Amelia cared more for fashion, she would have asked after the dressmaker. As it was, however, she thought the dress a tad ostentatious. Of course a girl of Hyacinth's tender age needed to feel pretty, so the choice was understandable. It was a need Amelia no longer worried about. She was a widow, a mother, and a writer. Fortunately, none of those roles required fashionable clothes.

Hyacinth sat primly on the edge of a chair. Her stiffness was out of place in the relaxed atmosphere. "You'll have to excuse my father's eccentricities, Lady Amesbury. Father adores his naval memorabilia. He misses his time on a ship."

"Not at all," dismissed Amelia, noting the girl's discomfort. "I like the room." She motioned to the maps. "He's a man of the world. I admire that."

The comment put Hyacinth at ease. "He certainly is. He was gone more often than not when we were children."

"That had to be difficult," said Simon. "I know your mother passed early, as did mine."

Amelia recognized the unrequited sadness in his voice. It

was the sadness shared by all people who suffered a great loss. Her heart went out to him.

"I was quite young, so I don't remember her." Hyacinth smoothed the ruffles of her dress. "Flora said I resemble her, though. Flora was like a mother to me—to all of us."

"I'm sorry for your loss." Simon reached out his hand to comfort her. "Flora's death must be difficult for everyone."

"Thank you," murmured Hyacinth, clasping his hand momentarily. "It is." She tilted her head, and the black feathers on her hat shook. "I still can't believe she's gone. Flora was so happy. How could something like that happen on such a joyful occasion?"

"I'm so sorry, too." Amelia couldn't imagine the pain of losing a sister; she and her own sisters were very close. "Your father said she wasn't feeling well."

"It was an upset stomach," Hyacinth explained. "Probably nerves or the champagne. Her maid was supposed to be watching her, in case she became worse. Can you believe she fell asleep? Lazy creature. I could kill that woman." Her tiny hands turned to fists, the youth shining through in her voice.

Amelia and Simon shared a look.

"Excuse my saying so, but really, she's slothful." Her eyes darted around the room. "I haven't seen her all day."

Simon laced his hands together over his knees. "I hate to be the bearer of bad news, but Charlotte Woods was found dead last night at St. James's Park. Drowned in the pond. I thought your father told you."

Hyacinth sat on the chair, blinking. Amelia wondered if they should fetch her some smelling salts. She'd heard women were prone to fainting, but it was not something she'd witnessed herself in Somerset. Women there were too busy for fainting.

"May I find you a glass of water?" asked Simon.

"No, I'm fine." An awkward bubble of laughter escaped her lips. "Actually, I'm better than fine. I'm glad she's dead."

"You blamed her for your sister's death," said Amelia. It wasn't a question. It was affirmation of what she already knew.

"Of course I did," Hyacinth confirmed.

Amelia noted a twitch in her left eye. The involuntary movement was brought on by the laugh. She was obviously prone to nerves.

"Everyone did, even herself," continued Hyacinth. "Why else would she drown herself in the park?"

It was interesting that suicide was the first place her mind went. Numerous explanations might have explained her death, yet Hyacinth jumped there.

"She shouldn't have fallen asleep on the job." Simon tapped his chin. "But is it possible, just possible, that someone . . . encouraged the idea?"

Hyacinth's nose wrinkled at the idea. "What do you mean? Someone told her to do it?"

"Someone pushed her into the water." Amelia didn't mince words. Hyacinth was happy about Charlotte's death; the time for smelling salts had passed.

Simon gave Amelia a sideways glance.

Hyacinth considered the idea. "I suppose it's possible. After Flora's death, the staff didn't trust Charlotte. Actually, they hadn't trusted her for some time. There was a to-do about a diary or list." She twisted her ear bobble, which had become entangled with a hair. "I can't say for certain. My father doesn't care for gossip. He protects me from most of it. He worries about my being frivolous. He's such a serious person, you understand."

"I understand," said Simon.

"Flora was *not* frivolous," continued Hyacinth, smiling. "She was like Father, a very studious person. The duke said he admired her intelligence." She tilted her head, a brown lock of hair coming loose from her earring. Her eyes held a faraway look. "But he admired my dresses. I know he did."

"I'm certain he did," agreed Amelia. "How could he not?" She shouldn't encourage Hyacinth's conceit, but the girl was young and perhaps a tad self-conscious. It might have been the reason she wore spectacular clothes in the first place. Growing up with an older, smarter sister was hard. Amelia knew because she had older sisters of her own, each one beautiful and talented.

When Edgar had asked for her hand, they weren't envious. They were delighted. The declaration was confirmation that good things happen, as their parents taught them, if only you believe in them. The day she left in the Amesbury carriage, their tears were of sadness but also joy. They were happy that, after inquiring about London to guests and tradesmen and anyone who would listen, she was finally going herself. And with a terrific husband besides. Amelia could still picture them waving, following the carriage all the way down the drive, her sister Sarah's satin slipper sailing through the window, after an exuberant throw, for good luck.

"The duke blamed himself for not being here." Hyacinth interrupted her reverie. "But what could he have done? Even if he'd spent the night with the rest of the guests, he couldn't have prevented the fall." Her eyes narrowed. "Only Charlotte could've prevented it, and she didn't." She cleared her throat. "More tea?"

"No, thank you." Simon stood. "We've taken up enough of your time. It's always good to talk to you. It's been an age since we've spoken."

Hyacinth stood also. "And you as well. Thank you for stopping by."

Amelia walked behind them while they chatted about a mutual acquaintance. As a seaman, Simon had a comfortable relationship with the maritime family. Hyacinth was more relaxed with Simon one-on-one. Amelia supposed the girl felt as if she had to act a certain way in the company of a countess. Nothing could have been further from the truth, especially in her case. But it explained some of Hyacinth's nervousness.

After Tibens retrieved her coat, Amelia scooted past Simon and Hyacinth, giving them a private moment. A footman was on the steps, talking to Simon's coachman. Amelia thought she heard Charlotte's name and hurried to join them.

"I wouldn't put anything past Lena. She has a memory like an elephant and is as ornery as one, too."

"Lena, did you say?" Amelia repeated. "Who's Lena?"

"So sorry, my lady." The footman rushed to open the carriage door. "I didn't see you come down."

"No need to apologize." Amelia waved away the comment. "Tell me about Lena. Does she have something to do with Charlotte? Miss Woods was an acquaintance of mine, and I'm trying to comprehend her death."

The footman tipped his chin, looking distinguished in his blue-and-white livery. "Charlotte was a good maid, honest and kind. I'm sorry about her passing."

Amelia nodded. "Does Lena work for the Edwards family?"

"She did. She was Miss Hyacinth's maid, but not anymore." The footman took a step closer. "Now she's a scullery maid for the Van Ackers."

Though Amelia was new to social hierarchy, she wasn't so new that she didn't understand what that meant. A scullery maid was not a sought-after position. It was the lowest work with the lowest pay. Lena had been demoted. But why? She took a guess. "Miss Hyacinth mentioned something about a diary."

"A list," the footman corrected. He waited for a carriage to pass before he spoke again. "A black list of the house. Lena Crane put to paper every untoward rumor she'd heard about the Edwards family. When Charlotte found it, she turned it over to the admiral immediately, and Lena was dismissed. He was much obliged, but he forgot the kindness after Flora's death, and I can't say as I blame him. Flora was his everything."

Simon was bidding Hyacinth good day, and Amelia rushed back to the statement she'd overheard when she first came down the steps. "Do you think Lena took revenge on Charlotte? For telling the admiral about the list?"

He lowered his voice. "I don't care for natter, but yesterday I saw Charlotte clutching a missive. When I asked her about it, she hid it, saying it was from a friend. But I wondered if Lena was threatening her. Charlotte was acting very suspiciously."

Amelia guessed it wasn't a letter from Lena but the letter to Lady Agony. Much as Charlotte had revealed the black list, she was about to reveal the murderer's identity in St. James's Park. Even though it would have been to her own peril, she had tried to do what was right.

Amelia felt a new appreciation for Charlotte swell in her chest. She was not only honest but courageous. Amelia must do everything she could to bring her murderer to justice.

Chapter 8

Dear Lady Agony,

My mum says conversations in carriages are to be avoided. I say carriages are optimum vessels for a private moment with a suitor. What do you say?

Devotedly,
A Carriage Conversationalist

. . . .

Dear A Carriage Conversationalist,

Your mum has a point. One wrong turn, and you and your suitor may have a scandal on your hands. That being said, carriages can make the perfect vetting places—just don't tell your mum I said that.

Yours in Secret,
Lady Agony

On the way back to Mayfair, Amelia told Simon about her conversation with the footman. He agreed it was a good idea to follow up on Lena Crane at the Van Ackers' house. Although he didn't know the family personally, he was confident Amelia could come up with a reason for visiting.

"You're a creative person." Simon smiled at a child who skipped past the carriage window. "I trust you'll think of something."

The carriage jolted forward, and the horses' hooves clicked a steady pace.

"That must have been quite a difference between you and Edgar," he continued. "He was a more logical person, not creative at all. He followed my advice about marriage to the letter."

Amelia crossed her arms, leaning into the velvet cushion of the carriage. The comment bothered her, and she wished to put some distance between her and Simon. "That's not the first time I've heard you say that. Explain what you mean."

Simon noted her action and leaned closer. "After his family died, Edgar was a very wealthy man, but a sick man. The *ton* only knew the wealthy part, so mamas pushed their daughters at him in droves." He paused, perhaps recalling a specific incident. "I couldn't let him put his life in their hands, and especially not Winifred's." His eyes took on a faraway look. "He deserved better."

"And what of me?" she asked. "What did I deserve?"

The question surprised him. Obviously, he hadn't thought through what the advice would mean for Edgar's bride. "Not two years of mourning garb, to be sure."

"This is not a joke, my lord."

"I'm not laughing."

But Amelia could see the twinkle in his eyes, and her ire got the best of her. "I was young. I deserved to know what I was getting into."

"Would it have changed anything?"

Amelia didn't answer right away.

"I didn't think so. Admit it: you fell in love with the adventure, not the man."

Amelia had had enough of his nonsense. Who was he to say such things to her? They'd met only two days ago. "You don't know me. How could you possibly say that?"

"I know you well enough." He reached over and touched her hand. "London was your adventure. It still is."

She jerked back her hand. *The nerve of this man*. He thought he possessed all the answers. Of course she loved London. She was moved by its movement. The bustle. After living in the quiet countryside for twenty-three years, the busy city streets were a welcome change. But it wasn't the reason she'd married Edgar. She'd cared for him very much.

"Don't feel bad," continued Simon. "I, too, love the city. I would have left years ago if I loved it any less. In fact I did leave—and came back."

"I feel nothing of the sort," declared Amelia. "Perhaps it's *you* who feels bad for duping me."

His cheekbones sharpened. "*I* did not dupe you."

"Edgar did," said Amelia.

Simon glanced out the window. Raindrops started to fall, a quiet pitter-patter as he formulated his response. "Any dissemblance belongs to me. I told Edgar to find a country girl, one who did not recognize his name or title, and make her his wife. Only then could he trust her with his niece and his fortune."

"And how can I trust a man who tells others to lie?" asked Amelia.

Simon didn't wait to answer this time. "Because I have been lied to."

She shook her head. "That does not suffice."

"What would?" His green eyes turned emerald in the cloud-covered carriage.

That's the question, thought Amelia, but remained silent.

Rain pummeled the roof like nails, and the driver called out to the horses to quiet their resistance. They did not care for the afternoon rainstorm any better than shoppers, who were scurrying for cover. But their hesitation continued, and when the carriage wheel hit a rut in the road, Amelia came off her seat just as Simon slid forward. The result was an awkward half embrace.

She froze, paralyzed by their nearness. They were so close, she could feel his breath, warm like his laugh, on her cheek. Her heart raced, and she hoped he couldn't detect it as she had his breath.

He reached for her hat, which had gone askew, and briefly his fingers brushed her neck.

Though she'd been Edgar's wife for two months, never had a touch felt so electric. And dangerous. She'd had no idea what she was missing—until now.

The thrill was like riding a horse or switching a drunk man's gin for water. Only better. If a touch could do this, imagine what his hands could do and where.

The carriage stopped in front of her house, and he plunked her back on the seat across from him, leaving her to wonder what had just happened. Her waist still burned where his hands had been. She blinked off the memory, but it was no use. His touch had scorched like a fireplace in January.

"Excuse me." His voice was husky. "It seems we encountered a bump in the road."

That wasn't exactly how she would describe it, but she nodded, unsure how to respond.

The carriage door opened, and Amelia took the footman's hand. She welcomed the cool, refreshing air. It helped lift the fog from her head. For a moment, she'd forgotten why she and Simon were together in the first place: to solve Charlotte's murder. She took a deep breath. A close encounter wasn't going to ruffle her petticoat or deter her from finding justice for her reader. Clearing her throat, she opened her parasol. "Shall we commence where we left off tomorrow?"

"I would like that," he said.

The look in his eyes told her he wasn't just talking about Charlotte. She swallowed and tried again. "Lena Crane works as a scullery maid for the Van Ackers. We could pay them a call."

"And what reason will we give?"

Amelia chewed her lip, thinking out loud. "You're a marquis. Everyone is thrilled by a visit from a marquis."

He crossed his arms, the black fabric revealing the large muscle beneath it. It was clear his work in the navy had been physical. "The same could be said of you. You're a countess. Or have you forgotten?"

Truth be told, she did forget, and quite often. She still thought of herself as Miss Amelia from Somerset. But now that he had reminded her, she realized she didn't need him to open doors. She could do it herself. An invitation to Kitty's ball should do the trick.

Kitty was incredibly popular, especially with the younger set. Everyone sought an invitation to the young couple's home. "Do the Van Ackers have daughters?" Simon should know. His family had resided in London for generations.

"One, and not popular. Why?"

"Perfect. I can extend an invitation to Kitty's costume ball." She smiled. "Mrs. Van Acker will thank me. Everyone who's anyone will be there. Her daughter's popularity will grow two-fold in one night."

Simon frowned. "I don't believe I've heard of it . . ."

The invitation was probably lying in a bin somewhere, properly ignored, or maybe not at all. He hadn't been in town long, and from what Amelia surmised, his return was unexpected, prompted by his sister's debut. Kitty would love to have him attend. She prided herself on her parties, and her guest lists. A marquis at a party was always a good thing. "Consider yourself informed—and invited."

"Thank you," said Simon. "I appreciate the invitation. But are you sure your friend will agree?"

"You must be jesting." The rain was coming down harder now, and Amelia took a step toward her front door. "As I said, everyone loves a marquis."

Simon ducked under the parasol. It immediately felt two sizes smaller. "Are you always this outspoken, Lady Amesbury?"

Amelia thought about it for a moment. She didn't consider herself outspoken; she considered herself honest. London's upper crust, however, didn't see conversation that way. They had a way of speaking without really talking. "Yes, I suppose I am."

He gave her a look of appreciation before bobbing out from underneath the parasol. "How absolutely refreshing. Good day."

"Good day." Amelia watched him leave before slipping inside the house, where she shrugged off her drab paletot and returned her parasol to the hall tree. Despite a chill, she wore a smile on her face. The day had taken several positive turns, the bumpy carriage ride not the least of them. A chuckle escaped her lips before she could snap them shut.

Aunt Tabitha was watching her from the bottom of the stairs, her pointed chin tilted upward. *That's it!* It was her chin that made her neck seem so long. Amelia finally figured out the root of her constant look of censure. "Good afternoon, Aunt. What a storm!"

Tabitha glanced out the window without moving her head. "Hardly. A small cloudburst, very typical for June."

"Regardless, I find it refreshing. A nice rain like that does wonders for the soul." Amelia started for the library. "Join me for a sherry before dinner?"

"Women like us should not drink alone." Despite her protest, Aunt Tabitha was following right behind her.

"Women like who?"

"Spinsters. Widows," answered Tabitha.

Amelia laughed, liking the sound of her own happiness. Inside the library, a roaring fire waited, taking the snap out of the cold afternoon. She had the best staff in the world. Her cordial glasses were polished and her decanter filled. If she wished for a glass of sherry before dinner, they would make certain it happened, regardless of Tabitha's protests. "Some might say the opposite, Aunt. They might say it's just these types of women who deserve a drink at the end of the day."

"No one says that. No one."

Amelia handed her a glass of sherry. "Well, they should."

Tabitha took her drink to one of the paisley chairs. Amelia took hers to the other.

"I saw you arrive with Simon Bainbridge," said Tabitha. "Where were you?"

Amelia sipped without responding. She had sensed this coming, but couldn't it come after they had enjoyed their drink?

She set her cordial on the table. By the look on Tabitha's face, it could not. "We paid a call on the Edwards family. Do you know them?"

"Admiral Edwards?" Tabitha was surprised by the information. "Of course I know the family. The admiral worked beside our dear late Edgar. A fine man, but followed by tragedy all his life. His wife died young, leaving him with three dim-witted daughters. Two now, I suppose, after the last one fell off the balcony." Tabitha took a drink.

"Aunt!" Amelia exclaimed. "How can you say that?"

"Because it's true." Tabitha stretched out her legs, warming her feet by the fireplace. "First her mother, then herself? Something is at work besides gravity."

Amelia shook her head. "I think you misunderstand. Flora Edwards was engaged to the Duke of Cosgrove. They were having a party."

"I misunderstand nothing. I know my history."

"Flora was a sleepwalker," explained Amelia. "That's why a maid slept in her room, even the night she died."

Tabitha's sparse eyebrows lifted. "I've lived here half a century. I came to live with my brother before Flora was even born. I have seen families move, babies grow, and people die. Mark my words. The Edwards family is cursed."

The word hung in the air like smoke from a gun. Amelia sipped her sherry. The mother, the daughter, and now the maid? Maybe Aunt Tabitha was right. Maybe the family had terrible luck.

Chapter 9

Dear Lady Agony,

My mother says I must not take soup twice. But I like soup. Why should I not eat what I like?

Devotedly,
Hungry for Soup

. . . .

Dear Hungry for Soup,

Your mother is right. It's vulgar to make guests at a dinner party wait for your second bowl of soup. When you are in the privacy of your own home, fine. Eat soup. Until then, dear soup sipper, move on to the next course. Your company will thank you.

Yours in Secret,
Lady Agony

Later that evening, Amelia went to Kitty's house for dinner. Kitty wanted to talk about the flower arrangements—Tabitha's contact had been in touch—as well as other preparations for her upcoming costume ball. Although Amelia wasn't looking forward to discussing floral particulars, she was anticipating dinner with her friend. Dining was always an event at Kitty's, and conversation was always interesting. Unless Oliver happened upon a subject that was decidedly *uninteresting*.

Oliver Hamsted was a scholar and writer and could be knowledgeable to a fault. Being a historian, he rarely encountered a subject he didn't know something about, which led to many side conversations that Amelia could have skipped altogether. Like the one about the recent mummy unwrapping. He'd gone on for at least a quarter hour describing the mummy's brain. Amelia shivered. How Kitty put up with it she didn't know. Actually, she did know. Kitty and Oliver were desperately in love. Even after two years of marriage, the two were inseparable. Except for Lady Agony's escapades, which Kitty joined in frequently. Those Amelia and Kitty still enjoyed together, in secret. If Oliver found out, he'd put an end to their fun. It wasn't that he was against their independence. On the contrary, he was unique in his attitude that women should enjoy the same rights as men. It was that he cared too desperately for his wife to allow her any danger.

When Kitty floated into the drawing room like an artfully drawn white cloud, Amelia understood his reservations. If knowledge was his fault, beauty was hers. Tonight, Kitty's hair was twisted around a single white flower that matched her light dress. Amelia glanced down at her own gown, deciding that if Kitty was a cloud, she was a thunderstorm. It was hard to remember, at times, they were the same age.

"*Amelia*," Kitty scolded. "Why didn't you tell me you knew the Marquis of Bainbridge? I was stunned this morning when he walked into your breakfast room. I could hardly think of a way to respond. Thankfully, conversation has always been my strong suit."

"Good evening, Lady Amesbury." Dressed in sensible black, Oliver walked in behind his wife. His cravat was sloppily tied but not from lack of effort. He tried very hard for his wife. His efforts just missed the mark.

"Good evening." Amelia turned her attention to Kitty. "I didn't have a chance. He recently arrived in town, and I only met him the evening before. He's a friend of the Amesburys."

Kitty looked to Oliver. "Can you imagine? Meeting Lord Bainbridge and not telling your best friend? Goodness. Those would have been the first words out of my mouth."

Amelia was missing something. The marquis was a marquis, but really, Kitty wasn't usually impressed by titles. She herself had a secure position within the *ton*. Amelia wondered why she was making a fuss now and asked her.

"A fuss?" Kitty's blue eyes widened. She and Oliver shared a surprised expression. "I think it's possible she doesn't know."

"Know what?" asked Amelia.

Oliver motioned to sit, and he and Kitty sat close on the flowered settee. Amelia chose the chair across from them.

"I went to school with Bainbridge," Oliver began, "and he has a past most interesting."

Oh no. Here we go. By the time the lecture was over, Amelia was certain she'd know not only Simon's history but his entire family's.

"He's a marquis of one of the wealthiest families in the area, but that's common knowledge. He has a sister, Marielle. They expect her to come out at the Smythe ball. It's a little-known fact that the Smythe family once owned land in Scotland, an equestrian refuge for their impressive steeds—"

"Let me tell it." Kitty patted his knee. "Oliver is right. Lord Bainbridge is all those things. However, the interesting part is that he was involved in a scandal a few years ago. He was engaged to Felicity Farnsworth, and with the marriage a week away it was abruptly canceled." She leaned in closer, as if the walls had ears. "They say he found her in a compromising position with his best friend."

"How dreadful," Amelia exclaimed.

"And that's not the worst of it," added Kitty.

Amelia didn't know how it could get any worse.

"There were letters, where she admitted marrying him for his title. She and her paramour planned to continue the affair, under the protection of his title, once they were married."

"He left for the Americas shortly thereafter," explained Oliver. "Poor chap. I don't think he could endure the talk—or the hungry mamas."

"Many mothers saw the broken engagement as a window of opportunity for their daughters, but they were unsuccessful at making a match." She raised a pretty blonde eyebrow. "Before he took off for the Americas, he quit attending events altogether. Some even say he became a recluse. People speculate he won't attend a single soirée this season, except for his sister's debut."

"Huh." Amelia shrugged. "That's interesting, because he told me he is coming to your costume ball next week."

Kitty jumped off the settee. "Simon Bainbridge is coming here? It cannot be true."

"It is," admitted Amelia. "When he asked about the event, I extended an invitation. I didn't think you would mind."

"*Mind?*" repeated Kitty. "Of course I don't mind. But you should have come here straightaway."

Amelia blinked. "It was a few hours ago."

"But don't you see?" She fled the room and returned with a long list. "I'm going to have to redo my entire seating chart!"

Amelia and Oliver shared a glance. It was quite possible that tonight's dinner would be late, which was disappointing because Amelia was starving. She'd worked up an appetite on the walk over. Despite the butler's dinner announcement, Kitty was inspecting the list, shaking her head, and saying, "It will never do."

But Amelia knew it would certainly do. Like Kitty herself, the ball was meticulously planned. It could accommodate Simon Bainbridge with a small revision on whom he would accompany to supper. Indeed, she could receive Queen Victoria herself if she so desired.

Amelia went to her. "You'll be ready, Kitty. It will be fine."

"Easy for you to say." Kitty pouted. "You are friends with him. Other women will swoon when they find out he's coming. Imagine the talk!"

"I wouldn't exactly call us friends . . ." considered Amelia. What would one call it when one falls into another's lap and wonders what happened? *A lonely widow, that is what*, Amelia chided herself. If she weren't five and twenty, she would have added the word *old*.

Kitty waved away the remark. "Oh, you're friendly. I saw the way you look at each other." She sighed, perhaps recollecting her experience with Oliver. "The banter is part of the game, isn't it, Oliver?"

If it was, Amelia didn't play it well, and she and Edgar hadn't played it at all. She was starting to realize their relationship had been very different from that of most couples. Edgar trusted her to care for him, and she had until the very end. But care wasn't what Amelia felt in Simon's carriage. Nor was it concern. It was curiosity and excitement. She had no idea another person could alight her in such ways. No wonder love letters were so often desperate. She'd felt a little bit desperate herself for something to happen. Exactly what, she couldn't say. But she could imagine.

Oliver joined them, clasping Kitty's hand. "Yes, dear. And I play the game so much better after I've eaten. Do you mind?"

Kitty smiled at Oliver with understanding, and they left for the dining room.

As they feasted on roasted lamb, Amelia considered the new information about Simon. He'd known exactly what he was doing when he told Edgar to find a simple girl, like herself, who would take care of him. He'd been jilted by Felicity and didn't want the same fate for his friend. Did he really believe all females were like Felicity? Kitty said Simon quit attending events after the breakup and, even now, might not attend a single soirée. Except Kitty's. She poked a piece of meat. Something had driven him out of his self-imposed isolation. Could it be herself? She chewed deliberately. *Doubtful.*

The person to ask about all this was Grady Armstrong, her lifelong friend and editor at the magazine. He would have the story on Simon as well as Flora Edwards. Plus, she could trust him. They'd grown up together with the same idea of leaving Somerset as soon as their legs were strong enough to carry them. Being a man, Grady had had an easier time of it. He took off for London the day he turned sixteen, working his way up in the penny papers.

Amelia would have done the same thing if it hadn't been for her parents and the inn. They had needed her help, at least until an offer of marriage arrived. Then it was miraculous how much they didn't need her help anymore. Reminding her they had other capable daughters, her parents encouraged her to accept Edgar's offer. When Amelia revealed that Edgar was ill, her father scoffed at the idea. *Modern medicine*, he boasted. *Don't discount its abilities. He shan't be sick for long.*

Amelia had either believed it or wanted to believe it because she accepted his proposal without another thought. She adored Edgar, and he *looked* healthy. He probably would be cured. He was an earl, after all, with a hefty fortune. He could afford the best. Unfortunately, the best wasn't enough when it came to his degenerative disease. He was much closer to the end of his life than either of them had ever imagined.

"Amelia, did you hear me?" Kitty asked.

Amelia refocused on the dinner conversation. Kitty was still discussing the fittings. Or was it the flowers? Something with an *f.* "Hmm?"

"*Flora,*" Kitty repeated. "Flora Edwards."

Amelia snapped back to attention. "What about Flora?"

"Oliver is familiar with the Edwards family." Kitty threw her a knowing look.

"They are a fine maritime family. I chronicled them in my latest book, *Maritime History*, volume three." Oliver took a sip of wine. "Really, the family could have their own volume when one considers their record . . ."

Kitty cleared her throat, coaxing him along.

"At any rate, they've weathered their share of tragedies. Which reminds me of poor Henry Cosgrove. A week ago, he came to the club, and I hardly recognized him. He looked a genuine pauper. I feel for the man, losing Flora before the wedding. A shame."

"So sad," agreed Kitty. "If he's not careful, he will be the next subject of gossip."

"And hungry mamas," added Oliver.

"Will he be at your ball?" Amelia asked.

"I invited him, of course," said Kitty. "But who knows if he will attend. He has the right to decline all invitations this season, and I wouldn't blame him if he did."

The footmen exchanged the lamb for small salads. Then dessert, chocolates, nuts, and coffee. Despite the intimate dinner party, Kitty didn't skimp on meals—or service. Her table gleamed with ivory and gold plates, twinkling in the warm candlelight of the polished candelabras. Every detail had been considered. From the fine crystal goblets to the embroidered napkins, the dinner was a testament to Mayfair's elegance.

After the footmen retired, Amelia asked Oliver about the Edwardses. "You mentioned tragedies, and Aunt Tabitha hinted at family troubles. She implied Flora might have taken her own life."

Oliver's answer was immediate. "Heavens no. Flora Edwards was smart, healthy, and happily engaged. A lot like the admiral, in fact. There was no reason for her to do such a thing."

"That we know of . . ." said Amelia.

"Flora's death was a terrible accident." Oliver lowered his voice. "Tabitha is a smart woman but growing older. You can't put too much faith in her memory."

"True." Kitty gave Amelia a secret wink.

Amelia took the hint. She and Kitty had gone on wild-goose chases before that led them down a path of trouble. Oliver was very protective of his wife, and when Kitty twisted her ankle while investigating a claim of infidelity from one of Amelia's readers, he became quite angry—and suspicious. They'd been cautious about what they shared with him since.

"If I were you, I'd put the matter out of my head altogether," said Oliver. "It's the most prudent thing to do."

Amelia agreed. It was the most prudent. Unfortunately, prudence had never been her strength.

Chapter 10

Dear Lady Agony,

I'm in London for the season, which is a happy miracle, considering the effort it took to bring me here. The problem is my chaperone, a disagreeable cousin five years my elder. She disapproves of my dresses, my hair, my dance partners. I worry she will chase off any attempts at my affection, which are few as it is. She follows me everywhere. Please help.

Devotedly,
Girl + One

. . . .

Dear Girl + One,

Many impasses, such as your cousin, remain immovable for two reasons: one, they are necessary, and two, they are unhappy. Despite personal objections, I must admit she is necessary, so *the question remains, How can we make her less unhappy, at least for the season?*

I have a simple solution. Find someone who isn't you to occupy her time. I understand this will be difficult, since she is so disagreeable. However, with a little subterfuge, it's possible. She may find interest in an older man, a lonely widower, or a disagreeable fellow like herself, with your encouragement. One nod in the right direction ("I see he's noticed you, Cousin.") is all it will take to set the plan in motion. An occasional "He's here again!" will keep things moving toward your goal of freedom. With persistence, I know you will prevail and have a good time in London. Everyone deserves at least three happy months in this splendid city.

Yours in Secret,
Lady Agony

The next day brought with it less rain and more letters. The season was in full swing, and Lady Agony was in high demand. Ill-fitting dresses, undesired matches, rankling relatives—they were all the subjects of today's batch of letters. Overhead, Tabitha's cane stomped somewhere. Amelia understood rankling relatives. They could wield crushing power in one's life.

Amelia had just finished her responses when Jones announced Simon was waiting for her in the drawing room. Good. She was eager to pay a visit to the Van Ackers. Lena was their scullery maid and Charlotte's adversary. If anyone had cause to kill Charlotte, it was Lena.

Amelia handed Jones her parcel. "Please see this goes to Mr. Armstrong right away. Thank you."

Jones took the package, and Amelia proceeded to the drawing room. Simon was facing the door. His eyes flicked to her neck, where she wore a pearl-drop amethyst necklace at her throat, small and not ornate, but enough adornment to highlight her olive skin. Black was the bane of her existence. It was nice to wear something pretty again.

Simon nodded in her direction. "The necklace is nice."

Amelia smiled at the compliment. She knew it was nice, but it was fun to be told. Tabitha's response had been a brief recital of protocol—as if it weren't already etched in Amelia's mind from the last two years. "Thank you." She crossed the room. "Kitty agreed to inviting the Van Ackers' daughter, by the way. And she agreed to your invitation as well."

Simon feigned seriousness, covering his heart with his hand. "I lay awake all night wondering if I would be allowed in or if I would be rejected."

Amelia tilted her head. "Rejected by your own actions. From what I've surmised, you haven't attended a ball for some time. Why is that?"

He crossed his arms. "The same could be asked of you."

"That's not fair," returned Amelia. "You know why I haven't been out, and besides, I attend plenty of events. I'm the splotch in the ballroom, the one that blends into the shadowy corner. And do not think I didn't notice the switch of topics. We were talking about *you*."

"I have a hard time believing you could blend into a corner." He followed the neckline where the amethyst lay. "At any rate, I confess I'm not much of a dancer. Ballrooms and I do not agree."

"I think there is more to it than that."

"So you have heard the rumors." Simon settled into his stance. "I suppose I will be the subject of your next inquiry."

"Rumors make no difference to me," she said. "I won't pry

into your personal affairs. Unlike some people, I respect a person's privacy."

He lifted his eyebrows. "Did you just take a jab at me?"

Amelia smiled. "When I take a jab at you, you will know."

"I believe it."

"Shall we get started?" She motioned to the door, and he dipped his head in agreement. Seizing her parasol on the way out, Amelia led the way.

It was nice to be out on the city streets. She liked the way the horses and people moved along the spring day. The hooves, the wheels, the chatter, the shoppers. She wasn't much for shopping herself, but she accompanied Kitty a good deal, mostly for the activity and street vendors. Tea shops, spices, and cakes—they were the lure for Amelia. London was a city of infinite variety, and though she'd lived here two years, she'd never tired of its diversity.

The Van Ackers lived a distance from Mayfair, which gave her and Simon time to talk, but, eager not to repeat yesterday's occurrence, Amelia continued to focus on the happenings outside her window. An omnibus zipped past them on Bond Street, where the raucous laughter of a peanut vendor reached her ears. She laughed at his laughter, and Simon inquired about the joke.

"It's nothing," explained Amelia. "Just the man outside." She turned in her seat. "In a sea of a hundred voices, his rides into the carriage on a wave. It's so poetic."

"Spoken like a true creative," Simon answered. "When did you start penning for the magazine?"

She folded her hands over the handle of her parasol. "When Grady Armstrong asked me to take up the job. He's my friend and editor."

"What happened?"

She told him about the previous writer's hasty departure, the influx of letters, and Grady's inability to answer them. Because agony columns were popular additions to any penny paper, he wanted to respond but didn't have the manpower—or woman-power, as it were—to continue the regular feature. Edgar had passed, and Amelia was despondent. That's when she took on the pen name Lady Agony.

"How do you know Grady Armstrong?" he asked.

Amelia was surprised at his interest in the subject. He was on the edge of his seat cushion, waiting for her answer. "Grady was our neighbor in Somerset. We played together as children and pored over the newspapers together. Mells is a small village, and the deliveries came directly to the inn. Later, he worked our stables. He worked everywhere, in fact, until he received his apprenticeship. A very diligent person—thoughtful, too."

He leaned back. "It sounds as if you have a history, not all professional."

A laugh sputtered from her lips. "I should hope not *all profes-sional*. We were children, for goodness' sake." By the upturn of his chin, Simon didn't like her answer. Her gaze returned to the glass. Men and their egos. As if they should be the only people in the world with a history.

The Van Ackers' house was a respectable walk-up on Gloucester Street. A curtain fell into place as the carriage slowed to a stop, and Amelia understood the shadow behind it. If the carriage size didn't give away their arrival, the Bainbridge crest did. The butler would know right away that someone of impor-tance was paying a call. It didn't surprise her that help came immediately. After giving their calling cards, they were ushered into the house with great efficiency.

They waited for Mrs. Van Acker in the drawing room, and

while they did, Amelia rehearsed the conversation in her head, still stumbling over her question about Lena.

If she were at the Feathered Nest, she wouldn't have this problem. One could go from the weather to the crops to the latest gossip in a span of five minutes. Strict rules and conventions were the only thing about London she didn't like. In the heat of the moment, she always seemed to forget some obscure tenet.

She shook off the concern. She would go with the same explanation as before at the Edwardses' house. Charlotte was her acquaintance; it wasn't a lie. They *had* corresponded.

Mrs. Van Acker entered the room speedily. Her cheeks, pink with excitement, were just a shade lighter than the red hair that framed her heart-shaped face. Her violet dress floated over the carpet as she hurried to greet them. "Good afternoon," she said, slightly winded.

"Good afternoon, Mrs. Van Acker."

"Good afternoon," added Simon.

"It's a pleasure to meet you both. I'm honored for the call." Mrs. Van Acker motioned for them to sit down, then fluttered to an aqua chair with well-worn arm cushions. Adjusting the skirt of her dress, she exuded nervous energy. Content with the placement of her frills, she took a breath and smiled. "Would you like tea?"

"No, thank you, Mrs. Van Acker," said Simon. "We appreciate you seeing us on such short notice."

Amelia started with Kitty's invitation. It was the best way to put the mother in a good mood. "When I told my friend Mrs. Hamsted I was paying you a visit, she asked me to mention her upcoming costume ball." She handed her an invitation. "She would like your daughter to attend."

Mrs. Van Acker's small eyes grew two sizes. A squeal of joy

could be heard somewhere upstairs. She glanced at the ceiling before replying. "Of course. She would be delighted."

"Wonderful," Amelia gushed. "That's excellent news." She cleared her throat. "The reason for our call is Charlotte Woods." Seeing Mrs. Van Acker's confused look, she explained. "I expect you aren't familiar with her but I was. She was an acquaintance of mine. Unfortunately, she passed two days ago."

Mrs. Van Acker's plump hand flew to her lips. "I am so sorry, my lady."

"Thank you," murmured Amelia. "I appreciate that."

"Your maid Lena Crane used to work at the Edwardses' house with Miss Woods," added Simon. "Lady Amesbury is hoping Miss Crane might be able to shed some light on her health."

"Of course," Mrs. Van Acker agreed. "Absolutely. Anything my staff and I can do to help the countess. Should I call in the girl?" She checked the clock on the overcrowded wall. "She'll be upstairs by now."

"Thank you." Amelia smiled. "That would be most kind of you."

Mrs. Van Acker disappeared without another word. A few minutes later, she reappeared with Lena, who looked very little as Amelia had pictured. Hardly sinister, her face was as bright and round as the moon. Her blonde hair was neatly pulled back, and her apron was crisp and white. When she smiled, a dimple creased her cheek, making her look young, but she must have been about thirty years of age.

"Miss Crane is happy to help." Mrs. Van Acker gave Lena a little nudge into the room. "I explained you're here about one of her former colleagues."

"Deeply appreciated," said Simon. "We'll ring if we need further assistance."

Amelia was glad for his comment. His statement indicated that they planned to talk to Lena in private.

Mrs. Van Acker took a step backward. "Let me know if you need anything at all."

When they were alone, Amelia asked Lena to join them. Lena was thrilled by the invitation if her pink cheeks were any indication. She sneaked a glance at Simon and blushed deeper. *Ah.* Maybe the marquis should do the talking. He had the attention of the girl, if not the admiration. Amelia hoped he would take the hint.

"Thank you for meeting with us, Miss Crane." Simon's voice was as smooth as silk.

The girl made a noise. It might have been a giggle or word.

"We're here about Charlotte Woods," added Simon. "Do you know her?"

"Yes, your lordship, I do." She leaned in. "If you're looking for a reference, though, I can't give it. Between you and me, she's nothing but trouble—with a capital *T*." Despite her fresh face, her voice betrayed her age and experience. It was a mix of grit and bitterness.

Simon feigned surprise. He couldn't hire Charlotte if he wanted to; she was dead. But for the moment, he and Amelia kept that fact to themselves.

"She's a talker, you understand, a real church bell," Lena continued. "Gossips about the workers. Gossips about the family. All around, a bad person you don't want to be associated with." She batted her eyelashes. "Especially someone of your *high* standing."

"You know her from the Edwardses' house?" asked Amelia.

"I was Miss Hyacinth's lady's maid. Wore her castoffs and everything." Her nostrils flared with pride. "I'd been her maid for five good years when Charlotte told the family a pack of lies about me. She was always jealous of me. I looked right pretty in those clothes, I did."

"And they believed her?" Simon asked.

Lena nodded. "One day they'll see *she's* the bad apple. Then they'll beg me to come back. I just know it."

One day when Charlotte was dead. If Lena had killed her, Charlotte would be out of the house—permanently.

"I hate to be the one to tell you this." Simon cleared his throat. "But Charlotte is gone."

"She quit?" Lena snorted. "Doesn't that beat all."

Amelia shook her head. This wasn't the time for euphemisms. "No, she's dead. She drowned in St. James's Park."

Chapter 11

Dear Lady Agony,

Do you believe it is better to be polite or honest? I cannot seem to be both, no matter how hard I try.

Devotedly,
Two-Faced Trouble

. . . .

Dear Two-Faced Trouble,

Honest. The answer is just that simple and just that hard.

Yours in Secret,
Lady Agony

From the time she was young, Amelia said what she meant and meant what she said. That was one of the reasons she had a hard time being the Countess of Amesbury. Aristocrats could be positively insipid when they wanted to be. Often, her gut reaction and swift tongue got her stern looks from London intelligentsia, not to mention Aunt Tabitha. Simon, however, gave her a knowing grin when she revealed the bad news straightaway.

"Balderdash!" Lena exclaimed. "It can't be true."

"It is." Amelia leaned in, in case Lena needed assistance. Her pale face was becoming more so, and she looked as if she would faint or throw a tantrum. Either would be detrimental, for it would surely gain the attention of Mrs. Van Acker. "She was found two nights ago. Some say she was overwhelmed by the death of Flora Edwards. That she blamed herself."

Her eyes narrowed on Amelia. "What are you saying? She done herself in?"

Amelia waited for a reaction and wasn't disappointed.

"You got it wrong, your ladyship. Charlotte might have been a church bell but she was a churchgoer, too. She wouldn't kill herself. She was too high and mighty for that."

"Then explain something to us," Simon broke in. "Tell us about the list."

Her face drained of the rest of its color. "What list?"

"The one you were making on the Edwards family—the one Charlotte discovered." Amelia studied her eyes.

"Like I said, it was a lie—"

"Come now," pressed Amelia. "We don't have time for dissemblance. A woman is dead, and the black list may have led to her demise."

"Lordy! Do you think?" asked Lena.

"It's hard to speculate without knowing what's on the list." Simon's face was calm and patient like that of an experienced sailor in a storm.

Lena's eyes shifted from side to side. Perhaps she was debating what to tell them.

Amelia thought about how to help her make the right choice. "And if they weren't afraid to kill Charlotte, they won't be afraid to kill you."

"Oh!" Lena exclaimed. "I see your point." The color returned to her cheeks, and she spilled the contents of the list posthaste. The list included details about the Edwards family, from the admiral's penchant for gin to Hyacinth's hysterics. It also included the staff. Although Tibens sounded more like a general than a butler, plenty of mischief was to be had by all in the house. Lena disclosed who gossiped, who lied, who drank, and who chased after others' beaus.

This last detail piqued Amelia's attention. "Who do you mean?"

"The Edwards girls are all of marriageable age." Lena lowered her voice. "There was bound to be some overlap in male interests, you understand."

"Could you be more specific?" Simon encouraged. "Who was interested in whom?"

"Miss Hyacinth, in particular. She always had eyes for the duke. And now, with Miss Flora gone, who knows?" Lena shrugged. "Maybe he will decide to marry one of the other sisters. Miss Hyacinth must be hoping so. He's a good-looking chap and well-off to boot."

"Money is not a concern for the Edwards family, is it?" Amelia inquired.

"Money's a concern for *all* families, unless you're . . ." Lena's sentence trailed off into nothingness. She obviously didn't want to mention their titles.

"You're right," Simon agreed. "Times are hard everywhere."

"Especially for me," Lena grumbled. "I'm back on the bottom rung, so to speak." She tossed up her apron. "A lowly scullery maid."

"It could be worse," interjected Amelia. "Look at poor Charlotte."

Lena ignored her, preferring Simon's affable words and smile.

"Thank you for the information." Simon stood and bowed. "You've been most helpful."

Lena blushed. "Anytime, my lord."

"Yes, thank you," said Amelia, joining Simon.

Lena's smile turned flat as she walked out the door.

With Lena gone, Mrs. Van Acker rejoined them in the drawing room and escorted them out. She fluttered around the butler as he retrieved their coats. The poor man looked just as flustered as she did by the time he had the items. "Please send my regards to Mrs. Hamsted for the invitation. We are deeply appreciative."

"I will," Amelia promised. "And thank you again."

Simon thanked her also before ushering Amelia outside.

On the way back to Mayfair, Simon told Amelia he'd heard rumblings of the Edwardses' financial distress before. The admiral was getting older, and the Royal Navy didn't provide as it should have. It was the reason he'd started his shipbuilding business, Fair Winds, in the first place. His business handled contracts for the navy, but contracts were becoming fewer and fewer. With three daughters to marry and no wife to help him, he had his hands full, and Hyacinth wanted the best of everything, despite her father's modest income. Respectability wouldn't be enough for her. She wanted what her sister had had: a proposal from a titled gentleman.

"It's silly, if you ask me," Amelia mused. "The house is homey, the family is healthy. If Hyacinth could find a gentleman half as kind as her father, she would be a lucky girl."

Simon adjusted the cuffs of his white shirt. "Kindness is a dying virtue, Lady Amesbury. It takes more than goodwill to get a girl."

Amelia wasn't ignorant; she knew it was true. But it shouldn't be. "I would take kindness over wealth any day."

"Said the countess to the marquis."

She smiled. "True."

His eyes met hers with a smile.

"For myself, I didn't set out to become wealthy," Amelia continued. "It just happened." She paused, wondering if she should continue. Like most times, she decided, *Why not?* "Have you found it to be a barrier in your relationships? Your wealth, I mean. I know you had that one problem, but I suppose there have been others?"

Lowering his chin to his chest, he crossed his arms. "You really have no fear, do you? If Aunt Tabitha could see you now, she would understand the color of your dress is the least of her problems."

"The color of my dress *is* the least of her problems," said Amelia. "I couldn't care less if she forced me to wear a paper sack for the next year. It makes little difference to me as long as I have my trusty parasol to protect me from London's rain." She tried to catch his green eyes again. "You, however, haven't answered my question. Did you encourage Edgar's action because of your own experiences?"

"I suppose I did. I didn't want him to repeat my mistake, so I gave him what I thought was good advice before I left. If London is your freedom, the sea is mine. It's the one place I don't have to worry about marriage or money."

She considered the admission. "You have found most women desire you for your money, then."

His eyes found hers. "'Desire' is a very strong word."

"Rather they . . . *pursue* you for your money. Rather than, say, your patriotism or humor or good looks."

"You think I'm good-looking?"

She blinked. "Dark hair, unique eye color, a robust build. All very appealing."

"I think you're good-looking, too."

"Thanks, but I'm rather ordinary. Reddish-brown hair, brown eyes, gray dress." She lifted the dull fabric. "Not much to recommend myself."

"On the contrary," he said. "You're one of the most interesting women I've ever met."

She glanced up from her dress. "Now you're just being complimentary."

"I've been called a lot of things, but 'complimentary' isn't one of them." His eyes held a challenge in them.

What that challenge was, she couldn't say, but she wasn't afraid to find out. She was not a girl anymore. She was a widow and a mother and bloody curious about what he meant. She'd been curious since yesterday, and twenty-four hours was the longest she'd ever waited for anything.

"I'm sure Edgar told you every day how interesting you are," he continued, his eyes tracing the outline of her face. "And how beautiful."

She let out a little laugh.

"He didn't?"

"Edgar was very ill," she explained. "You know that. My intellect and beauty were not his chief concerns."

"But you were married," he stated.

"In name, perhaps." She shrugged. "Ours wasn't the first marriage of convenience in London." She nudged his leg. "You've lived in this town long enough to know that. I was his helpmate. That's all."

He closed his eyes briefly. When he opened them, they betrayed his anger. At her or himself, she didn't know. "I owe you an apology." He cleared his throat. "About Edgar—about everything. I'm truly sorry."

"I understand," she said.

"I don't think you do," Simon clarified. "I should have never said what I said to Edgar. It was selfish. You were young. You're *still* young."

She tried to lighten the mood. "Then here's your chance to make up for it."

"I'm afraid I'm not the man to do that," he rebuffed.

She wasn't sure of his response or what question she'd even asked.

"I would be another disappointment, and you've had enough disappointments already."

Now she understood. *He thinks I need him.* She would make the situation crystal clear.

She clasped the handle of her parasol, glad for something to grip. If she could, she would have knocked him on the side of his head with it. "First, please stop telling me what I do and do not understand. I have a perfect grasp of my wants and needs. I *want* you to help me find justice for my reader. However, I do not *need* it. I work perfectly fine alone. I've been on my own for two years now."

"Amelia—"

"You mean 'Lady Amesbury.'" She turned to the window. "You seem to be more comfortable with formal relationships."

Chapter 12

Dear Lady Agony,

My friend tells me I must stop reading novels about crimes. She says they will lead to my moral downfall. But newspapers deal with the subject every day, and no one objects to them. Who's right, me or my friend?

Devotedly,
Reading Right

....

Dear Reading Right,

Many will tell you inviting a villain into your reading is like inviting a villain into your home. I will tell you nothing of the sort. If we had to read about people only like ourselves, I cannot imagine the boredom. Give me a good *crime any day. There's nothing better for the mind on a dull afternoon.*

Yours in Secret,
Lady Agony

Amelia poured herself a hefty glass of claret in the library. *The trouble with men is their egos.* They got in the way of everything, even a good time. Stung by Simon's rejection, she took a drink of the burgundy liquid, liking the way the taste got rid of the reminders of him. Well, almost. It was hard not to replay their conversation in her head. Even harder to believe was that chivalry—ha!—was Simon's reason for rejecting her. She glanced at the stack of letters on her desk. She couldn't wait to advise all those lovelorn women to find another hobby such as—she looked around the room—reading. It was much more satisfying than any interaction she'd had with men to date—and more fulfilling, too.

Tabitha appeared in the doorway. "If you must stomp and sneer, please shut the door, Amelia. I've told you a hundred times, servants talk."

Amelia crossed her arms. "*You* stomp and sneer."

"Yes, but I'm an old lady. I can get by with it." She pointed to the wine decanter with her cane, and Amelia poured. "Where were you and Lord Bainbridge?"

"Simon and I paid a call on the Van Ackers. Kitty wanted me to invite the daughter to the ball."

"*Simon?*" She sat down, hands crossed on her walking stick, waiting for her libation. She looked like a judge holding court. "Are we on a Christian-name basis now?"

Amelia placed the glass on the table and took up the chair

next to her. "It's just the two of us. I thought I could dispense with the titles." She felt a lecture coming and quickly continued. "May I ask you something?"

"You're going to anyway."

True, thought Amelia. "Kitty said Simon was engaged to be married once. Being old friends, you must know the story."

"I trust Kitty relayed the pertinent details of the affair." Tabitha exchanged her cane for the glass of wine. "She knows everything that happens in Mayfair. So what you really want to know is the effect it had on Simon."

Amelia took a sip of her wine, considering the question. "Yes."

"I don't think he ever recovered," Tabitha said plainly. "He was very much in love with Felicity Farnsworth, and she broke his heart. After what happened with his mother, he could not move past it." She brought her glass to her lips. "Who could blame him?"

Amelia leaned in. "What happened with his mother?"

Tabitha's open mouth betrayed her surprise—and regret. "Of course Kitty wouldn't know those details. Not many do. Perhaps I shouldn't continue."

Amelia remained silent, willing her to finish the story. It was getting late, and she still had those letters to return. Plus, she wanted to talk to Winifred about the music and perhaps Governess Walters as well. The hours for practice were dwindling as the upcoming recital approached.

"What I'm about to tell you doesn't leave this room. The Amesburys and Bainbridges have a long-standing history. We cannot betray that trust."

"I never would," Amelia promised.

"When Simon was young, in his teens, his mother died in a

train accident." Tabitha set her glass on the table. "That, in and of itself, was not spectacular for the time. Trains were a work in progress. They crashed frequently and spectacularly. What was concerning was with whom she was traveling—not her husband, but another man. The family was devastated."

"Poor Simon," said Amelia.

"Indeed, poor Simon." Tabitha sniffed. "When Simon's father found out about Felicity's infidelity, the two nearly came to blows. He accused Simon of repeating his mistake of becoming a cuckold. He promised not to give his consent again without prior approval. Edgar was angry about that, because it wasn't Simon's fault. Felicity had ruined the match. But Simon didn't care. He vowed to remain a bachelor until the end of his days. And despite pressure from his aging father, he remains so today."

Amelia sat back in the tufted chair. "It makes sense."

Tabitha shook her head. "It makes *no* sense. It's the silliest thing I've ever heard. Simon must marry, and because of an argument between him and his father, he has not."

But Amelia wasn't thinking of the bad blood between father and son. She was thinking of his comments in the carriage. Good Lord. Did Simon think their friendship would turn into a marriage proposal? Maybe he'd forgotten, but marriage hadn't turned out well for her, either. The last thing she wanted was to get into another fated relationship. *Thank you but no, thank you.* She'd had her fair share of attention from the three Fates who determined one's destiny: Clotho, Lachesis, and Atropos. Those temperamental women could stay away for good.

Amelia returned to the topic. "Must he marry?"

"Of course." The stress in her voice was palpable. "He's the only son in the family. The Bainbridge future depends on it."

A maid came in and added another log to the fire. Amelia waited for her to leave before continuing. "Simon will find the right woman in due time. Good things come to those who wait."

"Like me?" She stood. "No, dear, good things come to those who go out and find them. Remember that."

Long after Tabitha left, Amelia considered her words. There was truth in what she had said. Amelia had always been a woman of action. Waiting was not her specialty, and perhaps it wasn't Aunt Tabitha's, either. But that didn't mean Simon needed to find a wife. And she certainly didn't need to find a husband. Edgar's death and wealth had settled the question for now—and forever, if need be. She had Winifred and she had her letters. She even had a murder to solve. Her life was too full for another relationship.

And yet, she did think about her conversation with Simon as she responded to her letters. Despite her best attempts to focus, she felt her mind wandering back to it. She blamed her reverie on all the lovelorn missives scattered on her desk. With the sting of Simon's rejection on the tip of her pen, it felt good answering the letters with renewed vigor. When the last one was penned, she handed the stack to Jones and rushed to find Winifred, who was playing in the nursery.

With Winifred's flaxen hair shining in the sunlight, more gold than flax, Amelia realized Winifred didn't really *play* anymore. Not like she used to. Most days were spent studying, drawing, singing, or reading. Time was marching on, and Winifred was growing up. But she wasn't too grown up to give Amelia a hug. When she noticed Amelia in the doorway, she put down her book and rushed to greet her.

After they embraced, Amelia asked, "How was your practice?"

"Better," said Winifred.

"Good." Amelia took a seat on the small chair at the table. "I'd like to hear you play after dinner."

"Of course," agreed Winifred. "How was your . . . rendezvous with the marquis?"

"It was not a rendezvous," Amelia answered. Winifred arched a perfect Amesbury eyebrow, and Amelia tweaked her cheek. "It wasn't!"

"I have no objections to a courtship, by the way." Winifred kept her voice even, serious, and adultlike. "In fact, I find it rather interesting." She sat up taller. "Some children hate it when their mothers or fathers remarry, but I don't feel that way at all. I'm excited for you."

Amelia's heart skipped a beat. She and Winifred had been as close as two people could be, but never had Winifred called her *Mother* or indicated that she felt that way about her. It was a thrill and a joy, and Amelia blinked back the tears that moistened her eyes. She gave Winifred a smile. Nothing could touch the love that she felt for this child. To think that it was reciprocated was almost too much to hope for.

"It's nice to know I have your support if I should ever pursue that avenue." Amelia winked. "Speaking of the marquis, he promised to come to your recital. Isn't that generous of him?"

"Very generous," agreed Winifred. "Though it probably has more to do with you than me."

"Do you know he used to play?"

Winifred scrunched up her face.

"It's true." Amelia shrugged. "He said his mother was a terrific musician. He reveres the pianoforte a great deal."

"Does he still play?" asked Winifred.

"I'm not sure, but we could ask next time he pays us a call."

Winifred's dimple showed.

"What?" asked Amelia.

"I knew there would be a next time."

Amelia turned over a book on the table. "Has Miss Walters been slipping you romances? Is a Jane Austen novel tucked somewhere inside? It must be."

Winifred rolled her eyes. "Miss Walters thinks I'm a baby. She'd never sneak me a romantic book."

"Good. Because you're growing up too quickly as it is." Amelia pushed in her chair. "I'll see you at dinner. I need to dress."

Winifred waved a goodbye.

When Amelia entered her room, Lettie was arranging her jewelry. Her plump cheeks were flushed from hurrying about the room.

"I noticed your amethyst, so I laid out a few other options." Lettie held up a beautiful pair of ear bobbles. "These?"

"Lovely." Amelia sighed, admiring their sparkle. "I'll wear them tonight."

"Have you thought about your costume for Mrs. Hamsted's ball?"

Amelia held the jewelry to her ears. "I've thought about it, of course. But I've been dreadfully busy."

"With Lord Bainbridge," added Lettie with a smile.

The news was making its rounds in the house. "We have been working together on a . . . project." Amelia waffled. Lettie was not only her maid but her friend. She wouldn't lie to her, but she also couldn't tell her the whole truth—not yet, anyway. "Can I ask you a question? Have you ever heard of a black list?"

"A black list, my lady?" Lettie untangled the chain of a necklace. "Of course. Not in this house, mind you."

"Why would staff keep one? As a type of leverage?"

"Not exactly," explained Lettie. "It's more of a Who's Who and What's What for the serving class. Just like employers have references, we have ours, too."

"I see." Amelia digested the information. "Have you ever heard any complaints about Admiral Edwards's house?"

Lettie laid Amelia's evening gown on the bed. Then she sat next to it, her short legs dangling off the edge. She loved gossip even more than she loved clothes and dove into the topic enthusiastically. "I knew a girl who worked there once. She said the admiral's daughters were the dickens to work for, and the butler was a regular dictator. A man named Tibens. He forced the housemaid to fire a girl after a row. She's a *scullery* maid now."

"Because of the black list, I heard."

"That may be, but you have to ask yourself why she made the list in the first place." She fussed with the slim ruffle on Amelia's dress. "Was it insurance against the Edwards family, or the butler himself? One wonders with a man like that."

Amelia didn't know the answer, but it was a good question, one she planned on asking very soon.

Chapter 13

Dear Lady Agony,

I write to you not for advice but in hopes that you will print my letter in its entirety so that other women may avoid my folly. Recently, I went into a cosmetic store excited for a beauty solution and came out with eyebrows the color of coal, a half an inch wide, with a curl at the tip. When I tried to remedy the situation at home, with lemon juice, I was left with flaming red hair and irritated skin. Until my face returns to some sort of natural state, I am forced to wear a veil. To others who feel the pull of the vanity shop, I say this: Your God-given eyebrows are adequate. Do not let queen, country, or vanity tell you otherwise.

Devotedly,
Barely There

. . . .

Dear Barely There,

*Thank you for sharing your experience. I receive many letters
like yours each day and am happy to reprint yours in full.
Please know that while you have not saved your own eyebrows,
you have saved at least one woman from tears. This Author
thanks you.*

*Yours in Secret,
Lady Agony*

The next day, the mail didn't arrive by regular post but personal delivery. Like a breath of fresh air, Grady Armstrong was at Amelia's doorstop with a large envelope. Under his cap, his blond hair was mussed and his jacket was swept open, revealing a no-nonsense waistcoat. A crease at the stomach suggested he'd spent his morning leaning over a worktable at the office, and the tips of his fingers, like always, were a smudge of dry ink. It reminded her of home and their afternoons poring over the newspapers in the great hall of the Feathered Nest. Amelia smiled at the recollection.

"My apologies, Lady Amesbury." Jones pulled at his jacket, as if Grady's presence were physically bothersome. "I told Mr. Armstrong to wait in the drawing room."

"Not a problem. I thought I heard a familiar voice."

"Good day, mate." Grady gave Jones a salute. Jones sniffed in response and retreated. When he was out of earshot, Grady whispered, "He's a cantankerous little fellow."

Amelia led him into the library. "Just fastidious. He likes order."

"For you." Grady handed her a large parcel filled with individual envelopes. "That last answer garnered quite a few responses."

"Which one?"

"The one where you told Lady of Leisure to tell her suitor to stick it where the sun doesn't shine."

She laughed. "I never said that."

"Well, you might as well have." He fell into a chair. "It raised a ruckus at the magazine. People are debating whether you're right or wrong. And now these letters. Some from men, some from women. It's caused a bloody paper storm."

"The man was an impostor, vying for her money." She felt incensed all over again recalling the letter. "I'd stake my title on it."

He waved away the comment. "You'd stake your title on anything, but I agree with you. Still, the *ton* do not like to discuss money and marriage. It makes them nervous."

She took the seat across from him. "They should discuss it, in my opinion. They'd have happier marriages."

"Or fewer." Grady's shoulders shrugged in his too-large jacket. He was more concerned with words than his appearance, and no matter how long he lived in London, among the fashionable, he'd always look like a country squire. "Either way, their arguments make for titillating gossip."

"I suppose," she agreed. "At any rate, I am glad you're here. I wanted to talk to you about a letter I received."

"I'm all ears."

Amelia told him about the letter, the postscript, and the murder. Grady sat mesmerized, hardly saying a word. He motioned anxiously for her to go on when she paused to take a breath. He never could wait to hear the end of a story. He'd snatch the newspaper out of her hands if she read too slowly. She hurried along, and after describing the scene at St. James's Park, she explained she was following up on some leads with the help of Simon Bainbridge.

"Spoken like a true investigator." Grady rubbed his hands together. "But Simon Bainbridge? He's a member of the e-l-i-t-e. How'd you get him to help?"

"It's a long story, but he knows the Amesbury family and was there when I discovered the body. I guess I left that out." She lowered her voice. "He followed me after dinner. I had to tell him about my"—she looked around—"pseudonym."

Grady's blond eyebrows came to a point. "Interesting. Bainbridge left London for a couple of years on account of being jilted. Hasn't been seen since. He must be worried for your safety. He's a navy man. Duty and all that."

"Wonderful." Her voice held a healthy dose of sarcasm. "I knew there had to be a reason for his interest."

"You haven't gone and fallen for the bloke, have you?"

"Grady!" hissed Amelia. "Be quiet."

"Because you're blushing, and I've seen you run through the Feathered Nest in your knickers and not blush."

True. He had seen her run through the inn in her knickers, but she was seven years old, and he was chasing her. "You have no shame," she rebuked him. "Aunt Tabitha is in her room and Winifred's practicing the pianoforte."

Laughing, he put up his hands in a sign of surrender. "Just be careful. If this person murdered Charlotte, like you think, they could come after you."

"I know."

More quietly, he added, "And be careful of Bainbridge, too."

Amelia was confused. "Why?"

Hesitant, Grady tapped his fingertips together. "It's just a feeling. You don't have the . . . best of luck, and I don't want to see your feelings hurt. Especially after Edgar."

Next to Kitty, Grady was her closest friend and had known her the longest. They'd grown up together. They didn't keep secrets, and he understood about Edgar's disease and how much it pained her to know his days were numbered. To be so close to death made her feel powerless. The last thing she wanted was to get into a doomed relationship. She told him so.

"Maybe, but you need to guard yourself against his good looks and charm." He winked. "Like you do mine."

Amelia let out a laugh, and Grady joined in. With the seriousness of the last few days, it was good to share a chuckle.

"Lord Bainbridge to see you, my lady—" started Jones.

"Never mind," Simon interrupted, filling the doorway. He wore a jet-black double-breasted jacket and royal blue cravat that made his eyes waver between navy and emerald. "I just followed the laughter."

Amelia blinked. Was Simon Bainbridge in her library, or was it her imagination? They'd been talking about him, and *poof!* Here he was. She hoped he hadn't overheard their conversation.

"Are you going to introduce me to your friend?" Simon asked.

Grady stood. "Grady Armstrong. Nice to make your acquaintance, my lord."

Amelia recovered quickly. "Mr. Armstrong is with the magazine. Mr. Armstrong, this is Simon Bainbridge."

"Ah." Simon shook his hand. "The connection to the ever-elusive Lady Agony. It's good to meet you."

Amelia spoke to Grady. "I had to explain the connection."

"Understandably," said Grady.

"Don't worry. The secret is safe with me." Simon sat on the couch next to her. "So what's the news?"

She noted how close his knee was to hers. If she could have cut the sofa in half, she would have. She didn't want to get too close to him again, not after the fiasco in the carriage. As it was, she tried to ignore it. But it was a big knee. She inched toward the corner. "No news. Just letters. I told him about the note from Charlotte and our inquiries."

Simon nodded toward Grady. "Any ideas on who might have wanted Charlotte Wood—or Flora Edwards—dead?"

"Good questions." Grady removed his cap, smoothed his hair, and repositioned it higher on his forehead. "I haven't heard anything about Miss Flora, and if her death was suspicious, I should have heard something by now. It's been several days. I'll keep a lookout, though. I know a coroner who is willing to talk. Rumors have a way of finding my desk."

"Speaking of rumors, my maid told me the Edwardses' butler, Tibens, is a regular dictator." Amelia forgot about Simon's closeness now, as she forgot about everything when she was excited. She leaned into their small circle. "No one dares cross him. Lena's black list might have been insurance against him. Maybe Charlotte had no such protection."

"Staff have their own hierarchy, as you know," Simon considered. "It's possible he got rid of Charlotte if he saw her as a troublemaker, but what of Flora? He wouldn't murder the mistress of the house. How can there be a connection?"

"You think the same person who killed Flora killed Charlotte?" asked Grady.

"Yes," Simon answered. "If Flora was indeed murdered."

"Of course she was murdered!" Amelia thought they'd already agreed on this point. "Charlotte wouldn't lie."

"Everyone lies, and you didn't even know Charlotte," noted Simon. "How can you speak to her credibility?"

"I know my readers." Amelia would argue this point until it was safe to swim in the Thames. That's how adamantly she felt about her correspondents. "They write to me for help. Lying would defeat the purpose."

"I agree with Amelia." Grady's warm brown eyes remained steady and dispassionate. "She knows her readers best. If she says Charlotte wasn't lying, then she wasn't lying."

"Thank you," Amelia said with a polite nod of her head at Grady.

"So what's next?" Simon's voice cut to the point. Their agreement seemed to nettle him, and Amelia was glad it was he rather than she who was now on the edge of his seat.

She turned to him with a smile. "I'm so glad you asked. I think we should return to the Edwardses' house and ask the butler a couple of questions. See what we can find."

Simon quirked a brow. "I don't know how many times I can go back there without the family becoming suspicious."

"I thought you were friends with the family," Amelia prodded. They needed to explore the new rumor.

"I am, but I don't see them on a daily basis."

"I take your point." Grady scratched his sandy-blond chin whiskers. "How else could you find out?"

The library went quiet as they considered the question. Outside, horse hooves clopped past and carriage wheels creaked. Amelia saw a hansom cab roll by. The city was always moving, even when she was still. Now *she* needed to move, to find a way into the Edwardses' house.

Grady snapped his fingers. "The Edwardses put an advertisement in the paper for a lady's maid. They're receiving applicants between the hours of two and six this afternoon. With a decent disguise, like the ones you used to wear at the Feathered Nest, you could apply for the job. Talk to the staff yourself."

Many families, including the Amesburys, hired by word of mouth. Some used the city registry. The admiral must have liked the direct route of advertisement that the newspaper provided. Silently, Amelia praised his action. "That's an excellent idea!"

"Now, wait a minute—" said Simon.

"I have my costume trunk upstairs." Amelia explained to Simon what Grady already knew. "My parents put on plays at the inn, and my siblings and I performed—and Grady a few times, too. I can do this with my eyes closed. Trust me."

Simon crossed his arms. "I don't think it's a good idea."

Amelia checked Grady's response. He seemed just as puzzled as she was. It was a great idea. She had not only performed in plays but worked at the inn. A disguise would give her the perfect opportunity to talk to the staff. Tibens, as the butler, would be aware of the interviews. "Why not?"

"What if someone recognizes you? What possible defense would you have?"

Amelia scratched her head. He had a point. If she was worried about her secret identity being found out, she was doubly worried about herself being involved in a scandal, dragging the Amesbury name through the mud in the process. But who else would fight for Charlotte? It must be her.

"Amelia here is a master of disguise." Grady winked. "No one will recognize her. I promise."

"Countess of Amesbury, you mean," corrected Simon. "And all that title implies."

"I understand your concern," said Amelia. "But I've gone out incognito before. Kitty, too. Sometimes Lady Agony must do a little sleuthing herself. To help a reader, of course."

"Of course," repeated Simon. "I can see there's no talking you out of it." He stood. "So where do we begin? Your face? Your hair? I don't see how the devil you'll ever hide that mane."

Amelia stood, too. "I have the perfect black wig. It changes everything."

"The one you wore as Nerissa in *The Merchant of Venice*?" asked Grady.

"The very one." Amelia started toward the door. When she saw Simon following her, she stopped. "Where are you going? To my bedroom?" She could have sworn his face flushed, and she laughed. "Stay here. I'll be back in a jiffy."

She took the stairs two at a time, hoisting her stiff gray dress above her ankles. It would be lovely to get out of the gown, if even for a half hour. Now if she could just get past Tabitha, who was finishing her correspondence in her own bedroom . . .

Amelia entered her bedroom and flung wide a hope chest, searching for the long black wig. It was under the green silk frock she'd worn. "Perfect!"

She called for Lettie, who was always eager to help her out with a request. Though she didn't know the reason for Amelia's sometimes odd appeals, Lettie understood it to be part of something exciting. About the same age as Amelia, Lettie knew the value of entertainment and was always encouraging Amelia to seek out fun.

"You want to wear one of my dresses?" Lettie's smooth face wrinkled in surprise. "It will be too big."

"Don't worry about that." Amelia waved off the concern. "Just fetch one, and be quick, please."

Lettie was right. It was big around the middle. But with a properly placed apron cinched at the back, the dress suited the part just fine. Amelia donned the wig, and Lettie pinned it, carefully placing a white cap atop. Amelia dusted her neck and face with powder to disguise her warm complexion. She gave her reflection a satisfied nod and started for the stairs.

She tiptoed past Tabitha's room, pausing to hear a soft snore. *Thank heavens.* Tabitha rarely napped, but when she did, it was after a big breakfast and the morning's papers.

Simon was astonished by the transformation; Grady not so much. He had a good laugh while Simon circled her like a shark sizing up its next meal.

Grady congratulated her. "I knew you could pull it off."

"I agree." Simon's eyes flicked over her costume. "It's quite convincing. Still, your face is your face." He walked over to a side table and found a pair of Tabitha's reading glasses. "Here. Put them on."

She slipped the round spectacles on the end of her nose.

"Ha!" laughed Grady. "You look like a regular schoolmarm."

"Better." Simon nodded, satisfied with the addition.

Amelia checked her reflection in the window. The glasses definitely aged her, but as long as she didn't look like herself, she didn't care. Giving the dress a little swish, she decided she could live in the practical attire. It was nice to be free of stiff undergarments—for one afternoon. "I'm going to start off right away, while my family is occupied."

Grady held out his arm as he had done so many times before. This time, however, the performance wasn't in Mells but the largest city in England. Amelia's nerves bubbled to the surface, and she took a deep breath. *Better.*

"Good idea," Grady agreed. "You can catch a cab with me."

Simon reached for his hat. "I'd be happy to accompany you."

Amelia and Grady shared a chuckle.

"What's so amusing?" asked Simon.

"Nothing. It's just you are not the cab-riding type of fellow."

"And you are?" he quipped.

She gestured to her costume. "In this I am."

"Don't worry, Marquis." Grady nodded. "Lady Amesbury and I have a long history. I'll take good care of her."

As they scooted out of the library, Amelia heard Simon mumble, "That's what I'm afraid of."

Chapter 14

Dear Lady Agony,

I spend my days at school and my evenings writing plays. My heart belongs to the theatre, but my parents say I must focus on the future. They wish me to become a governess, but, oh, my heart! It longs for another path. What should I do?

Devotedly,
A Playwright in Disguise

....

Dear A Playwright in Disguise,

"All the world's a stage, / And all the men and women merely players; / They have their exits and their entrances; / And one man in his time plays many parts," writes Shakespeare in *As You Like It*. What the great bard does not say is that many parts are played at the same time, and yours may be governess

and playwright. Sometimes the answer is not one or the other.
It's both. Do not limit yourself to one possibility.

Yours in Secret,
Lady Agony

Though Amelia had put on performances at the Feathered Nest, this was her most challenging role yet. To go into a house and pretend to be someone else? It would be a test of her abilities. Yet, she felt comfortable playing the part. Donning the costume seemed like an extension of her childhood, and she breathed easy moving about the city in the crowded cab.

Perhaps even easier than the Countess of Amesbury. Her title brought certain expectations she wasn't prepared for when she moved to London. When Edgar was alive, life was simple. No one looked to her to uphold the family name. But with him gone, her actions were scrutinized, and not just by Aunt Tabitha. Everywhere she went, she felt eyes upon her. But now? Now she was invisible, and it felt nice.

Better than nice.

Wonderful.

At her stop, she bid Grady goodbye and walked boldly up the front steps of the Edwardses' house, studying the edifice. It looked taller and more impressive than it had appeared two days ago. But that was her nerves talking. Determined not to let them get the best of her, she took a deep breath and knocked.

Butler Tibens was the first—and most formidable—obstacle. In some respects, Tibens was an extension of the house, which functioned much like the admiral himself. Order was demanded, and Tibens's steps resembled a march. If she could get past him, she could get past anyone.

Tall as a tree and as broad as one, too, he sized her up with a glance. As she well understood, he was not the typical wan butler. He was young and stern. By the width of his shoulders, Amelia wouldn't be surprised if the admiral had found him at the shipyard.

"Name?"

"Penelope Pinkerton." The name came out easily, for the character was one of her favorite roles as a child. Penelope was a curious girl in the Pinkerton family and part of an original skit created by Amelia's mother. Amelia imagined the inquisitive character had grown up and was looking for work. She would make a fine lady's maid. Actually, she would make a fine anything, if she put her mind to it. She was a bright, daring person.

"References, please." Tibens held out a large hand.

Dash it all! Amelia could have had Simon pen her a reference if she'd thought ahead, but in the flurry of activity she'd forgotten. She responded in the most innocent voice possible. "I'm new to London. I'm afraid I don't have any references."

Tibens let out a disappointed breath. "The admiral is only interested in *experienced* help. He'll be assisting with today's interviews."

That was interesting, since many times butlers and housekeepers interviewed male and female candidates respectively, but not altogether surprising. The admiral was the type of man who took matters into his own hands. Perhaps he'd even heard the rumors about Tibens and didn't want to take any chances with his daughter's care. Hyacinth's maid would be busy. Nonetheless, Amelia needed to leave before having to speak to him personally. She didn't want to take the chance of him recognizing her. "I have experience," promised Amelia. "I'm a hard worker."

Tibens didn't budge. He was the ultimate gatekeeper. It was yet to be seen whether or not he would allow her past the foyer. "Where?"

She went with a revised version of the truth. "I served at a respectable country inn and helped guests with their daily activities. I know how to take orders and follow rules."

His shoulders relaxed. "Have you experience, personally, with being a lady's maid?" he pressed.

She didn't dare lie to the man. "No." She lowered her voice. "But I understand discretion is of the utmost importance, especially with three young women in the home. Excuse me, two."

"The admiral does value discretion—and loyalty. I expect it." He marched forward, and she followed. They stopped at a waiting area of sorts, where one other woman sat with her hands primly folded. "Stay here," he instructed. "I don't know if you'll be interviewed or not."

Amelia gave the woman next to her a smile. She was a couple years younger than herself. "Here about the position?"

The woman turned to Amelia. Her face was bright and open, and she was eager to talk. "Oh yes. I'm excited to work for Miss Hyacinth. She's very popular. Her sister was engaged to a duke, you know."

"What about *him*?" asked Amelia, nodding in the direction that the butler left.

"Tibens?" The woman giggled. "I heard he's dreadful, but he's nice-looking, too. Lots of girls think so."

He was good-looking in a rugged sort of way. He might have turned some women's heads. Did that include Charlotte's, or even Flora's? Amelia tucked away the thought for later. She didn't have time to consider it now. "I heard the last girl made some kind of trouble for the house. Now she's working as a scullery maid."

"I heard, too." The woman lowered her voice. "But I also heard the chit had it coming. It's best not to cross Tibens. He's not known for second chances."

Tibens returned and called the woman forward. Amelia watched her enter a room with a spring in her step. She didn't know whether or not to cross her fingers for the woman and didn't have time anyway. A knock happened at the door, and a moment later Tibens greeted Henry Cosgrove, Flora's former fiancé. Tibens apologized for the interviews, but Henry said not to worry. He wasn't bothered by the commotion.

"I only need a moment of the admiral's time," the duke explained. "I can wait here."

"Of course." Tibens gave him a short bow.

"Thank you." Henry remained in the entry, eyeing a piece of naval memorabilia on the wall. As he turned, he spied Amelia looking at him.

She lowered her gaze. Never having been formally introduced, she was trying to soak in as many details as possible: brown hair, small eyes, distinguished chin, lean build. She didn't realize she was being so obvious.

"Hello there," Henry greeted.

Amelia kept her head down. "Hello."

"It's warm out today." His voice was cordial and unassuming. "Summer is almost here certainly."

Thankfully, their conversation was cut short when the admiral entered the foyer. The two men enjoyed a brisk handshake before entering another room. Amelia could almost hear their conversation—almost. *If only she were a little closer.* She glanced up the steps. No one was around, so she stood and stretched. When that went without incident, she inched a few toe lengths toward the room. It sounded as if Henry wanted to create a commemorative garden for Flora.

"I appreciate the gesture, I truly do." The admiral was talking. "And no one deserves it more than my Flora. But the pomp of it, Cosgrove. It doesn't sit well with me. The ostentation."

"I understand." There was a slight hoarseness to Henry's voice. He cleared his throat. "If it is a matter of cost—"

"It's not." The admiral was adamant and perhaps a little incensed.

After a moment, Henry added, "It just feels as if I should be doing something. I *need* to do something."

"Yes, you do," the admiral agreed. "You need to move on with your life. It will be hard, but you must. Remember, I lost my wife when I was quite young. I have experience with grief."

Outside the door, Amelia winced. The words were true but perhaps a little harsh, especially for a recent death. She knew from her own experience it took much longer than a couple of weeks to move on.

"How can you say that?" Henry was incredulous. "She was your eldest daughter, the heart and soul of this house. Do you not care?"

"Of course I care, but what can I do? No amount of mourning or flowers or gardens will bring her back. Time marches on. We must do the same."

The room went silent. A creak came from upstairs. Should she return to her seat? The seconds ticked by without another occurrence.

"The garden will go forward with or without your approval,"

continued Henry. "It's the right thing. To do nothing looks un-caring at the least, unaffected at worst."

The admiral let loose a harsh chuckle. "Is that what this is about? The way her death *reflects* on you?"

A curse escaped Henry's lips, and Amelia covered her mouth. Death brought out the best in people, but unfortunately it also brought out the worst. When Edgar died, she'd bitten her lip many times. People could say the stupidest things that cut to the bone. And tensions were high, especially among people who were hurt the most. She had to assume that was what this spat was about. Still, part of her wondered if it was something more. Could one of them be right, or both?

"Explain yourself, miss."

Tibens's heavy hand was on her shoulder, and Amelia tensed. "I was . . . uh . . . wondering if it was my turn to see the house-keeper."

Tibens spun her around, his lightning-blue eyes piercing hers. "Wrong room. Tell me what you heard."

Amelia tugged out of his grasp. "Nothing. I didn't hear a thing."

Tibens grabbed her wrist. "If a word of gossip gets out about this, I'll find you."

"And do what?" Amelia held her chin high. Even though she was playing a role, she was incensed for Penelope. Why should Penelope—or any woman—have to subject themselves to this treatment for work? It wasn't fair, and it wasn't right. Who knew what Charlotte had been put through?

Tibens pushed her toward the door. "Utter a word, and you will find out."

Amelia straightened her apron and walked shakily down the steps. Inside a cab was the last place she wanted to be just now.

She needed to clear her head before returning home. Winifred would be waiting for her, and right now Amelia was too upset to see her.

The bustle of the streets and the movement of people was salve to her soul. She peeked in store windows, said hello to street vendors, and watched babies and their nurses stroll along Hyde Park. After a half hour, she felt her shoulders relax. It was always that way with the city. The pulse, its lively heart, restored her own.

When she returned to Mayfair, she felt better and was glad for the new information. Avoiding the front door, she sneaked in the servants' entrance. It was normal for a maid to use it. But Amelia felt odd, like a guest in her own house.

She made a mental note to talk to her staff about how much they meant, how her home was their home. Working at a family business like the Feathered Nest was different because the inn *was* truly her property, the employers her family. Until she walked up the back steps dressed as a maid, she hadn't completely realized the implications for her help. She did now.

Inside, she took off her wig and stuffed it under her arm, glad to be rid of its extra warmth. She was preparing to do the same for the apron when a familiar voice froze her stiff.

"Amelia Amesbury! In the name of God, what are you doing?"

She had no choice but to turn around and face the wrath of Aunt Tabitha.

Chapter 15

Dear Lady Agony,

Clear up a disagreement between my sister and me. She says all lies are evil. I say some lies are necessary. What do you say?

Devotedly,
No Two Lies Are the Same

. . . .

Dear No Two Lies Are the Same,

There is the lie you tell your friend about the ruffles on her dress, and the lie you tell your mother about her singing voice. Then there is the lie you tell the shop owner about the missing banknote, and the one you tell yourself on your wedding day. Thus, I say you are right. No two lies are the same. Just be careful which lie you allow to pass your lips.

Yours in Secret,
Lady Agony

Amelia had faced Aunt Tabitha's disapproval before, but it didn't make it any easier. She hated disappointing the older woman. With each wrong move, Amelia imagined Tabitha ticking off a point. The misspoken words, the faux pas, the occasional brandy—Amelia couldn't have many more points to spare. At least in the past she'd had a reasonable excuse for her behavior. Someone had offended a person or cause for which she cared deeply. Standing in the back entry, dressed in Lettie's uniform, she couldn't think of a single reason for being in disguise. So she decided to ignore the obvious.

"Good afternoon, Aunt Tabitha." Amelia took off the apron and folded it under her arm. "I've been out walking."

Tabitha wore a lavender-gray dress with stiff ruffles at the neck and sleeves. The color made her face almost alabaster. Her eyes, looking more gray than blue, narrowed on Amelia. "In a maid's uniform."

It wasn't a question, and Amelia couldn't deny it. Why would she be dressed in a maid's costume? There was only one reason she could think of, and it was solid. "I'm trying out a costume for Kitty's ball. You know the party is the day after next, and I still have nothing to wear. It looks as if this dress is passable as a disguise. And good news, it's black."

Tabitha gripped her jeweled cane, the one that Amelia thought would hurt the most if she were ever conked over the head with it. "You cannot attend the ball in *that*."

"Why? You couldn't object to the color."

Tabitha harrumphed. "What are you hiding?"

"Before we continue this conversation, I need to change." Amelia smiled. "I'll be back in a moment."

"Meet me upstairs," instructed Tabitha. "I need my tea, and Winifred is going to perform."

Amelia proceeded to her bedroom and flopped onto her bed

with a sigh. "Amelia Amesbury, how do you get yourself into these messes?" For several minutes, she stared at the carved birds on her heavy, ornate bedstead. They had no answers because there was no answer to give. It was just who she was. You could take the girl out of the Feathered Nest, but you couldn't take the Feathered Nest out of the girl. Some parts of her would always be as nonsensical as the countryside.

She slipped out of Lettie's dress and into her own gray frock. She smoothed her auburn hair, fixing the loose strands. Then she hurried to meet Tabitha, who was waiting stiffly in a floral chair. Amelia chose the settee, waiting for the maid to finish with tea before she spoke. "Ah! Lemon cakes, my favorite."

Tabitha lowered her gaze, willing her to speak.

Amelia had a feeling if she reached for the tart, Tabitha would bang her fingers with her cane. She leaned back into the settee, noting how soft it felt in contrast to Tabitha's hard stare. "Aunt Tabitha, I'm sorry. I don't know what else to say. I always disappoint you."

Her face changed to one of surprise. "You do not disappoint me. I never said that."

"You didn't have to."

Tabitha let the information settle for a moment. "I have my duties, and the Amesbury name is one I take very seriously. I do not want to see it jeopardized. That's all."

"I would never," promised Amelia, and she meant it. "I know how important it is for Winifred. Edgar entrusted her to me. That must mean something to you."

"It does. Of course it does." She took a tart from the tray, dusting off a smudge of powdered sugar. "But I have seen a change in you, and not just the jewelry. It concerns me."

Amelia reached for a lemon cake. "I'll never change in my love for the Amesbury family. You can count on that."

They enjoyed their sweets in silence. After a few minutes, Tabitha continued. "I understand the need for a costume at Kitty's ball. You've been in mourning two years now. I considered you might not want to wear gray to the fete."

Amelia quit chewing.

"Still," she added quickly, "you must be careful in your attire. You should wear something that fits your station, and before you argue, I don't mean that in a pretentious way."

Tabitha stood and walked over to a table behind the settee. Amelia noticed the lamp was gone. A large box replaced it. Tabitha pointed to the package with her walking stick. "Shakespeare's Titania, for example, would be quite appropriate." She lifted the lid to reveal a beautiful fairy's costume.

Amelia rushed over to look. The dress was white gossamer, with a swath of pastel flowers encircling the skirt, and wings as delicate as the flower petals. The crown was a stunning achievement of gold and matching flowers.

"I don't know what to say. Thank you, Aunt!" Caught up in the excitement, she embraced Tabitha. The older woman's spine went stiff with shock.

"Do not thank me, dear." Tabitha patted her back. "Thank Lord Bainbridge."

Amelia released her. "What?"

Tabitha held up the crown. It glinted in the sunlight. "He sent the package by personal messenger."

"Simon Bainbridge?" Amelia shook her head. "How could he know my size?"

Tabitha dismissed the question. "It's easy enough to ascertain. He *is* a marquis and has the best tailor in the city. It would be as simple as one dressmaker contacting another."

Simon really doesn't like my gray dresses.

She *had* joked about him taking up the task of convincing Tabitha it was time for a change. He'd obviously taken the jest to heart. Amelia picked up a satin slipper. White as snow and as soft as silk, it was the loveliest thing she'd ever seen or owned. Her wardrobe had been drastically abridged by Edgar's death. Since then, she'd worn black frocks and sensible shoes. And even before, if she were being honest. His health problems made fancy clothes seem silly and unnecessary at the time, and she'd never been one for fashion anyway. She was too active as a child and young adult to fuss with clothes.

Tabitha handed her a small black locket with a wisp of Edgar's hair. The memento would represent Edgar's passing. "You might attach it to a necklace or pin."

"An excellent idea," Amelia agreed. "I shall wear it always."

Winifred and Miss Walters joined them in the drawing room. When Winifred saw the dress, she squealed and rushed over to inspect it. Miss Walters stood by the pianoforte, patiently waiting.

"Is this yours?" asked Winifred, her voice full of wonder and curiosity.

Amelia nodded. "It's my costume for Mrs. Hamsted's ball."

"May I?" Winifred's hand hovered over the box.

"Of course." Amelia took out the wings and held them to Winifred's back. "Now you can fly."

"They're lovely!" Winifred giggled. "After the ball, may I try them on?"

"If you're careful, you may borrow them. They're expensive and should be used again."

Winifred nodded. "I will be careful. I promise."

"Aunt Tabitha tells me you're going to perform for us." Amelia motioned toward the pianoforte. "We're eager to hear you play."

Winifred gave the gown one more longing look before walking to the instrument.

Governess Walters pulled out the bench, and Amelia and Tabitha took their seats. Winifred threw them a glance over her shoulder.

Amelia smiled encouragingly.

Winifred began to play, and Amelia's mind was transported to Somerset. Singing, dancing, performing—she loved music in a house. It made a home come alive, and she couldn't wait for Winifred's recital. It was going to be more than a recital; it would be a celebration. Which reminded her: she needed to talk to the baker about the special sweets she'd ordered for Winifred's young guests. She also needed to talk to Cook about the punch. Winifred loved cherry, but red would not go over well with mothers of younger children. She made a mental note to find a substitute.

Amelia's attention returned to the room. The notes were coming faster and faster. Watching Winifred's fingers fly over the keys, Amelia felt her heartbeat increase. Winifred had not slowed her pace. Was it Aunt Tabitha who had her spooked? Amelia gave her a side glance. Playing for her would be hard, but many older women like Tabitha would be at the recital. Winifred needed to overcome her fear of playing in public if she was going to be a musician.

Winifred missed a few notes. Then she missed a few more and stopped. She turned a teary face toward them. "I'm sorry!"

Amelia walked to the pianoforte and patted Winifred's

golden head. Winifred was holding back her tears with sheer willpower, and Amelia was worried for her. "There's nothing to be sorry about, dear. Take your time. I'm not going anywhere, and neither is Auntie."

Winifred shook her head. "I can't do it. You'll have to cancel the recital."

"Don't be foolish, Winifred," scolded Aunt Tabitha. "It will be fine."

"A concert cannot be canceled." The governess's normally bland face pinkened with embarrassment or irritation. It was hard to tell which.

Winifred gaped at Amelia in fear.

Amelia sat down on the bench so the girl didn't need to crane her neck. "*Anything* can be canceled. I'm not going to force you into something you're not ready for. It is my decision."

Miss Walters sucked in a breath. Aunt Tabitha coughed.

Amelia ignored them. She clasped Winifred's hand. "The thing is, I know you are ready. I've heard you play. You are meant to share your music. Whether it's today, tomorrow, or next year does not matter to me."

"A year!" exclaimed Winifred. "I could not wait that long. These songs will be too easy by then."

"True," said Amelia. "But maybe easy is good. Maybe that's what you want." Amelia knew very well it was not what the girl wanted. Once she progressed past a piece, she rarely played it again. Whatever went on in her mind was between her and the instrument.

Winifred squared her shoulders. "Let me try again."

"Of course." Amelia stood. "Aunt Tabitha and I will be over there having tea and reading the paper. Don't mind us."

Amelia grabbed the morning's paper before returning to her chair. She made sure to rustle the pages as she sat down.

Winifred began playing the first measures, timidly at first, then more assuredly. Amelia turned a page, but she was keenly listening to Winifred. They all were. When Winifred played, it was hard to ignore her. She had a gift for music, and it poured out of her like an angel. It should be shared with others and would be—but not until Winifred was ready. Amelia would make certain of that.

Chapter 16

Dear Lady Agony,

I have been invited to one of the most anticipated balls of the season and require a dress to match. When I inquired at my usual dressmaker's, they informed me the number of flounces I need cannot be done in time. What am I to do? Should I put my faith in another dressmaker, who promises it can be done? Or should I demand the dress from my own seamstress, risking offense and hasty workmanship?

Devotedly,
A Troubled Dancer

....

Dear A Troubled Dancer,

If you go through with either plan, you risk more than poor workmanship. You risk a young girl's health. Would you feel good in a dress sewn with the bloody fingers of a girl who got no

sleep or meals because of it? I should hope not. Besides,
flounces are cumbersome things when it comes to dancing. Forgo
them and be satisfied with what is available. If you decide
otherwise, please do not write to me again, for I do not corre-
spond with vain fools.

Yours in Secret,
Lady Agony

The day of Kitty's ball, Amelia couldn't decide who liked the costume more, she or Lettie. Lettie flitted around the room, gathering undergarments, stockings, and pins like a fairy herself. Her face reminded Amelia of Mrs. Addington's when she tight-laced a corset. Determined, officious, and a little bit smug, she was definitely her mother's daughter. When Amelia tried to help with the tissue paper that shaped the skirt, Lettie insisted on doing it herself.

Lettie pulled the dress out of reach. "Let me, my lady. The gown is white, and you're used to wearing black. You might smudge it."

Amelia laughed. "You do realize that *I'll* be the one wearing it, don't you?"

"I know," Lettie grumbled. "And you need to be careful. One step in the wrong direction, and you'll be covered in punch."

"I'm not an ogre," said Amelia. "I think I can manage."

"But it's been so long," Lettie fretted. "What if you've forgotten?"

"Forgotten what? How to avoid the punch bowl?"

"No. How to dance."

A spike of terror pierced her heart. *Dance.* She wouldn't be dancing, would she? Not so long ago, there wouldn't have been a question. Of course she would dance. At the Feathered Nest, her family would push back the chairs after dinner service, her sister Sarah (the best pianist of the four girls) would pull up a seat to the well-worn keys, her father would get his violin, and they would dance and sing the night away. Amelia could still hear the laughter of her youngest sister, Margaret, as she spun her around to "Home, Sweet Home!" Margaret was as light as a balloon and just as fun. How they'd enjoyed themselves.

But now.

Amelia sat down on the side of the bed. She loved to dance and was good at it, but Lettie was right. She hadn't danced in a long time. Things had changed, including the dances. Suddenly she felt much older than twenty-five years.

"Don't you worry," encouraged Lettie. "You can practice on me. I'm a good leader. All my women friends tell me so."

"Thank you, Lettie, but I'll be fine." Amelia unlaced her boots. "I'm just glad to be going. Chances are, I won't be dancing. I am a widow and a mother. I'll be with the other matrons, talking about the weather or soup or whatever it is they talk about." A boot dropped to the floor. "I guess I'll find out."

Lettie put the boot aside. "Come now, Lady Amesbury. You aren't like them. You'll never settle for the weather. Besides, you're only a few years younger than I am."

"There are certain expectations . . ." started Amelia.

"Nonsense." Lettie pulled at her stocking. "You don't care a fig about expectations. You never have. But it's okay to be afraid, my lady. I would be, too."

"I'm not afraid," Amelia declared, because she never was. As she uttered the words, however, she heard their falseness. Lettie was right. The thought of dancing terrified her, for it was one she had needed not consider when she was draped in black. No one dared ask her.

Face it. It was easier to tell Winifred not to be afraid than to admit her own fears. Dancing at the Feathered Nest was a distant memory, a mélange of the flickering stone fireplace, the well-worn pianoforte, and her father's rich timbre. She had been a wife, a caretaker for her dying husband, and was now a widow and mother. Could she be those things and young, too?

She wasn't sure, and it didn't matter. Simon was the only man she'd been in contact with lately, and he certainly didn't want to get close to her, if his actions in the carriage were any indication. Like her, he hadn't danced in years. Maybe he was right to close himself off altogether. Balls were popular with the young and inexperienced, which didn't exactly describe either of them. They weren't there to see or be seen. But one person Amelia could not wait to see was Kitty. When her friend spied her costume, she would be undone.

Lettie helped with the other boot. "If you change your mind, you know where I'll be. I know all the popular dances."

Amelia smiled. "You are a good friend, Lettie. I appreciate it."

Lettie gave her a nod. "Friend or not, if you spill on this costume, I'll send my mother to scold you, and you know she will."

"Cross my heart, I will not spill."

After Amelia was dressed, Lettie started on her hair. She piled Amelia's auburn locks on top of her head, in the opening of the fairy crown, allowing a few natural tendrils to escape around her face. Glancing in the mirror, Amelia was amazed at the result. If fairies were real, she imagined this is what they would look like. The fabric, the flowers, the fantasy. If she could live it for one night, it would be worth Lettie's efforts—and Simon's. She had rushed off a note to him immediately but couldn't wait to thank him in person. Without his thoughtfulness, she might be in her gray dress, or Lettie's black one.

She didn't have to wait long, for soon Simon was downstairs, talking to Tabitha. She recognized his voice immediately. The deep tone, the easy chuckle. He was there to escort her and Tabitha to the ball, but he might also have news about Charlotte. After giving Lettie a quick hug, she hurried to join them, or hurried as much as she could in wings and a crown.

"Good evening, my lord. Aunt Tabitha."

Simon sucked in a breath when he saw her. Recovering quickly, he gave her a short bow. "You look stunning, Countess."

"This dress is beyond compare," said Amelia. "I don't know how to thank you."

"It fits well," added Aunt Tabitha. "Please send my regards to the seamstress."

"I will." Simon was clothed in his Royal Navy dress uniform. The deep blue jacket framed his broad shoulders, and the brass buttons shone brand-new. He looked like a marquis, all hints of a seafaring pirate erased by the authority of the uniform. Except for his playful green eyes. Creased from squinting into the sunlight, they told the story of a man who spent his time on deck with his men. And drank rum.

"Your suit is handsome as well," Amelia complimented. Tabitha, dressed appropriately as a bumblebee, shot her a look, and Amelia realized the poor word choice. "I mean gallant—respectable. And, Aunt Tabitha, your costume couldn't be any better. It suits you."

"It does." Tabitha had exchanged her cane for a black walking stick with a faux point at one end and held it to the side to show off her mostly black dress with thin gold stripes. Two antennae were pinned in her hair. Though pretty, like a bee, she could sting if she or the Amesbury name was threatened.

Simon held out his arm. "Shall we?"

Amelia took Simon's arm, strong and warm, and Tabitha trailed closely behind them. Too closely. When they got to the carriage, she sat squarely next to Amelia, placing her walking stick in front of her, as if drawing an imaginary line between Amelia and Simon. Feeling like a young girl, Amelia tried not to giggle.

Instead, she focused on the city outside the window. When it came to social etiquette, Tabitha could be downright archaic. Though as for that, many widows remarried quite quickly. Without their husbands' wealth or property, usually given to other male relatives, they had to. Fortunately, Edgar understood the dilemma perfectly and accounted for it in his will, leaving Amelia everything that wasn't entailed. Regardless, Tabitha's strict adherence to convention wouldn't tamper Amelia's fun tonight. For the first time in over two years, she felt like herself, and it was wonderful. If an opportunity to disappear presented itself, she would take it.

Disappearing would be easy, if the flowers at Kitty's house were any indication. Tabitha's florist had come through splendidly. Pink roses were on display in every room, festooning the stair railing, the balcony, and the ballroom entrance. Everything was lovely, including Kitty, who was at once recognizable as Queen Elizabeth. Her husband, Oliver, was also dressed as a royal, if his crooked crown was to be trusted. Though, to be honest, he looked pretty much the same as always, with shinier buttons.

Simon handed off their cloaks to a footman, and Tabitha excused herself. She needed to use the ladies' dressing room to redo a pin in her bee's bonnet.

"Your costume!" Kitty gave Amelia's hands a quick squeeze. "I don't dare risk a wrinkle." She twirled Amelia in a circle. "It's perfect." Then, glancing in Tabitha's direction, she added, "How did you manage white?"

"It wasn't me," whispered Amelia. "It was Lord Bainbridge. He had it sent over. Aunt Tabitha had no choice but to agree."

"Smart," Kitty congratulated.

Oliver shook Simon's hand. "Bainbridge. It's nice to see you again. Thank you for coming."

"You as well," said Simon. "By the way, I read your recent book on naval history. Very thorough and educational. Well done."

"I'm glad you enjoyed it." Oliver indicated the twittering group of girls near the entrance of the ballroom. "It looks as if your attendance has been duly noted. Thanks to you, our fete will be talked about all season. My wife will be pleased."

Amelia realized the *ton* must be shocked to see Simon out in public. If he was on the marriage market again, mothers and daughters weren't going to miss an opportunity. Poor Simon. No wonder he avoided dances. Until now, she hadn't thought about the enormous pressure such an event placed on bachelors.

"It's not me they're talking about," Simon corrected. "It's Lady Amesbury. They had no idea she knew another color but black."

"Very possibly," agreed Oliver. "She's been stuck in it too long, if you ask me."

Kitty gave her husband a smile, linking her arm in his as they walked into the ballroom. Simon and Amelia followed. "No one is asking you for fashion advice, dear."

"It's warm in here." Simon wiped his brow. "What would you like for a refreshment?"

"Punch," Amelia requested. "No, wait—champagne, please."

"Good choice," said Simon.

"If I spill on this costume, my maid will never forgive me."

"Champagne for me, too," Kitty told Oliver, and the men went off to fetch the drinks. When they were alone, Kitty turned to Amelia. "Thank Tabitha for me, will you? If it weren't for her, I don't know what I would have done about the flowers. After a word from her, these arrived as if by magical wand." She motioned to the rose bouquet near the refreshments.

"I will."

"And thank the marquis," added Kitty. "Without his intervention, you might have been in mourning garb for the rest of your life—maybe longer." She fluttered her eyelashes. "I wonder at his motivation?"

Amelia smirked at her friend. "Sympathy, I'm sure. Nothing more."

"Oh, it's *something* more." Kitty's gaze followed the direction of the men. "The last time Oliver bought me a dress was . . . well, never. Though I must say, I don't mind." She cleared her throat, where a chuckle had stuck. "He does not have the sharpest eye for fashion."

Love must make one dumb and blind. However, Kitty's ignorance was the most enduring aspect of her and Oliver's relationship. Kitty cared about fashion to a fault. She loved expensive clothes and looked good in them. Amelia had known her to spend two hours in Lock & Co. Hatters, selecting between a blue and a periwinkle bonnet. Oliver, on the other hand, always looked a little—Amelia followed his steps with her eyes—slapdash. Despite Kitty's best efforts, he often had a shoe untied or shirt collar folded over. The consummate distracted scholar. Yet Kitty was oblivious to his fashion faux pas.

Simon returned with her champagne. "You'll never guess whom I saw."

"Whom?" asked Amelia.

"Henry Cosgrove." Simon nodded toward the refreshment table. From the look of his bright red coat, heavily embordered in gold, and blue sash, the duke was dressed as Louis XV.

"The poor fellow." Kitty took her champagne from Oliver. "Two weeks in mourning, and already the mamas are after him. I have seen him shrug off two inquiries." She took a dainty sip. "They ought to be ashamed of themselves."

"My question is: Why attend at all?" asked Oliver.

"Indeed," agreed Simon.

Kitty swatted Oliver's arm. "My parties are quite popular, if you didn't notice. It's the only costume ball of the season."

Kitty was right. Costume parties were dwindling, which made Kitty's ball even more special—and popular. No one wanted to miss the opportunity to imitate their favorite kings, queens, and royalty, especially the *ton*. Amelia had counted three Marie Antoinettes, two Queen Elizabeths, and one Queen Victoria already.

"I'd wager it was Cosgrove's mother who gave him a shove." Oliver's eyes trailed Henry into the crowd. "I've heard she's adamant the tragedy does not affect the season. Her husband died young, and she's anxious for more grandchildren."

"It very well may have been," said Simon. "Parents present their own set of challenges and expectations."

Amelia sneaked a glance at Simon's face. The change in his jawline, tense and rigid, told the story. As a firstborn son, he could relate to Henry's challenges. Death was tragic, but life moved on, and wealthy sons were expected to move with it. They had to fulfill their obligations at all costs, putting their own feelings and desires aside.

Kitty smiled, nodding toward a grouping of chairs. "Aunts, too."

Amelia followed Kitty's indication. Aunt Tabitha was walking a straight line in their direction, the firm plunk of her walking cane clearing a path. Amelia sighed. In a matter of moments, she would be whisked away to talk about all the things she didn't want to talk about. She didn't entertain, she loathed embroidery, and she could think of nothing worse than her cooking skills. What would she have to discuss with the other matrons? She supposed she was about to find out.

Simon set down his glass of champagne and held out his hand. "I believe now is the perfect time for a dance. Lady Amesbury, would you do me the honor?"

Amelia blinked. "I haven't danced in years."

"We shall make a proper pair, then, because neither have I."

"She's getting closer . . ." Kitty said under her breath.

Amelia waffled. She would like to dance, very much, but felt as if she was pushing her luck. First the dress, now a dance? Aunt Tabitha would lecture her from now until kingdom come about what widows did and did not do. She was fairly certain dancing was on the did-not-do list.

Simon arched a dark brow. "You're not going to refuse a marquis, are you? What would Aunt Tabitha say?"

Amelia took a drink of her champagne and handed it to Kitty. "You leave me no choice, my lord. Consider your toes forewarned."

Chapter 17

Dear Lady Agony,

I need to know. Is it best to talk to one's partner when dancing or not? I've heard many differing opinions but trust yours. May I have it?

Devotedly,
A Sparkling Conversationalist

. . . .

Dear A Sparkling Conversationalist,

I surmise from your signature that you like to talk, which gives me pause, for I have found most people who like to talk do so incessantly. Though it is always best to follow your partner's lead in this matter, I would advise caution in your case. If you talk too much, you might just talk your way out of a second dance, and that would leave you nowhere but the perimeter of the dance floor.

Yours in Secret,
Lady Agony

Simon might have been out of practice, but Amelia wouldn't have known it by the way he twirled her around the dance floor. His moves were as effortless as walking. Strong and assured, his hands told her which way to turn, and soon her shoulders relaxed and her feet lightened, and she forgot to worry about stepping on his toes. Instead, she enjoyed the perfumed scent of roses as they passed under a particularly large swath and the sound of the orchestra, happy and blissfully loud. It was easy not to hear the whispers of other dancers while the music played. Still, she caught pieces of them as they weaved in and out of dance-floor traffic. Of course, she expected it. Simon was the Marquis of Bainbridge, after all, and hadn't attended a ball in an age. And while she attended events sporadically, she hadn't been seen on a dance floor in London . . . ever. Edgar had been too ill to attend events, and partygoers were eager to see the elusive Countess of Amesbury in action.

"I hope you don't mind my speaking." Simon twirled her. "If you find it too difficult to dance and converse at the same time, please let me know."

Amelia noted the mirth in his green eyes as he guided her around a corner. If fairies had magic, she was starting to feel their power. "I think I can manage."

"Your presence is causing quite a commotion in certain circles," he murmured.

"Me?" Amelia shook her head, then remembered her fairy crown and checked the action. "It's you they are whispering about. I understand you are quite popular with the female crowd."

"My *title* is quite popular," Simon corrected. "There's a difference."

"I'll admit I've never understood the obsession myself," she said. "Certainly, wealth makes life easier. I will say that. But it doesn't guarantee happiness. Sometimes, it's just the opposite. It makes a muddle of everything."

Simon was quiet for a moment, and she wondered if she'd been too outspoken. Too forthright. Amelia hated censoring herself; she thought they could be honest with each other. Their motives had been laid bare. Couldn't their words, too?

Simon pulled her a hair's breadth closer, his hand warm on her waist. "You're a brilliant dancer—too brilliant to be stuck in the matron's corner, drinking punch. You should dance at every opportunity."

Amelia was glad for the sound of his voice and the change of topic. "I haven't had many opportunities. It wouldn't have been proper to partake during mourning."

His jaw tightened, and she wondered if the admission bothered him. Did he still blame himself for encouraging Edgar's marriage to a young innocent? She hoped not. The decision was hers alone. Even if she could have, she wouldn't have changed it. Edgar's illness had taken the romance out of their marriage. But it had also given her maturity and motherhood, two aspects she never expected and now greatly appreciated.

"You will have many opportunities tonight." His eyes narrowed on a man as they passed him. "That ruffian has not been able to take his eyes off you the entire waltz."

Amelia glanced over her shoulder at the young man in spectacles. "Him?" She laughed. "I wouldn't exactly call him a ruffian. Besides, Kitty strictly forbids ruffians in her ballrooms. Trust me."

"Ruffians come in many shapes, sizes, and titles."

"And glasses?" Amelia chuckled. "That man looks no older than a schoolboy."

"A schoolboy with desires," added Simon. "Remember what I said."

"Um-hum." As they turned, Amelia noticed another man, this one talking to Henry Cosgrove. If a ruffian did get past Kitty, it was he. Dressed in a pirate's costume, the man was shaped like an oak tree and probably as strong as one, too. His tight breeches and torn shirt revealed the extent of his muscles. The men weren't exactly arguing, but there was something menacing in the pirate's attitude. "Who's he, in the pirate costume?"

Simon checked her direction. "That's Jacobus Stephens, but don't call him that to his face. It's Jack to everyone but those who want their jaws broken. He served under the admiral for many years. His older brother is a captain with several years of service in the Royal Navy. A good family with many sons. I believe he is the youngest."

Simon drew her closer as they passed the crush of people, expertly leading her out—or into—danger, depending on how one looked at it. His hands steered her to an empty alcove, where dancers seemed to dissolve like snowflakes on the warm ground.

She fumbled her feet, not speaking for a moment. The press of his chest and the scent of the sea briefly muddled her senses. Somehow Simon smelled like the ocean, and it was thrilling. She couldn't remember the last time she had danced this close to a man before remembering she hadn't, not like this. His touch was fire. It sparked something in her she didn't know existed, a feeling that had lain dormant until he brought it to life.

Their eyes met, and for a moment she wished they hadn't. She was certain hers betrayed her intoxication. A youthful curiosity. It wasn't right for her to feel this way, and in the middle of a London ballroom, no less. Refusing to repeat her previous mistake, she dropped her gaze over his shoulder and perused the ballroom anew.

Henry and Jack were walking toward the balcony. She needed to see where their conversation was headed. "I feel warm. Let's get some air."

Taking her cue, Simon quickly led her off the dance floor, but when he spotted Henry and Jack, his concern changed to chagrin. "Ah. I understand. You mean to eavesdrop on Jack and the duke."

"Shh," she quieted him. "Not so loud."

The night was clear, and a wide ribbon of stars dusted the sky. The heady scent of honeysuckle wafted up from the colorful gardens, inviting guests to descend the stairs and enjoy a stroll through the well-manicured lawns. Some pairs did. Some disappeared behind the hedges, undetected. Years ago, she would've wished to join them. Whom was she kidding? She still wished to join them. But where were Henry and Jack? They couldn't have traveled far.

"Do you feel better?" asked Simon, his voice filled with mirth.

Despite his teasing tone, she nodded. The cool air was nice on her shoulders, and she felt more like herself, or at least more clearheaded.

She scanned the area, listening for Jack's or Henry's voice. Simon said Jack worked under the admiral's command, and Henry was engaged to the admiral's daughter. Could there be a connection? "Do you think they could've been arguing about the Edwardses earlier?"

"I doubt it." Simon's voice held a note of surprise. "Jack's combative by nature. Think of him as a rooster with his tail feathers up."

"But they both know the admiral."

"In different capacities, yes," Simon conceded.

"So they could have been discussing him."

"Jack Stephens is a navy man. Henry Cosgrove isn't. What business would Jack have with him?"

Amelia folded her hands on the cool stone of the balcony. "It's just a feeling I have. When I was at the Edwardses' house, the admiral and Cosgrove exchanged words about a memorial garden in Flora's name. The admiral did not take to the duke's suggestion. He was strongly averse to it."

Simon leaned his back against the railing. "I'm afraid there's nothing suspicious about the admiral's reaction. Your feelings are perhaps best reserved for your letters."

The statement lighted her internal fuse. "What makes you say that?"

"Because," Simon explained, "the admiral is a man who cherishes privacy. A memorial garden and pretentious ceremony would upset that. Cosgrove's heart is in the right place. It's just not how it's done with navy men."

"Of course, it's not how it is done with navy men. Why didn't I think of that?" She tapped her chin, feigning perplexity. "All those *feelings* of mine must be getting in the way." Rolling her eyes, she turned toward the steps.

Simon was fast on her heels.

She froze on the first landing. It was Jack and Henry. They were arguing near the hedge. She and Simon ducked out of the light.

"I don't know what you want from me, Stephens," said Henry. "I've told you everything I know."

"It isn't enough," Jack shot back. "No one falls ill from a glass of champagne."

"Ask the admiral yourself, then." Henry's voice rose in defense. "You were present. I don't know what else to tell you."

"You must have seen something. *Something* made Flora sick."

Silence shot through the air like a bullet, and Simon and Amelia exchanged a look of understanding. Things were about to get heated.

"What did you say?" Henry asked.

"I said something made her sick," repeated Jack.

"No." The word was a hammer, shattering the calm night. "You said '*Flora.*'"

"So what if I did?" Jack was unconcerned about etiquette. His voice didn't budge an inch. "I've known her all my life. She went with the admiral to the shipping yard since she was a girl. Excuse me, *Your Grace*, for forgoing the title."

"You bastard," Henry spat. "You loved her, didn't you?"

A moment beat past, betraying the truth.

"I ought to kill you." Henry ground out the words. "She was my fiancée. *Mine.*"

Jack laughed, a dark, angry sound. "Name the time and place. You'd be dead before your hand reached your pistol, and you know it."

Amelia looked to Simon. He nodded, and she understood what Jack said was true.

"I'll let you get by with that this once because you were her friend. But if you ever come near me again—if you so much as say her name—I will come after you with all I have," warned Henry. "Do you hear me? You will not disrespect her memory."

Jack grunted, shuffling his feet.

With the movement, Simon pulled Amelia farther into the darkness, and a breath caught in her throat. She hadn't been this close to a man in a dark corner—well, ever. For a split second, she forgot all about the argument and wondered what might have happened under different circumstances. Letters from readers gave her plenty of ideas.

Then Henry walked past them, and she was back in the present. Jack stalked away in the other direction, toward the garden, perhaps leaving for the night.

When they were gone, Amelia released the breath she was holding. "It looks as if you owe me an apology."

Simon's brow furrowed.

"My hunch was right," she explained. "There *is* something between them. Admit it."

Simon gave a slight nod. "I concede the point. I will never underestimate the power of female intuition again."

She flung him a smile over her shoulder as she walked up the stairs. "Wise decision."

Chapter 18

Dear Lady Agony,

My mother says I shan't kiss a man until I'm married. That it will ruin my chances of a decent match. But what if the boy I would like to kiss is the match? Is it acceptable to kiss him before marriage? You're a modern woman. What are your thoughts?

Devotedly,
Longing for a Kiss

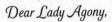

Dear Longing for a Kiss,

I've devoted many a response to kissing, near kissing, and longing to kiss. Personally, I do not see all the fuss. This putting one's lips to another's has ruined far more girls than it has satisfied. Why risk it? My advice is this: do not kiss that

boy until your wedding day. Until then, he may welch on his
promise and leave you with nothing but wet lips.

Yours in Secret,
Lady Agony

Upon returning to the ballroom, Amelia was hailed by Kitty, who swerved in and out of clusters of people to reach her. Simon bid her goodbye before clapping a friend on the back, greeting him with a hearty hello. And just like that, the adventure was over, and she was back to ordinary life, which had taken an extraordinary turn. Not only did she understand the personal nature of Flora and Jack's relationship, she finally understood why so many readers were obsessed with ballrooms, balconies, and beckoning gardens.

And what about the question Jack Stephens had asked Henry Cosgrove? What had made Flora ill the night of her death? Both men had cared for Flora. That much was revealed by their conversation. But had Jack cared too deeply? He *had* used her Christian name, which meant they were familiar, perhaps too familiar for Henry's liking. She needed to find out in what capacity Jack knew Flora. But not now. Right now, Kitty was approaching, wearing a look of dread on her face, and Amelia saw in a moment why. Behind her was Aunt Tabitha, parting the crowd like the Red Sea with her walking stick.

"She's coming," whispered Kitty. "Get ready. I said you were in the water closet."

"I'm a grown woman, for goodness' sake." Amelia straightened her shoulders. "I do not need to be looked after like a child." But her courage faded as the elder woman came into sight.

Tabitha's perseverance was marked by every line on her face. "Hello, Aunt. I was in the water closet."

Tabitha shook her head. "Never mind that. I need you to come with me."

"What's wrong?" asked Amelia.

"Remember that woman you asked me about, Flora Edwards?"

Amelia nodded.

"One of the matrons you've been so successfully avoiding has told me an interesting tidbit about the night of her death." Tabitha leaned in on her cane. "That evening, Miss Flora had an argument with one of her sister's suitors. If she hadn't stopped him when she did, the situation might have been devastating for the young girl."

"How?" asked Kitty.

Tabitha ignored her. "Just come with me, Amelia. I think you will be interested in what she has to say."

Amelia did as she had been told.

As they got started, a gentleman stepped in their path. "Excuse me, may I interrupt for your dance card?"

It was the man in glasses, the young person Simon had warned her about. *Maybe he's right*, Amelia thought with a chuckle. The look in the man's eyes was decidedly more hazardous up close.

"Not now, sir." Tabitha waved him away. "We're in the middle of something important. Catch up with her later."

Amelia bit her lip to keep from laughing as Aunt Tabitha left the man staring after them. She hurried to keep up as Tabitha led her to a group of women with curious faces and gray hair.

"Lady Sutherland, this is Edgar's widow, Lady Amesbury."

"It's very nice to meet you," said Lady Sutherland, who had

a shock of hair that rivaled any young woman's in the ballroom. Twirled in an extravagant chignon, it was gray with strong streaks of snow white. Her chin was soft, however, and made her appear more amicable than the other women.

"And you as well," greeted Amelia. "Your costume is stunning." Lady Sutherland was dressed as a mermaid with a pretty blue fishtail, pinned up high, with iridescent gills.

"Never mind fashion." Tabitha waved away the compliment. "Tell her what you told me."

Aunt Tabitha could get by with dismissing the manners she insisted upon because these were her closest friends. Similar in age and disposition, they'd earned the right to cut to the chase at the appropriate time. Evidently, now was one of those times.

"I was at Flora Edwards's engagement party. It was quite a fete, with many titled gentlemen present." Lady Sutherland thought back a moment before continuing. "As you know, Flora Edwards was engaged to His Grace, which meant much pomp and circumstance. More than the admiral would have normally allowed."

"The admiral detests pomp," another woman chimed in. With her rounded shoulders, she wasn't more than five feet, but despite her diminutive stature, her voice was clear and succinct. Her perfume was lavender, soft and grandmotherly.

Lady Sutherland nodded before continuing. "As I was saying, guests packed the house, and many men who knew the admiral were in naval uniform, including the man pursuing Flora's youngest sister, Rose. Flora knew him in an instant."

"Flora was a clever child," said the short woman, pressing a finger to her temple. "Always could calculate difficult math equations in her head."

Tabitha gave her a look that said, *Quit interrupting.*

"Who was the man?" asked Amelia.

"A young clerk from the shipping docks." Lady Sutherland's voice relayed the nugget of information with disapproval. "Mr. William Donahue. Flora knew him from her work with her father."

"Flora helped the admiral with the books of his shipbuilding business, Fair Winds," added the woman.

"Lady Sutherland is telling the story, Mrs. Grover," Tabitha huffed. "I think she can manage."

Lady Sutherland cleared her throat. "Flora happened upon the couple in a dimly lit hallway, and I don't have to tell you that's not where a young, unchaperoned woman belongs. Flora was very upset with her sister."

Amelia bet she hadn't been the only one. The admiral had to have been livid as well.

"Of course, nobody witnessed the encounter except Flora, but I heard about it afterward. Everyone did. Thank goodness Flora came to her sister's rescue. She was always the responsible one of the girls. The rest of them . . ." She shook her head. "Well, it is not Christian to gossip."

Mrs. Grover stifled a laugh. "That's never stopped you before."

"And you are a pillar of virtue?" said Tabitha.

Amelia was seeing a new aspect of Tabitha, and she liked it. Finally, it felt as if Amelia and Tabitha were on the same side of something. She let the feeling of camaraderie wash over her as the women argued among themselves, debating who was the least Christian among them.

Kitty caught her eye, and Amelia was glad for the opportunity to duck out of the discussion. "It looks as if Mrs. Hamsted needs my assistance. Thank you so much for the information, Lady Sutherland. I appreciate it. And it was good to meet all of you."

"And you as well, dear," said Lady Sutherland. The rest of the women were too enthralled in the conversation to notice Amelia's departure.

"Do tell." Kitty linked her arm with Amelia's. "What were you and Lord Bainbridge *really* doing all that time? I didn't see you dancing."

"We danced," insisted Amelia.

"Oh, I know you danced," said Kitty. "But I also know you took a detour to the balcony. Tell me everything."

Amelia caught Oliver's eye and waffled. He was so protective of his wife. Maybe Amelia shouldn't divulge more than she already had. She and Kitty had been involved in plenty of exploits but never anything as dangerous as murder. Plus, Kitty had been planning this event for months. It wasn't right to dampen the mood with talk of death.

"Oh no you don't." Kitty pulled her arm tighter. "I know that look in your eye, and you are not putting me off this time. I've waited two years. I'm not going to wait another minute."

Kitty had waited two years? Ha! Amelia had waited forever. "I'm sorry to disappoint you, but the detour had nothing to do with me or the marquis."

Kitty's pretty blue eyes clouded in confusion. "What, then?"

"We saw Henry Cosgrove arguing with a man and followed them out."

"It was about your investigation, then." The statement was tinged with disappointment and perhaps a little irritation. "Why is it always your letters with you? When will you put aside your readers' exploits and have an adventure yourself?"

The question stung. "How can you say that, Kitty? A woman is dead."

"And that woman isn't you."

Amelia felt her jaw slacken.

"I apologize for my bluntness, but it's true, and you know it." Kitty let go of her elbow and crossed her arms. "You live vicariously through your letters. It's time you start living yourself."

Kitty was right, of course. After Edgar's death, Amelia had postponed her own adventures, putting away the dreams she had for a new life in London. The last two years had been spent deep in her readers' lives. Maybe it was time she devoted as much energy to her own concerns as she did to theirs.

The dance changed to a quadrille, and Kitty added, "This is the worst."

"It wasn't *all* bad." Amelia's brow wrinkled in confusion. "We did hide in a dark corner, if that makes you feel any better."

Kitty's eyes didn't leave the dance floor. "I'm not talking about that. I'm talking about *her*."

Amelia followed her gaze to the woman Kitty's eyes were boring holes into. She was tall yet curvy, with raven locks that rivaled the color of the bird by the same name. As her costume suggested, she was a queen, with a tiny waist and ample bosom. If there was a more beautiful woman at the party, Amelia dared her to come forward. Indeed, Amelia looked like a woodland nymph compared to her. "Who is she?"

Kitty turned to her. "Felicity Farnsworth."

"*The* Felicity Farnsworth who broke Simon's heart?"

"The very one," said Kitty.

"What is she doing here?" asked Amelia.

"I have no idea. She certainly wasn't on my guest list, but then again, neither was Simon Bainbridge." Kitty lowered her voice. "It had to have been my wicked mother-in-law's idea. The woman is friends with the worst people in London."

By "worst," Amelia knew she meant the best—or at least the most popular. Lady Hamsted was the *ton*'s favorite person. Kitty was favored by association, but she was also well-liked in her own right for her attentive ear. Kitty knew what people needed because she listened—and cared.

But Kitty couldn't fix what was happening before them. Unaware, Simon was crossing the space to greet an acquaintance, and Felicity noticed the action. She stepped in his path, her presence unavoidable. Amelia forced herself not to shield her eyes.

She watched in horror as Simon froze for a moment before recovering. He bowed. What else could he do? Felicity offered him her hand. Amelia was astonished at the brazen move. Who did she think she was? She might be nice-looking, but that didn't give her the right to flaunt their history in his face. Amelia was disgusted for him and looked forward to his slight. Instead, Simon not only took Felicity's hand but kissed it, leaving Amelia to gawk in disbelief.

Chapter 19

Dear Lady Agony,

There's an insufferable woman in the village who inserts herself where she doesn't belong. She makes eyes at men wherever she goes. I cannot help but feel uncomfortable when she enters the room, and it's not just indigestion. Many women feel likewise. But what can we do? I see few options and hope you may know an alternative. I always appreciate your original advice.

Devotedly,
A Pain in My Side

. . . .

Dear A Pain in My Side,

That feeling you cannot quite put your finger on, the one that burns like indigestion? It's called jealousy, and it does no one any good. My suggestion is simple but honest. Ignore said woman, or better yet, make friends with her. Perhaps if she had *more female associates, she might be more inclined to talk to them instead of their male counterparts. You know what they say: if you cannot beat them, join them, or in this case, befriend them.*

Yours in Secret,
Lady Agony

The nerve of the man. Amelia fumed as she watched the spectacle, and she wasn't the only one. Half the room turned to witness the interaction. She told herself not to be jealous; she reminded herself of the advice she'd dished out so easily in her responses. But it was impossible. Moments earlier, those hands had been leading her around the dance floor, and now they greeted a woman who looked like a Greek goddess. Amelia stomped her tiny white slipper beneath her dress. *Poor Simon indeed!* He didn't look so poor right now. Head high, shoulders back, he looked like the commander of a ship, not a hardened man with a broken heart.

"What's the matter?" asked Kitty.

Amelia huffed. "Nothing."

"Is it Miss Farnsworth?"

"The raven-haired beauty with porcelain skin and statuesque silhouette, the one draped over the marquis's arm, smiling and laughing?" The compliments were like curses on Amelia's tight lips. "Not at all."

Kitty smiled, showing her cute dimple. "You are just as pretty."

"Ha!" Auburn hair, wide eyes, and olive skin weren't exactly the height of fashion.

"I've never known you to be jealous."

"I'm not—" Amelia didn't finish the sentence. That's exactly what she was: jealous. Which was silly because she and Simon weren't in a relationship. They were partners on a mission to catch Charlotte's killer. She had nothing to feel jealous about. What was happening to her? One night at a ball in a fairy gown and she was acting like a petty schoolgirl. Astonishing.

"He has no other choice, you know," said Kitty. "What else could he do? Crumble like a cookie? Cut her like a piece of bread? Crush her like a berry?"

"Are you hungry, Kitty?"

"Actually, yes I am. It's almost suppertime." Kitty clasped Amelia's hand. "The point is, he's a gentleman and a fine one at that. He's not going to let Felicity rattle him, at least not in public."

Amelia smiled at Kitty. "You're pretty smart, do you know that?"

"Of course I am," said Kitty. "That's why I'm friends with you. Now tell me what Aunt Tabitha said. She was being so secretive."

Amelia supplied her with details of their earlier conversation. As Kitty listened, Amelia couldn't help but notice Henry Cosgrove was still there, looking miserable. He should go home straightaway, especially after the argument with Jack. Why didn't he?

A moment later she had her answer. His mother, a portly woman with dark hair and an angular face, introduced him to a waifish girl of no more than seventeen. Amelia peered closer. She recognized the girl. How? Yes, now she remembered. The girl was a neighbor of hers. It was the girl's first season out, and she was much anticipated because of her decent looks and large dowry.

It was obvious Henry's mother was putting her in front of

Henry for these very reasons, but while polite, Henry wanted nothing to do with the girl. Anyone could see that from his forced smile and cool stare. But his mother would not retreat from the idea, and Henry eventually asked her to dance.

They made a perfect match in height and form, and that was about it. Amelia felt pained watching them. Henry's arms were stiff and square. The girl kept her back straight and her gaze over his shoulder. Perhaps she was counting the minutes until the dance was over. She'd best get used to the problem. The girl would be spending much of her time on the dance floor with men who had ulterior motives.

Ironically, that was the last thought Amelia had to herself before being asked to dance for much the same reasons. Gentlemen, lords, and barons asked after her dance card, and it wasn't all kindness driving their actions. She was the Countess of Amesbury, after all, and one of the wealthiest women in the room. Now that she was out of mourning, she would be one of the most sought after as well.

Amelia had no pretense about their encouraging words, slow steps, or warm smiles, but that didn't mean she couldn't enjoy them anyway. She hadn't danced for years, and she didn't care if she danced with the Hunchback of Notre Dame himself. She was going to enjoy it.

Her heart was light and so were her feet. The faster the orchestra played, the better she felt. It was as if she were coming out of a deep sleep, slowly at first, blinking and stretching, then jumping out of bed entirely.

After supper, she lost herself in the spell created by the flickering candles and heady-scented roses, the hours passing like minutes. It wasn't until a particularly wide turn that she realized many pairs had disappeared from the dance floor and the room had opened up. She checked the crowd and noticed Aunt Tabitha yawn. It was getting late. They should return home.

She found Simon standing nearby, finishing a refreshment. "For a while, I thought we would be here all night," he said. "I didn't think that last dandy would ever let you go."

Amelia tilted her head toward the dance floor. "Lord Wupple was a surprisingly good dancer." She lowered her voice. "He even taught me a few new steps."

"Wonderful." Simon's voice was dripping with sarcasm.

"It *is* wonderful," said Amelia. "I haven't danced in two years. I'm out of practice."

"It didn't seem that way to me." Simon's dark eyes, combined with the dark room, gave him a crafty look.

She refocused on Tabitha. "We should take Aunt Tabitha home. She's tired."

"I'll find our coats."

When he turned, Felicity was at his elbow. "You don't plan on rushing away without introducing me to your friend, do you?"

Amelia swallowed. The Greek goddess had appeared before them like Aphrodite from the foaming sea. It was hard being this close to her without staring. Her face was as porcelain as a doll's.

Simon glanced between them.

If you're looking for a resemblance, you won't find one.

While Felicity was all beauty, Amelia was mostly brains. Sure, she had a decent head of hair and a nice figure, mostly due to walking, but that was it. Standing next to the paragon, she keenly felt her deficiencies.

When he answered, his tone was curt. "Of course not. This is Lady Amesbury. Countess, this is Miss Farnsworth."

"I remember you," Felicity said. "Your husband passed away directly after you married him."

Her words are so much less attractive than she is. Amelia chose not to respond to the comment. Instead, she gave a slight dip of her head. "Miss Farnsworth."

Felicity looked to Simon. "Didn't her husband have some sort of disease?"

"Yes, he did," answered Amelia. "It was degenerative."

Felicity wrinkled her pretty nose. "Does that mean contagious?"

Amelia didn't trust herself to respond. "I must find my aunt. Good night, Miss Farnsworth. It was nice meeting you."

"I need to go as well." Simon dipped his chin. "Good night, Miss Farnsworth."

Miss Farnsworth. Amelia hated the sound of her name on his lips. The woman was a dunce. How could Simon have been engaged to her? She was pretty, no doubt, but what else? Was he *that* superficial? She wanted to believe otherwise, but Felicity's conversational skills were definitely lacking. Then again, maybe they didn't do much talking. The thought irritated her more than she liked to admit.

They found Aunt Tabitha, and after a quick thank-you to Oliver and Kitty, they were in the carriage on the way back to Mayfair.

Simon congratulated Amelia on the evening. "You were in high demand. I don't think you left the dance floor but once."

"As were you," countered Amelia. "Though I cannot imagine anything worse than dancing with Miss Farnsworth. I've had better conversations with birds."

Aunt Tabitha looked between them but said nothing. Her

eyelids were heavy, and she might have nodded off except for the conversation.

Simon smiled. "Luckily, dancing does not require conversation."

"You would know," Amelia mumbled.

"As would you."

Amelia played with the tulle of her skirt. "Conversation or not, the dancing was fun, if only for the exercise. I can't remember when I had such a good time."

"When Edgar was alive," added Tabitha, not opening her eyes. "That's when."

Amelia winced. "Of course."

They kept silent the rest of the way to Mayfair, and when the carriage halted, Amelia tapped Tabitha's shoulder to wake her.

"I'm awake," Tabitha insisted. "No one could sleep with all those ruts in the road."

Amelia nodded, despite the fact that it was exactly what Tabitha had done.

The door opened, and Simon was quick to help Tabitha down the steps. When she was safely inside, Simon took Amelia's hand. "Thank you for the nice evening. I enjoyed it."

"I did, too."

With the moonlight on his face, Simon looked like a captain, and all the excitement that image conjured up. His jawline was outlined in dark stubble, a hint of a shadow that deepened his features. The night, and its suggestion of danger, suited him. Spending another hour with him would be an adventure, one she shouldn't—and couldn't—speculate on right now. "Tomorrow we should talk to Jack Stephens. See what the trouble was between him and Henry Cosgrove. It might lead down another avenue."

"I will check around at the docks," promised Simon. "He works for Andrews & Sons."

"Excellent idea. What time should I expect you?"

"No." Simon shook his head. "The docks are no place for a lady."

His answer left little room for debate, but she didn't need his permission. If she wanted to go to the docks, she would find a way without him. She would figure it out—after a good night's rest. "As you wish, marquis."

His face turned to a scowl. "Do not *marquis* me. What are you *really* saying?"

She smiled. "I'm saying good night—and thank you, again, for a lovely evening." With that, she turned toward Amesbury Manor, leaving him to stare after her.

Chapter 20

Dear Lady Agony,

What advice would you give a young writer? Is there money to be made in the profession? I have heard it's a dismal business, so why go into it at all? I understand your situation is hardly similar, but what keeps you writing?

Devotedly,
A Wondering Writer

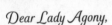

Dear A Wondering Writer,

If you are you looking for monetary reward, my blunt advice is take up another profession, for you will find none in the literary world. Write for the joy of it and nothing else. You will find your cup full, but not your wallet, when your pen is moving. Take care not to expect both.

Yours in Secret,
Lady Agony

The next day, Amelia eagerly awaited the afternoon post. She hadn't slept well and needed something to take her mind off murder. The more she learned about Flora Edwards and her maid, Charlotte, the larger the mystery became. She'd gone from thinking no one wanted Flora dead to believing anyone could have plotted her demise, so easily done with Flora's penchant for sleepwalking. First there was Hyacinth, her sister, who had a crush on her fiancé and, of course, said fiancé. Then there was the admiral, who was surprisingly cool about his daughter's death. Not to mention the young man Flora found with her sister Rose, as well as Jack Stephens, whose connection she couldn't make out—yet. And that didn't even touch on Charlotte's murder, which might have involved other members of the staff, including Lena, the now scullery maid, or Tibens, the butler, or any of the others who found out Charlotte knew the identity of the murderer. The web was growing ever more complicated.

Despite waiting for the sound, Amelia started when the knock came at the door. She took a breath, relaxed her shoulders, and waited for Jones to bring her the post. Parcel in hand, she took the letters to the library, where she donned her imaginary writer's hat. The good women of London were waiting for her advice. And she was counting on them for a distraction.

She settled into her green leather chair, feeling like a captain herself commanding a ship. It was the place in the house she felt she most belonged. Although Tabitha sometimes joined her, it was on a conditional basis. No one entered the library without Amelia's unwritten permission. It had become her sanctuary—and her connection to vicarious adventures. Today, she looked forward to them sweeping her far away from murder and mayhem.

The ivory letter opener felt heavy and important in her hand;

the slice of the paper was a welcome sound. Men might deem the task frivolous, but she knew that communication was as essential as any physical duties. What problem needed solving today? Where could she be of service?

She unfolded the sheet of paper. She felt the smile slide from her face as she scanned the words. It was no ordinary letter, and her hand trembled as she understood its meaning.

> *DEAR LADY AGONY,*
> *I KNOW WHO YOU ARE. IF YOU KEEP ASKING*
> *QUESTIONS, I WILL REVEAL ALL.*

Letting the note drop, she leaned back in her chair. Someone had found out she was asking questions about Charlotte's murder, but who, and how had they connected her to Lady Agony? She rocked her chair. The only persons who knew her identity were Grady, Kitty, and Simon, and none of them would have told. The postman might be curious, or perhaps an employee at the magazine. But they'd been so careful. Grady disseminated the letters in batches, in an unmarked parcel. No one but Grady and Amelia saw the actual missives. Who could have found out their secret?

It was a secret she didn't want to share. Not just for her sake—she cared little what the *ton* thought of her—but Winifred's. Amelia had made a promise to Edgar. She was Winifred's mother now and closest kin. She couldn't jeopardize her reputation. It would reflect poorly on Winifred. Or would it? Maybe it was best to consider the worst that could happen.

First off, Lady Agony was fairly popular. The women who wrote to her admired her advice. The men, on the other hand, were another story. They called her advice cheeky and cavalier.

Even reckless. If they knew she was the Countess of Amesbury would it make any difference?

It would, but perhaps not in the first way that came to mind. Having an alter ego was fun. It allowed her to shrug off the mantle of her title, at least for a short while. If readers knew her real identity, it would affect the way she responded to the letters. And the way readers wrote them. It would no longer be a fun escape. She would be forced to quit writing.

She glanced at the rest of her letters. The thought was unbearable. She liked this job—she needed this job.

She picked up the folded paper, a mix of bad penmanship and poor spacing. She resented its presence and the implied threat. She refused to quit investigating Charlotte's murder. Charlotte was a reader and deserved justice, the same justice she herself sought for Flora Edwards. She'd had courage, and now Amelia must, too. Amelia had to be close to making a connection. Otherwise, there would be no reason for the letter. She couldn't stop now.

She turned over the envelope, once sealed with cheap red wax. The magazine's address was written in the same handwriting and revealed little about the writer, except he or she had poor penmanship and perhaps lacked formal education. Still, if the writer did know her identity, why not send the letter directly to her address? Why send it to the magazine?

Outside was a warm June day, waiting for her to find out. She needed to talk to Grady about the letter. Maybe he would have a clue as to who had sent it. Quickly, she sent a note asking for a meeting in Hyde Park. Then, glancing at her gray morning dress, she decided to change. This time, the thought was a pleasant one.

For the first day in two years, she would be wearing regular clothes. Silently, she thanked Simon for nudging Aunt Tabitha in the right direction.

Thirty minutes later, Amelia was practically skipping to Hyde Park, her green walking dress a welcome change. It wasn't the latest style, or even that pretty of a hue, but it felt beautiful to wear color again. No longer did passersby frown at her with pity. She, like the green trees, blended into the park quite handsomely, and she took an open bench close to Oxford Street.

Listening to the rush of the city, she waited for Grady, who would be coming from Fleet Street. Though she longed to march directly into his office, the hub of London's newspaper world, to do so would most certainly connect her to the magazine. Especially now, with the arrival of the threatening letter, she could not take the risk.

In a cap and hastily thrown overcoat, Grady looked every bit the busy newsman he was. The slightly hunched shoulders, the ink-covered fingertips, the tired eyes. He clutched his cap as he walked quickly toward the bench where she sat.

As he came closer, Amelia noticed the concern on his face. It wasn't a look she was accustomed to seeing, and she quickly went about setting his mind at ease. "Hello, Grady," she said, waving. "I'm fine, as you can see. My note wasn't meant to worry you."

"Blimey, you caused me a scare." Grady plopped onto the bench. "What's this about?"

She told him of the threatening letter and its contents. When she finished, she gave him a moment to think before adding, "Did you note anything unusual in the day's mail?"

He smoothed his dishwater-blond hair. His brow was sweaty from hurrying, and he waved his hat in front of his face a few times before returning it to his head. "Nothing. It was the same as always. The mail sorter brought me the letters. I packaged the parcel and dropped it at the post."

"Do you think the writer really knows who I am?" asked Amelia.

Grady didn't answer right away. Instead he watched a young boy hurrying with his toy boat to the Serpentine. Trying not to run, he skip-galloped toward the water, his nurse pushing a pram steadily behind him.

Amelia watched, too, reminded of Winifred and all the days they'd spent playing in the parks. Now that Winifred was getting older, those days were few and far between. She still loved a walk as much as any other girl, but she also loved her books and music. Playtime was becoming a thing of the past.

"It's hard to say," Grady finally answered. "On one hand, why not send the letter directly, to prove they know your address?"

"Exactly."

"On the other, the letter might be traced back more easily that way," added Grady. "The person might be protecting their *own* identity."

"True." Amelia hadn't considered that. Arriving in bulk, the letter would be disguised by the sheer quantity of other letters. But sent directly, it would be more conspicuous.

"Did the envelope have any distinguishing marks or clues?"

Amelia shrugged. "The seal was red, suggesting a male writer. The penmanship was sloppy. He might not be formally educated. Or he could have been in a hurry. Or just have bad handwriting." She looked at him. "So in other words, no, nothing distinguishing."

"You've stumbled on something about the maid's death you

shouldn't have." Grady tapped his two index fingers together. "I'd bet my last quid on it. The letter was a notice to mind your own business, and if I were you, I'd heed the warning."

Amelia was surprised. She and Grady thought alike, especially where justice was concerned. She never considered he wouldn't want her to pursue the truth behind Charlotte's death. "And let the murderer go free?"

The intensity in his blue eyes was underscored by his furrowed brow. "And let Scotland Yard do their job."

She'd let Scotland Yard do their job *if* they understood the full extent of it. But they didn't know about Charlotte's letter. Only Amelia did. She, therefore, must be the one to find justice for Charlotte, and it wasn't a task she took lightly. She would get it, one way or the other, anonymous letter or not.

Chapter 21

Dear Lady Agony,

What advice can you give about hats? I love hats, I have hats, I want more hats, and yet, when I buy one, I look like a dodo bird. Why is that?

Devotedly,
Hatless in Hampshire

. . . .

Dear Hatless in Hampshire,

There's nothing like the vexation of a hat, as proven by the number of letters I receive on them. Hats are my third-asked question, and yet I know not how to answer. My only conclusion is this: Some heads are made for hats. Others are not. Try to pick one that highlights yours least spectacularly.

Yours in Secret,
Lady Agony

Though Grady advised retreat, Amelia went straightaway to Kitty's house. Never mind it was the day after the ball and her friend deserved a rest. Despite her long night and many afternoon well-wishers, however, Kitty looked as fresh as a woman on holiday. Clothed in a gray dress, with a waterfall of rich purple ruffles arranged over a modest crinoline, Kitty had a style that was both contemporary and chic. Her feathered hat, newly purchased in Paris, was amethyst silk and made her eyes appear more violet than blue. How Kitty had time—or energy—to arrange such an ensemble, Amelia couldn't understand. She had a feeling that fashion came as easily to Kitty as breathing.

"You look stunning," Amelia greeted her. "And here I thought I was smart in my green satin."

"You know that you are." Kitty perched on the blue velvet chair across from her. "It's so good to see you in color, but you're one caller I did not expect to see today. How was the carriage ride home with Lord Bainbridge?"

Amelia rolled her eyes. "Aunt Tabitha snored beside me the entire way."

Kitty sighed. "Love thwarted once again by a badly placed relative. Same old story." She arranged the hem of her skirt. "So, tell me why you're here. I know it's not to gush about my new dress. You have never been one to 'waste time' on clothing."

Amelia winced at the sound of her own words coming back at her. "I didn't mean it that way. I was in mourning. I was out of touch with fashion."

"I know." Kitty swatted her knee. "I'm just teasing you. You have the best parasol in the world. I'll give you that."

"It has come in handy a time or two." Amelia tapped it gently on the floor.

"So what is it you need?"

"Your ear."

Kitty stood and closed the door. "You've got it."

Amelia told her about the anonymous letter.

Kitty was aghast. She paced back and forth. "This person, then, is warning you against finding out the truth about Charlotte's death."

"It would seem so."

Kitty stopped in front of Amelia. "This person is not just a person; he or she is *the murderer*."

"Very likely."

"We cannot allow this." Kitty shook her head. "The murderer knows who you are. We must find him; your safety depends on it. Do you have any ideas?"

"I have one," said Amelia. "It occurred to me last evening."

Kitty joined her on the sofa.

"Lady Sutherland told me Flora Edwards confronted a man at her engagement ball, a Mr. William Donahue. He's a clerk for Admiral Edwards. Apparently, he was trying to seduce the admiral's youngest daughter, Rose. Flora knew him from her time at the docks, where she occasionally picked up the books. I thought we might investigate that avenue."

"How?"

"By inquiring after Mr. Donahue."

"At the docks?" Kitty's violet eyes were wide with excitement.

"At the docks."

"I've been wanting to peruse silks in the area. A friend of mine picked up a lovely cashmere there, but Oliver won't let me near the warehouses. Now I have my chance." Kitty clasped her hands. "I'll fetch my jacket."

Amelia envisioned Kitty donning her brightest coat for shopping. She referenced her own gray knit. "Something dull will do. You need to *blend in*, which means you might want to leave the hat behind."

"This hat?" Kitty gasped. "Oliver says I look *ravishing* in it."

"That's the problem," Amelia muttered. "Other men will, too." The London Docks were an amalgam of every man, sailor, and worker imaginable. She and Kitty would stick out as it was for being women of a certain class. But time was of the essence, and one quick stop at the silk shop couldn't hurt. Kitty should get something out of the meeting, too. "Fine, keep the hat on, but let's get moving. Find your coat and inform your footman. Can he be trusted to keep our whereabouts a secret?"

"Mr. Topper has never let us down before, has he?"

Actually, he had. Once, he'd called Oliver home from the club because Kitty had twisted an ankle trying to squeeze through a gate. A reader had written to Amelia, informing her that the seamstresses of a popular dressmaker were sleeping three to a bed. Amelia was so outraged by the accusation she had to confirm it was true before revealing it in her response. When she couldn't squeeze through the narrow gate, she engaged Kitty, who was as thin as the day was long.

The good part was Kitty didn't twist her ankle until after discovering the truth. The poor seamstresses were indeed sleeping in a bed no better than a thinly lined crate. Amelia outed the dressmaker immediately, and after being shunned by many shoppers she was forced to improve the conditions of her laborers. It was the highlight of Amelia's year.

But Oliver was upset and wondered what they had been doing to put Kitty in physical danger. It was the second time Kitty had come to harm in her company, and Oliver was growing suspicious. Amelia hoped he never found out. Otherwise, it might be the end of their duo adventures.

"Never mind," Kitty said, waving aside the topic when she noticed Amelia mentally replaying their exploits. "I will be right back. Wait here."

Ten long minutes later, Kitty returned in a drab gray paletot. It concealed most of the dress, except the regal purple ruffles and, of course, the magnificent hat. But Amelia supposed this was the best she could do in a pinch. Kitty was gorgeous, and even a flour sack couldn't hide her good looks.

Then they were on their way to the London Docks, which brought wine, tobacco, rice, and brandy to the fine citizens of London. Soon the streets took on a maritime feel, and shops displayed shiny sextants, compasses, and chronometers. Kitty scanned windows, looking for the much-talked-about store that sold cashmere and silk imports right off the boat, while talking about last night's ball. She worried about the tense moments, but Amelia assured her, like all her events, it was a success.

"But that awkward moment between Simon and Felicity." Kitty groaned. "I wanted to disappear into a rosebush."

"You might have," joked Amelia. "The bouquets were large enough." When Kitty still looked tense, Amelia gave her a nudge. "Don't worry. Simon wasn't bothered at all. He's obviously used to women throwing themselves at him."

"True," Kitty agreed. "I heard Felicity's father has doubled her dowry by including his equestrian estate in Sussex. It's much coveted and sure to attract wealthy suitors right away. He thinks another season will wreck her chances for a good match."

"Simon wouldn't fall for that," Amelia declared a little too quickly. Then added, "Would he?"

"It's doubtful." Kitty pressed her face closer to the window. "Still, he was in love with her once. It's hard telling the heart what to do." She pounded on the carriage roof. "Mr. Topper—stop, please!"

Amelia peered over her shoulder at the red-and-blue-flannel-clad window. She'd been to a lot of shops with Kitty, but this did not look like one of them. It was small, perhaps able to hold a handful of shoppers. Above the door it read FINE SILK. "Here?"

Kitty clutched her reticule. "Yes! My dear friend Lady Morton told me of it. Their silk is unparalleled to any in the world. You must see for yourself."

Amelia wasn't in the mood for shopping but would not be letting her best friend go in alone. Nearby, a man sat on a bench, hunched over a flask. He looked well on his way to finishing it if he hadn't already. "Promise you won't be long."

"I promise. I know just what I want."

Thirty minutes later, Amelia agreed Kitty knew just what she wanted: everything. They'd been through stacks of silks, racks of silks, and rolls of silks. Besides the colorful bundle Mr. Topper carried, Kitty held a sack of individual scarves in her hand. "That was incredible!" she exclaimed as they left.

Incredible, indeed, that we found our way out with any money left at all, thought Amelia. Her eyes adjusted to the light outside the store. The afternoon was much brighter than the dim shop. Even with the black clouds of smoke bursting from nearby chimneys and the large masts of the boats cluttering the Thames, the day was bright silver. A FAIR WINDS sign hung off a wharf not far from where they were. She pulled Kitty's coat sleeve. "That's it. Just ahead."

Kitty cleared her throat. "Mr. Topper, Lady Amesbury and

I are going to take a little walk . . . stretch our legs. We'll be along shortly."

Mr. Topper, a large fellow of fifty, with a stiff face and a thick beard, didn't move. He held the parcel like a statue.

Kitty held up her gloved hand. "Five minutes. Ten minutes, tops."

"I'll drop these off, Mrs. Hamsted." Topper glanced at the carriage. "Then I'll be back."

"Thank you." Kitty lowered her voice to Amelia. "Move, sister." They weaved in and out of clumps of dockworkers, who were eating oranges and drinking pints of beer. Others smoked, their pungent tobacco tingeing the air with its distinctive scent. Nearby, boats stirred the muddy bottom of the river, and the wind turned brisker, colder, and wet. Kitty held on to her elaborate hat as they approached the dock.

They took the steps carefully to the offices below. Inside were three men, one poring over a blueprint, another scanning a map of the river, and still another with his nose in a ledger. Amelia assumed the last must be William Donahue. A handsome fellow with a fancily tied cravat and neat trousers, he looked more gentleman than clerk. No wonder he'd fit in so well at Flora's engagement party.

And no wonder Rose was besotted with him. Taking off his round spectacles, he came to his full height. He was a tall man, lean also, with a wave of blond hair that he pushed back from his forehead. It immediately returned to his brow, as if it was used to falling forward from his work over the books.

"Good afternoon, ladies." His voice was as sweet as licorice. "This is a pleasant surprise. How may I assist you?"

"Are you Mr. Donahue?" Amelia surveyed the office, which

was neat and orderly and comfortably outdated. Just like Admiral Edwards.

He tipped his chin. "Why, yes. Who, may I ask, is asking?"

Amelia wagered he could enchant a woman younger and less experienced with the look. Fortunately, that did not include Amelia or Kitty. "I'm Lady Amesbury, and this is Mrs. Hamsted. Perhaps you have heard of her husband? He's the maritime scholar Oliver Hamsted?"

"I apologize. I have not." He slipped his hands in his trouser pockets. "I'm afraid I spend more time with boats than I do books."

"No matter." Kitty fiddled with her hat, which was askew from the wind. It was impossibly large and hard to refasten. "To be honest, his books are rather obscure. I've yet to get through one of them." She jammed a pin through a flower. "But we were in the area." She held up her dainty sack. "And I said to my friend, we must stop at Admiral Edwards's shipyard. My husband speaks nonstop of him."

"And with good reason." William's chest inflated two sizes. "I served under the admiral in the navy for many years, and he's an outstanding commander. When he began this enterprise, I was the first person he asked to assist him." He leaned toward them conspiratorially. "He needed a man with brains for business."

"And that was you," said Amelia, stroking his ego.

William liked the attention. "Yes, it was. I've always been good with numbers. My grandfather was the famous cartographer Sir Wendel Donahue. Maybe you recognize the name?"

"Unfortunately not." Seeing his disappointed face, Kitty batted her eyelashes. "But I'm sure my husband would."

Amelia gave Kitty a silent cheer. Kitty was getting better and better at investigation all the time.

"Certainly," agreed William. "Since he's an author."

The smoothness of his voice did not go unnoticed by Amelia. "It looks as if you have a great deal of books here."

"Not books but blueprints," corrected William. "Is your husband in need of a boat?"

"I am widowed," Amelia informed him.

William had the good manners to look chastened. His head dipped lower than necessary. "I apologize, my lady. I should have noticed your pin."

Amelia put a hand to her throat, where the new onyx jewelry rested. "That's quite all right. It's been two years since he passed."

"I would like to look at them." Kitty gave Amelia a conspiratorial nudge. "I'm always on the hunt for a new enterprise."

William called to an employee. "Albert, would you show Mrs. Hamsted some of our work?"

Upon finding out Amelia's availability, William desired a private conversation, which suited her perfectly. She could ask him more personal questions without onlookers.

When Kitty and Albert were engaged with a book, William continued. "I cannot apologize enough for misspeaking about your late husband. Please accept my apology."

"Of course I do." Amelia smiled. "These tragedies happen more often than we acknowledge. We only have to look to the admiral's recent loss to understand that."

"Flora Edwards." William nodded knowingly. "Yes, her death was a tragedy. The admiral hasn't been quite the same since."

"I understand they were close," said Amelia. "I heard she was like him. That she enjoyed mathematics and ships. Did she spend time here?"

William smoothed a small wrinkle in his waistcoat, perhaps forming an appropriate response. "The admiral . . . indulged his daughter. She did spend time here, of course, but did no real work."

Amelia noted the slight edge to his voice and tried to soothe it. "The admiral wouldn't want to heave such responsibility on a *daughter*. I imagine power like that could go to one's head."

"Could and *did*." William shortened the distance between them. "Some days could be a challenge with her playing accountant."

"Donahue!" hollered a man from above.

Irritation flashed in William's eyes at being summoned like a deckhand, but the smile didn't leave his face. "I apologize for the interruption. If you'll wait for me a moment?"

I'll do nothing of the sort. But Amelia nodded, deciding to continue her interview with those left in the office. She needed to talk to as many employees as possible with the short time they had left.

As soon as he was gone, she joined Kitty and Albert, who was showing Kitty a sketch of a boat. "Mr. Donahue and I were just talking about Flora Edwards. I'm so sorry about her passing. Did you know her?"

Albert was older than the other two employees. The creases around his eyes were deep, and a tremor in his hands was visible as he held the sketch. If he wasn't drinking, he had been. He smelled of rum. "Sure, I knew 'er, God rest 'er soul. She was a fine lass. Came 'ere often, she did."

"She was good with numbers, I understand," encouraged Amelia.

"Yes, milady. The admiral was proud of 'er smarts, and rightly so. She could've handled the whole operation, she could've." He flung out his arms and wobbled on his feet.

"Whoa there, Bert." The other employee looked up from his work. "You're still burning off a long night."

Albert steadied himself, holding on to the table. "They just don't like that she pointed out the problems with Donahue's bookkeeping," Albert snickered. "Kept 'em honest, she did."

"She thought she knew more than us. Pretentious female," the other man muttered as he walked out of the office.

"She probably *did* know better," whispered Albert. His breath was a combination of tobacco and alcohol. "She found an error once and 'eld Donahue's feet to the fire. He didn't like that. No, sirree." The other man returned with a ruler, tapping it impatiently against his palm. Albert took the cue and switched topics. "Now, this schooner." He pointed to another print. "Any man would be proud to call it 'is own." His trembling fingers traced the lines of the sails. "She's beautiful."

"Keep dreaming, Bert," teased the man.

William returned from the dock. "So sorry. That took longer than I'd hoped."

"Not at all." Kitty opened her reticule. "Thank you so much for your time." She handed him her calling card. "In case my husband and I decide to invest. It's been enjoyable learning a little bit about the business."

"The pleasure has been mine." William turned his attention to Amelia. "And your card, my lady?" It was a bold request, but she acquiesced. She wanted to know more, and if he did call, it would give her an opportunity.

Bidding the men good day, she and Kitty hurried up the stairs.

On the dock, they scanned the area for Mr. Topper. Amelia spotted him several yards away, talking to another man, so she and Kitty started toward the carriage. They hadn't gone far when a gust of wind took Kitty's fetching hat, and before she could snatch it, the hat skipped down the dock, snagging on a wooden pole. Kitty, of course, skipped after it, and Amelia after her, hollering for her to let it alone. Just when Kitty had almost reached it, another gust blew it farther down the pier.

By now, Mr. Topper had seen them—many men in the boatyard had—and was hurrying in their direction. When Amelia caught up with Kitty, she was leaning halfway into the river, where her hat dangled from an outcrop of rocks. A red-eyed pigeon was poised to pick a pretty purple feather.

"Oh no you don't," warned Kitty, extending an arm.

"Kitty, no!" Amelia hollered.

But the words came too late. Kitty retrieved the hat, but not before falling into the river.

Chapter 22

Dear Lady Agony,

Mother says I am getting to the age where I must make better choices, which means not challenging boys to races. But how am I to say no to a boy I can outrun? Especially when he says I can't. Mother says I must marry someday, but I'd rather break a leg than marry one of these blokes. Yet I must obey. Can you tell me how to start acting like a lady?

Devotedly,
A No-Good Rabble-Rouser

. . . .

Dear No-Good Rabble-Rouser,

First off, I must correct your signature. Much good has been done by rabble-rousers. We only need to peek into a history book or the Bible to know it. Second, I take offense, and you should, too, at the phrase "acting like a lady," for herein lies the *problem. If one must quit being herself to be a lady, then being a lady is no fun at all. Navigating new relationships is difficult, and being a real lady takes courage. However, I am certain you are up to the task.*

Yours in Secret,
Lady Agony

Oliver is going to kill me. That was Amelia's first thought when she saw Kitty fall into the Thames. The water was knee-deep here; Kitty herself would be fine. Amelia checked Kitty's soaked gown, drenched from the waist down. It, on the other hand, was another story. She squinted at the hat, which Kitty held up like a gold medal. Surprisingly, the hat looked undamaged. Amelia clapped. It was the one thing that survived the harrowing event.

She tiptoed near the water, holding out her hand for Kitty. Kitty stood, the heavy material of her dress, not to mention her petticoat, weighing her down. It was a short distance, but would she be able to walk it constricted by the cumbersome gown? Not alone. Amelia checked her own dress, lighter and less ornate. She should be able to reach her without a problem. With the extra hand for support, Kitty would be fine.

"Stand back," came a deep voice behind her.

Amelia startled and almost fell into the river herself. But the deep voice also had hands, and they were around her waist, lifting her up and placing her several feet from the water's edge. She spun around to see Simon wading into the water. "Simon! What are you doing here?"

"Same thing as you, I imagine." He pointed a finger. "Wait here."

She didn't have any other choice. Mr. Topper, who had come

running seconds after Simon, was standing so close to her that any movement toward the water would have been put to a stop. *Men.* They were always around when you didn't need them.

She watched as Kitty tried, and failed, to walk out of the water herself. Simon gave her a hand, yet she still stumbled, which left him no other option than to pick her up and carry her out of the river. *Fine, so we do need him.*

Simon paused at the water's edge. "Would you like me to help you to your carriage?"

"No, I can manage," said Kitty, dangling from his arms. "Thank you."

He placed her on her feet, holding her steady. "Of course."

"Thank you, my lord." Mr. Topper wore a worried expression, twisting his handkerchief. The square looked minuscule in his large hands. "I'm sorry for the inconvenience. I would've gone after her myself if you hadn't arrived."

"No apology necessary. Happy to help." He motioned toward the carriage. "Shall we?"

They began walking up the embankment, Simon helping Kitty with the extra weight of the dress. Amelia realized he would be accompanying them and cringed at the thought of the conversation. If his stony silence was any indication, the ride would be tense indeed.

It was silly, if you asked Amelia, which nobody did. Sure, Kitty had fallen into the water, but it was not the end of the world. Despite a wet dress, she was perfectly fine. Amelia didn't see what the fuss was about.

Amelia was tired of women being placed on a pedestal. *Like figurines not to be touched*, she thought as she marched up the incline. She herself had plunged into waters headfirst many times when she was younger. Thank heavens no one rescued her.

Of course this was different, but it wasn't grave, which was how it was being treated. If Simon tried to lecture Kitty on safety, she would stop him in a minute.

In the carriage, Amelia waited for him to say something. At the first horses' clops, she anticipated the lecture would begin, and she was ready to pounce. But what happened was Kitty's dress began to dry, and the stink of the Thames filled the carriage. An awkward quiet ensued.

Kitty broke the silence with a cough. "It's the dress, isn't it?"

Amelia cleared her throat. "I'm afraid so."

"Would you mind if, ahem, I open the window?" asked Simon.

"Of course." Kitty swallowed. "Go ahead."

A chuckle escaped Amelia's lips. To see the paragon of fashion wearing a rotting dress was almost too much to take. How Kitty kept her composure, Amelia did not know. She obviously couldn't keep hers.

"You find my foul-smelling dress amusing?" Kitty arched a blonde eyebrow, looking impossibly pretty despite the soaked gown.

Amelia straightened her shoulders. "No, of course not."

Kitty's face fell, and she broke down laughing. She held up her hat in between giggles. "At least I saved my hat. If that was lost, it would've all been for naught."

"Never underestimate the power of fine millinery," Amelia proclaimed. "It can move mountains—and rivers!"

Simon looked on, not saying anything.

"Oh, come, now, you have to find it just a little bit funny," teased Amelia.

"It's hard to find humor when people I care about place themselves in harm's way." His face was void of amusement.

"That's what you did today, Lady Amesbury. You put yourself and Mrs. Hamsted in danger by going to the docks when I explicitly told you not to."

"I have not been a child for a long time, my lord." Amelia's voice dipped lower. "I won't be told what I will and will not do."

She heard Kitty inhale.

"You would rather jeopardize your friend's safety?" pressed Simon.

"She was not in jeopardy," Amelia snapped. "She was with me—and Mr. Topper. I had it under control."

"Up until you didn't." The wind and the water had mussed Simon's dark hair, and he looked rakish with it dipping over his brow. His next words were as rough as the rocky shoreline. "I've spent most of my life on the water. Do you not think I've seen its ravages? Or worked with men who live day in and day out in isolation, who find women as necessary as a pint of ale?" He let out a harsh breath. "If you thought you were in control, you were sadly mistaken."

A moment passed, the severe words hanging in the air like the smell of Kitty's dress. Yes, he'd been a sea captain. He knew the ocean as well as she knew her favorite book. But his voice dripped with condescension, and that was the part that bothered her. "Point taken. I'm thoroughly and humbly chastened. I bow to your all-knowing wisdom and authority."

Kitty quickly changed the topic. "The important thing is Amelia got the information she was looking for."

Simon held Amelia's eyes for a moment. They posed a challenge and perhaps a warning as well.

A beat passed. Amelia refused to give an inch.

Finally, he asked, "What did you find out?"

"Plenty." Amelia steepled her fingers. "Flora discovered a

mistake in William Donahue's bookkeeping, and from an employee's retelling, it was a sizable one."

"Was it intentional?" asked Simon.

"That's the question," said Amelia. "If William was stealing from the admiral, and Flora knew, it changes everything. William was present the night of her death."

"Their argument might not have been about her younger sister Rose, after all," Kitty surmised.

"Exactly," agreed Amelia. "It might have been about the missing money."

"But William seems so *pleasant*." Kitty's nose wrinkled. "Do you think he would steal from the admiral, his superior?"

Simon weighed in. "William Donahue might *be* pleasant, but he's also a dandy who cares very much about his clothes and looks. It takes money to sustain appearances, and from what I know, he comes from a respectable but humble family. The income is not coming from them."

The carriage stopped at Kitty's house. "I suppose I'll find out more if he pays me a call." She bit her lip. "How will I keep Oliver from finding out about today?"

Simon nodded toward the window. "From the looks of it, that will be impossible."

Oliver was rushing toward the carriage, acting very unlike . . . Oliver. He was the consummate scholar, always a little untidy and distracted, and never athletic. Amelia and Kitty had quietly discussed many troublesome reader letters while he was engrossed in a book, and he never suspected their nefarious plotting.

But marching toward the carriage, his cravat undone and his hands in fists, he looked little like that scholar now. He was a man on a mission, and Amelia knew what that mission was. Kitty, on the other hand, pretended to have no idea what the matter was.

"Oliver dear," greeted Kitty as Topper helped her out of the carriage. Her dress was stiffening at the edges. "What are you doing home so early? I thought you would be at the library all afternoon."

Oliver hugged her tight to his chest. "Thank God you are unharmed."

"Of course I am." Kitty eyed Topper over Oliver's shoulder. "Who told you otherwise?"

He held her at arm's length, looking her over for bumps or bruises. "Half the shipyard, Kitty. They said you fell into the river."

"Pish." Kitty waved away the comment. "An exaggeration. I was merely retrieving my hat." Then she added with a wink, "I know how fond of it you are."

Oliver smiled and squeezed her hands. He turned to Amelia. "*You*. It's always *you*. Pray tell how trouble follows you like"—he sniffed—"the smell of this dress. You are a countess, a mother, and a role model." He shook his head. "It does not compute. I am missing something, and you are going to tell me what that something is right now."

"Calm down, Hamsted." With the motion of his hands, Simon suggested he lower his voice. "Let's take the conversation inside."

"Calm down?" Oliver repeated. "Kitty's my wife! She could have been killed."

"I understand you are upset," said Amelia. "But death was not imminent. Kitty was perfectly safe. Right, Mr. Topper?"

Topper had turned to go and had to double back. He stood tall, chin pointed upward. "Mrs. Hamsted was, for the most part, safe."

Amelia mouthed the word *Thanks* at him.

Oliver let out a cry of exhaustion. "See?"

Kitty stomped her boot. "Inside, all of you, right now."

They followed her like a line of chastened schoolboys. Kitty rarely lost her composure, but when she did, she could be fierce. Her legs were like soldiers' legs, marching forward in the drenched gown. She refused to let it—or their argument—weigh her down.

When they were inside, Kitty's maid rushed to assist her up the stairs. Kitty held out her hand to stop her. "I'm fine for the moment, Miss Younger. Thank you. Please inform Mrs. Cutter we would like tea immediately."

"Please, Kitty, go change," pleaded Oliver. "I'm sorry I got upset."

She pointed toward the drawing room. "In a moment."

They sat. Kitty did not. *Thank goodness*, thought Amelia. If her rotting dress touched one ounce of the beautiful floral chintz, she would be remiss. It was bad enough to have it in the same room with all these pretty things.

Kitty lifted her chin. In her soaking skirt, she was a pillar of strength, holding up the heavy fabric and undergarments with sheer willpower. "If you must know why I was at the docks, it was a surprise. For you. And now you've ruined it."

Oliver blinked. "A surprise?"

"I know you hate surprises, but this one is different." She tossed her untidy head. "It's . . . special."

Special, as in silk, thought Amelia. Kitty had bought him a silk scarf that would look the same as everything else did on him: silly, sloppy, and adorable in her eyes.

Kitty turned toward the door. "If there are no further questions, I'm going to change my clothes. And, Oliver?"

"Yes, dear?"

"See to it that Lord Bainbridge gets a brush for his trousers."

Chapter 23

Dear Lady Agony,

Why are secrets so hard to keep? A friend confided in me, and now I am eager to talk. What do you think it is that makes us want to tell? How do we not?

Devotedly,
Secret Keeper

. . . .

Dear Secret Keeper,

Secrets are like fire. The longer you keep them, the more they expand, until your chest is full and your mouth is, too. It's only natural to want to release the pressure. For your friend's sake, however, you must keep quiet. She confided in you, and you cannot betray her trust. It's the foundation of a good friendship.

Yours in Secret,
Lady Agony

Upon leaving Kitty's house, Simon asked Amelia when she was going to tell Oliver her secret identity. It was obvious the three of them were good friends. They had an easy camaraderie, even if it included frequent sparring. Maybe now was the time to reveal the truth.

"Never," answered Amelia. A lady pushing a pram walked by, and Amelia peeked at the chubby-cheeked baby. All smiles and bubbles, the girl reminded Amelia she needed to purchase a gift for Winifred's recital. She wanted to give her something grown-up, a locket or bracelet. They weren't far from the Burlington Arcade, on Piccadilly. If Simon agreed to the detour, she could stop. The arcade had a fine jeweler, whom she knew from purchasing her mourning jewelry. Mr. Jacques Allard would know exactly what she needed.

"Never is a long time," said Simon.

"Not when it comes to Oliver." Amelia waved at the baby. "If he found out, he'd never let Kitty come near me again."

"You're not giving him enough credit. Oliver is a logical man, methodical in everything he does. Once he weighs the pros and the cons of the relationship, he'll see Kitty needs you in her life."

Amelia wasn't so sure.

"Think about it," continued Simon. "Kitty can only purchase so many hats and dresses."

She laughed. "You don't know Kitty very well. She could shop for years and years and years. It's no chore to her." They stopped at a crossroad. "Speaking of, would you mind taking a detour to Burlington Arcade? I need to find a gift for Winifred's concert."

"Not at all." Simon motioned in the direction of the arcade. "I'd like to get her something myself."

Amelia was surprised by his enthusiasm. She didn't think a

young girl's recital was something he'd shop for personally. So many well-to-do families had tradesmen come to their homes, but Amelia liked to shop for herself when she could. The colorful stores, the smells of baked goods and roasted nuts—they were luxuries not afforded in a small village. She absorbed the city every chance she had. "That's very kind of you. We'd best not dally if we both need time to select a gift."

As she quickened her pace, her foot caught on a cobblestone.

"Whoa." Simon steadied her with a hand, looping his arm with hers until they were safely across the street.

She recovered quickly. "Thank you."

He smiled, and the earlier tension between them passed. They were partners, so to speak, on the same side of justice. No matter Simon's motive, guilt or fairness, they both wanted to bring Charlotte's killer to light. She just wanted it a little bit more.

Amelia's stomach rumbled as they drew closer to the scents of the shopping arcade. Even after a scrumptious tea at Kitty's, she longed for something more substantial, and her mother's pot roast came to mind. Served with potatoes and smothered in gravy, the meal had satisfied many guests, not to mention Amelia herself, who had a hearty appetite, more inclined to country fare than London delicacies. It was the thing she missed most about home. That and the large stone hearth, which was the center of the inn and the apex of family entertainment. When the night was over and the fire no more than a flicker, she and her sisters would cross the footbridge, over the pretty lily pond, and walk into their honey-colored manor house, still talking about the evening as they drifted off to sleep.

Her eyes stopped on a sweetshop, and she slowed her pace to gaze at the confections behind the glass. They weren't pot roast but certainly looked delicious. Toffees and chocolates were lined up in perfect brown rows, and customers waited their turn to purchase the famous candies. Dressed in black with a white apron, the clerk helped patrons while his assistant boxed and wrapped packages, tying each one with the store's signature ribbon.

"Would you like to stop?" asked Simon. "I'm happy to oblige."

Longingly, Amelia looked at the display case. "No, I'm—" She was just about to say she was fine when she spied Henry Cosgrove inside the store. She gave Simon a smile. "I would love to."

The decadent smell of chocolate filled the air as Simon held open the door. *Why did I hesitate? Chocolate is always a good idea.* She promised never to question it again.

"Oh, you fickle creature." His mouth was close to her ear, but his eyes were on Henry. "I see your ulterior motive."

"We're here," whispered Amelia. "We might as well talk to him."

Simon gave her a sly wink and called to him from the line. "Cosgrove, indulging your sweet tooth?"

Wearing a weary smile, Henry stepped out of line to greet them. He looked physically drained. Even in a well-tailored coat, his shoulders drooped, and his eyes were small, absent from the moment.

Amelia knew that look. It was the look one had to wear out on the London streets, pretending to be fine when, on the inside, one was falling apart. She understood the feeling well. After Edgar died, she played the part of Lady Amesbury even though her mind was somewhere else, mourning all the moments with Edgar she'd anticipated but hadn't lived. Had she been at the Feathered Nest, she would have been able to shutter herself in her room and cry herself to sleep, and it would have been acceptable. Grief was allowed in a small village. But here, among the elite, it was almost frowned upon. Mourning clothes, yes. Sadness, no. The season marched on, and Henry must march with it, his feelings be damned.

"Not *my* sweet tooth," answered Henry. "My niece's. She adores this place, and I promised her a treat."

"You give me an idea, Cosgrove. I could buy a box for Lady Winifred." He indicated Amelia. "This is Lady Amesbury. Winifred is her charge. Her concert is in three days."

"It's a pleasure to meet you." He gave her a reverent bow. "Allow me to bring Lady Winifred the chocolates. I went to school with Edgar. He was a respected friend, and I imagine his niece is a very talented girl."

"The pleasure is mine, Your Grace." Amelia beamed with pride. If it were up to her, she would go on about Winifred's many talents for the duration of their visit. Mothers, not dukes, were better listeners of praise, however, so she abridged her response. "And thank you. We'd be honored to have you attend." She put a finger to her chin. "But a duke and a marquis at her first performance? It might go to her head."

They enjoyed a chuckle.

"It was good to see you at the Hamsted ball," continued Simon. "I wasn't sure you'd make it."

Henry inched forward in the line. "To be honest, I would've rather been home, by myself, but my mother was insistent on the point. And as you know, it doesn't matter if it's today or six months from today. I'll receive the same stares, hear the same whispers. A duke must keep up appearances." He turned to Amelia. "You experienced a loss. You understand what I mean. Does the gossip ever go away?"

Amelia thought for a moment. "Yes, it does. And quite honestly, the longer you wait, the harder it gets to face it." She turned to Simon, thinking of his mother's passing. "Wouldn't you agree?"

"I would."

A deep crease appeared between Henry's brows, and he seemed more present. "We've weathered our fair share of storms." The corner of his lips twitched with a small smile. "No wonder we find ourselves in a chocolate shop, taking solace in sweets."

"It makes the difficult days more palatable, certainly." Amelia smiled.

"How's the admiral holding up?" asked Simon. "I've heard there has been some trouble at his house of late, with the help. That's the last thing he needs."

Henry scanned the confections in the display case. "He has had some trouble. He's down two maids, from what I understand."

Amelia knew he meant Lena and Charlotte. He must not have heard that Charlotte was found dead at St. James's Park, and she wasn't going to be the one to tell him. Not yet, anyway. He wasn't coping well with Flora's death. If he thought she was killed on purpose, it might devastate him completely. When she knew the full truth, including the murderer, then she would reveal it. Until then, she was keeping her summations to herself.

"In fact, I believe that's why the admiral went to his estate in Dartford," Henry continued. "It's Rose's first season, and she needs a maid posthaste. He might be able to recruit from there." Henry sniffed. "His advertisement was a dismal failure. Those things always are. But the admiral is stubborn. Once he has an idea, he follows it."

"That's the admiral for you," Simon agreed. "But you wouldn't think he'd have to make a special trip to find help."

"One cannot underestimate the value of a good maid," Amelia put in. "She's worth her wages twice over, especially to a young girl without a mother. After the rumor of a black list, he cannot be too careful."

"What's that?" questioned Henry. "A black list at the admiral's house?"

Amelia waved away the question. The information was a slip of the tongue. "Simply a rumor."

"At any rate, the trip might have a dual purpose," Henry added after a moment. "From what I understand, the sister of his late wife lives there."

Simon blinked. "I didn't know his sister-in-law lived with him."

"I have the distinct feeling nobody does." Henry leaned closer. Amelia could smell the mint on his breath as he continued more quietly. "I only met her recently. An interesting woman but not quite what I expected. She and Flora argued about our wedding date the night of our engagement party. Flora dismissed the fight, saying that her aunt was old and confused." Henry pointed to his temple. "Maybe she *is* senile. If so, I'm sorry for her. But it doesn't excuse the way she treated Flora."

"What was the disagreement about the wedding date?" asked Simon. "It seems a silly reason for an argument."

"The admiral told me his sister-in-law was once to be married on the same date." Henry slipped a hand in his trouser pocket. "For whatever reason, the marriage didn't occur, and she thought the date was . . . cursed. Though if you ask me, the man dodged a bullet." He shook his head. "Seeing her that night . . . any thinking man would have run in the opposite direction."

The clerk called on Henry, and Henry started, so engrossed

were they with the side conversation. He approached the counter, leaving Amelia and Simon to ponder the new information. The admiral's sister-in-law was clearly confused. Why else would she think the wedding date was cursed? But was she touched? If so, maybe she did something to Flora to prevent the wedding from happening.

The idea was extreme but not implausible. Henry was bothered by the incident, if not haunted. The troubled look in his eyes said it all. Maybe he didn't appreciate the way Flora was treated, or maybe he thought, in some odd way, the aunt was right. The date was cursed. After all, he, too, was left without a bride.

Finished with his purchase, Henry held a large chocolate box in each hand. For the first time in a quarter hour, he looked genuinely cheerful. Amelia understood the happy feeling. Giving a child a treat brought joy to the giver as well as the recipient. It was what made children so easy to spoil.

"I'm looking forward to bringing Lady Winifred these chocolates." Henry winked. "As long as I don't eat them before then."

"We look forward to it as well." Amelia smiled. "Take care of yourself, Your Grace."

"Goodbye, Cosgrove," added Simon.

It was Amelia's turn to order, and she indulged her curiosity. One didn't endure such a line and the delicious smells, too, only to skimp on the purchase. After ordering two of everything in the display case, she turned to Simon and asked him if he needed anything.

"I think you've ordered enough for both of us." Simon lifted his chin toward the man tying a ribbon on the oversized rectangular box. "I didn't realize you were so hungry."

"They're not just for me." Amelia paid and retrieved the

package. "They're for Winifred and Aunt Tabitha, too." She thanked the clerk, and Simon held the door as they returned to the London street, which was almost as busy as the chocolate shop.

Like Amelia, many women had made purchases and were hurrying to finish their shopping. One could feel the change in pace as the street traffic became more frantic, coachmen waiting to leave before the city became harder to navigate. But Amelia loved the busyness of it. Years of idyllic country life made the activity vital. She stopped to take a breath. Yes, she loved it a good deal.

"Careful, you might burst a lung in this smoke."

"I was just thinking how much I love the city." A hackney coach whizzed by, a man hollering something, and she followed him with a frown.

"It goes to show you one never knows what a lady is thinking." Simon took her arm as he hurried her across the street. "I thought you'd be devising the fastest way to Dartford after our conversation with Cosgrove."

"Everyone knows horseback is the fastest way to travel, but it's no longer an option for me, I'm afraid." She sidestepped a large crevice in the road. "Do you think Flora's aunt had something to do with her death?"

"It's hard to say without knowing the woman, or even knowing of her. If she thought the date was cursed, she might have done something rash to prevent it." Simon released her arm as they approached the shopping arcade. "But kill her?" He shook his head. "That would mean the woman is deranged. Unless an argument became an accident . . ."

That could be the case. If Flora met her aunt on the balcony, long after the crowd had left, they might have argued again. Without Henry to protect her, the aunt might have gone too far.

There was only one way to find out, and Simon was right. It included a trip to Dartford. Amelia stole a glance at him. Maybe he did know her mind after all.

Chapter 24

Dear Lady Agony,

Is it acceptable to talk to strangers if they are handsome? How about if they are kind? Really, I see no other way to meet men outside my circle. If he is agreeable, what's the harm?

Devotedly,
Meet in the Street

. . . .

Dear Meet in the Street,

What's the harm? Plenty, including your reputation. But my greatest concern is your safety. Do you think thieves and murderers make themselves mean and hideous? On the contrary. They may be sweet and kind and deceitful. Silly girl. You'd best stay home until you wise up.

Yours in Secret,
Lady Agony

After selecting a necklace for Winifred, a stunning peach cameo inlayed in gold, Amelia and Simon started for Amelia's house. Amelia was satisfied with her purchase and knew Winifred would think it very grown-up. Amelia paused. Winifred *was* growing up, and as she matured, would need the advice of a mother. Amelia hoped she could fill that role as aptly as a birth mother. But like all mothers, Amelia was learning as she went. The concert would be a test, she supposed, of her skills. Had she helped Winifred overcome her fears of her first performance? Would she not only survive the day but enjoy herself? That was the goal. It was soon to be seen if it was achieved.

Amelia had been surrounded by music at the Feathered Nest, and her young life played back to her like the tune of a cheerful dance. Performing for guests never made her anxious. It made her happy to be able to help others forget their troubles, if even for an hour or two. Winifred's performance was decidedly different, of course. Winifred had the added pressure of the elite assessing her performance and her talent. Still, Amelia understood how much music meant to her.

Her musing was interrupted by a man who came up suddenly on Simon's left. He wore dark trousers and a white shirt, blown open at the collar, revealing a tan throat. Amelia recognized that throat; it belonged to Jack Stephens, the man at Kitty's ball who had argued with Henry.

"Glad I caught up with you, mate." Jack looked past Simon, noticing Amelia perhaps for the first time. "Sorry for interrupting, milady." He tipped his soft hat and gave her a crooked smile. "Good afternoon."

"Hello, Stephens." Simon introduced her.

"Nice to meet you." Amelia returned his smile.

"What's the news?" continued Simon.

"At the docks, you asked me about Flora's engagement party. About her maid? Something came back to me." He pulled up a suspender strap, which had slipped low on his sleeve, and gave his shirt a tuck, perhaps trying to look more presentable.

That's why Simon was at the docks. He was talking to Jack. Jack was Flora's friend—perhaps too good of a friend. He'd used her Christian name, anyway. Henry assumed he loved her, and the use did suggest familiarity. Maybe she could find out just how close they were.

"Flora *did* have a discussion, but not with a maid. She had words with a man. A bit of a dandy. When I asked her what it was about, she said, 'Money.' I thought it was strange, but she laughed and said we'd discuss it later. But later never came."

An idea came to Amelia. "I think I know what she meant."

Both men turned to hear her explanation.

"Flora caught her younger sister Rose in a private conversation with such a man. As you know, it's Rose's first season, and being in a young man's company without a chaperone might ruin her chances for a decent match."

"Of course." Simon switched the box of sweets to his other hand. "But what does that have to do with money?"

Amelia walked toward a private corner, under the awning of a nearby smoke shop. "William Donahue clerks for the admiral at Fair Winds. He made a miscalculation in the admiral's books, and Flora found it. Whether or not the error was intentional, I could not say. Regardless, he wouldn't want the problem reported to the admiral."

Jack squinted, as if trying to see the explanation in his head. Simon waited for more information.

"William might have used his indiscretion with Rose as leverage. If Flora didn't tell the admiral about the error, he wouldn't let the word get out about Rose. A quid pro quo, so to speak," she added.

Jack closed one eye. Now he really looked like the pirate from Kitty's ball. "The lady might be onto something. If she's right, he'll rue the day he threatened Flora. Nobody treats a friend of mine like that and gets away with it."

Amelia gave him a sympathetic look before she continued walking. A new batch of shoppers flooded the street, and she was anxious to get home. "You and Flora must have been good friends for you to talk of her so affectionately. Had you known her a long time?"

"All my life." Jack took long strides, his legs used to exercise. Amelia upped her speed to keep pace. "Flora was an admiral's daughter, to be sure. She was smart and liked ships. The admiral never cared a wit for propriety. I suppose the shipyard was no place for a lady, but the admiral's wife died young. There was no one to tell him otherwise, and maybe he wouldn't have listened anyway."

"Knowing the admiral, probably not," Simon agreed.

The men shared a laugh.

Amelia skirted around a pair of matrons who seemed very curious about her walking beside two men, no chaperone in sight. Their eyes followed them after they passed. "I've only recently met the admiral, but he seems very attached to rules."

"Rules, yes. Society, no . . ." Jack's voice trailed off. "You know the first time I met Flora was on a boat? She was standing in front of her father, and I didn't see her at first. She was a wisp of a young woman. But her eyes . . ." He inhaled. "Standing at the wheel, she could have been a captain in her own right. She had that look about her. You know the one, Bainbridge. The one that tells you who's in charge."

"I do." Simon nodded. "Were you surprised when she became engaged to Cosgrove?"

Jack took a few steps before answering the unexpected question. "No. He was a duke. She had to say yes. She would have been mad not to. She had her younger sisters to think of. A match with a duke would put them in better positions to marry well."

What Jack said was true. The Cosgroves were titled and monied. A connection to the family would bode well for future offers. "But she did *care* for the duke, didn't she?" asked Amelia.

"How would I know?" Jack grumbled. "She must have. She agreed to marry him. She wouldn't just marry for prestige, would she?"

Amelia knew the question was rhetorical. What she didn't know was if his feelings for Flora were clouding his judgment. He seemed upset.

"Regardless, Cosgrove should have been looking out for her. It was his duty, and he failed. She died on his watch." Jack clenched his fists at his sides. "I'll never forgive him for that."

They were at Amelia's house now, and Simon stopped a few steps shy of the entrance. He didn't want the servants hearing the remainder of their conversation, and neither did she. "I understand duty. We both do. But how could've Cosgrove protected her from an accident?" asked Simon. "Even if he'd stayed the night, he wouldn't have been able to save her."

Jack faced them, his black eyes narrow, like slits in a fence. "Don't you see? She got sick and left the party early. Why? He should know, but he doesn't. He was too busy entertaining his distinguished friends." He spat out the word *distinguished*.

"Do you have any guesses?" Amelia prodded.

Jack dropped his head. "I wish I did. She was occupied most

of the night, and I only saw her a few times, including the one I mentioned. She held her own in that crowd. I wish I knew what happened to make her disappear."

Amelia had a few ideas, including the argument with her aunt. The sooner she found out more about the trouble, the better. She needed to travel to Dartford tomorrow, which meant she should make plans tonight. "You're welcome to join me for tea. Both of you."

Jack took two steps in the other direction before answering. "Thank you, but I'd best be on my way. I've taken up enough of your time."

"Not at all," said Amelia. "I'd love to have you stay."

Jack shoved his cap lower on his forehead. "Good day, milady. Bainbridge."

Simon and Amelia watched him make tracks in the opposite direction. When he was out of sight, Amelia turned to Simon. "Do you think he loved her, like Henry said?"

"As clearly as the nose on your face."

"I think so, too." Amelia scratched her head. "She must not have reciprocated Jack's feelings. Otherwise, she wouldn't have accepted Henry's proposal. Correct?"

"People marry for all sorts of reasons, not always love."

Amelia felt the sting of his words. When she accepted Edgar's proposal, she thought she was in love with him. Later, she conceded she might have been in love with the *idea* of him. The possibility of moving to London had enticed her like a hot cup of tea on a cold day. For years she'd heard about the city from lodgers at the inn. Mells was the stopping point for travelers on the way there. With Grady making the move a year earlier, sending her letters describing the wonders of the metropolis, the idea became more thrilling every day. When Edgar arrived, eager to propose, it seemed like *destiny*. Which was exactly the word her mother had used, confirming the trill in her heart must be followed.

"Had I been in love with someone else, I wouldn't have accepted Edgar's proposal," she said to no one in particular. "I was very much alone at the inn, however, with my family. The boys in the village were imbeciles, and my only male friend in the world, Grady Armstrong, had left for London."

Simon blinked. "I didn't mean to imply otherwise."

"Maybe not." Amelia shrugged. "But I did care. I cared for Edgar a good deal."

Simon spoke more quietly. "Care and love are two different things."

"Says the expert on relationships."

"I'm more of an expert than you."

"You have more *experience*," corrected Amelia. "That's something different entirely."

"I'm experienced enough to know your desires." He glanced at her lips. "Don't try to deny them."

Amelia walked toward the door, then turned on her heel. She couldn't deny them, and she wasn't going to. Hers were normal, natural feelings that might have been aimed at any young man in the London area. Unfortunately, they'd landed on Simon. He was different, and she was curious about the difference. That was all.

She poked her parasol in his direction. "What I desire from you, Lord Bainbridge, is help finding justice for Charlotte. Are you going to accompany me to Dartford tomorrow? Time is of the essence."

"I have a morning appointment. I can leave at noon." He glanced toward an upper window. "What of Aunt Tabitha? Will she grant you permission?"

Amelia followed his eyes. Tabitha stood like a portrait in a frame. "I do not need her permission. I'm a widow and beyond the reach of rules made for maidens and debutantes. No one is in search of a match, least of all you, and I would be foolish to give up my independence."

"Very well, then." Simon gave her a short bow. "I'll see you tomorrow."

Tomorrow. Despite her outward protests, her heartbeat doubled with anticipation.

Chapter 25

Dear Lady Agony,

Do you think love is planned, like parties or gardens? Or do you think it's spontaneous, like flowers or rain?

Devotedly,
What Says You

. . . .

Dear What Says You,

I think love is like a flower that blooms twice. Before love, we have one heart. Afterward, we have two.

Yours in Secret,
Lady Agony

The last thing Amelia expected the next morning was a visitor. She was scurrying to get ready for the recital, the day after tomorrow, and had much to do. Winifred's dress was being fitted, and, to the dressmaker's dismay, one of the seams had to be let out. (Children grew so fast at this age!) It would be finished on time, but it was a complication they didn't need right now.

Thankfully, the music was coming along swimmingly, and Winifred hadn't rushed the ending when she performed it last evening. Aunt Tabitha was in charge of the food and flowers, which was fortunate for Amelia, if not for the caterer and florist. Tabitha expected perfection, and when it came to her grand-niece, she would get it—no ifs, ands, or buts.

So when Jones interrupted the fitting to tell her she had a visitor, Amelia was surprised and a little irritated. Until she found out it was William Donahue, from the docks. Then she shot off Winifred's bed like a rocket. "Please show him to the drawing room."

Winifred swished her peach and cream dress back and forth. With her fair skin and hair, she was a vision in the gown and so grown-up. Her bright blue eyes were a striking contrast to the warm, delicate tones. "Isn't it lovely?"

"Very lovely, but please hold still for Miss Boucher. She's almost finished." Amelia gave the dressmaker a patient smile. Winifred's exuberance was nearly contagious, except to Miss Boucher, who didn't bother looking up from the material. But Amelia was happy Winifred was enjoying the moment. She wanted the concert to be a day of celebration, not stress. "Excuse me."

Amelia smoothed her auburn locks before walking down one flight of stairs and into the formal drawing room. Dressed in a well-tailored jacket and carrying a long, tasseled walking stick, William was gazing out the window when she entered. Obviously, he'd taken much more care with his dress than she had.

But when he turned around, he rushed to compliment her frock, which was nothing short of plain. The color was nice, cobalt blue and, against the gray day, was the only thing to recommend itself.

"Thank you, Mr. Donahue." His intentions didn't deceive her. She was a widow, and perhaps the wealthiest one in town. He would try every trick in his hand to gain an attachment. Maybe it was the reason he'd come.

"Please excuse the intrusion. I had no idea I'd have the pleasure of seeing you again so soon, but I wanted to deliver these myself." He held up a shopping bag. "I believe you left these behind that day at the dock."

Amelia felt herself frown as she took the bag from his well-manicured hand. Realization hit when she peered inside. Kitty's colorful—and expensive—silk scarves lay folded one atop the other in a colorful stack. She must have lost the package while trying to retrieve her hat and, after the argument with Oliver that ensued, forgotten all about it. "I owe you a debt of gratitude, and so does Mrs. Hamsted. These are hers, but I will make certain she receives them."

"My mistake."

William's warm smile told her he hadn't made a mistake. He was exactly where he wanted to be. Which was fine with her. She wasn't going to refuse the meeting. His unexpected visit gave her another opportunity to press him on Flora's involvement with the business, ergo another opportunity to investigate Charlotte's murder.

She reciprocated his smile. "Would you like tea?"

"Yes, thank you."

She gestured to the settee, and he made an ordeal of not sitting on his long-tailed jacket. After ringing for service, she took the chair opposite. "I'm glad you have time for a refreshment. I imagine the admiral keeps you very busy."

"Quite so." Satisfied with his coattails, William folded his hands on his lap and met her eyes. "The admiral is getting older and leans heavily on me to conduct the daily business, as he should. He's earned a respite."

"Having no sons, I imagine he relies on your solid know-how." A little flattery never hurt a man. In fact, Amelia found it was the surest way to a fickle heart.

His chest expanded with the pleasure of the compliment. "He was unfortunate in that one aspect of his life. His daughters are fine people but a bit . . . empty-headed. Excuse the description."

No, I won't excuse it. She was incensed at the comment but checked her emotion, keeping her voice agreeable. "I heard his daughter Flora was adept with numbers, however."

"She thought so." William's response was smug, his lips twitching with a grin. "She was proficient with figures but such a nuisance at the docks. Always thinking her way was the best way, poking her nose where it didn't belong. A nosy female."

Two words that made Amelia's blood boil.

A tray rattled, and the maid swiftly recovered, placing a tray on a nearby table. Her cheeks bright red, she bobbed a word of apology.

"No need, Miss Mead. Thank you." Amelia stood to pour the tea and, after Miss Mead departed, continued the sensitive conversation. "You knew Flora and the Edwardses well."

"I served under the admiral in Her Majesty's Royal Navy," explained William. "No better way to know a man. He considers me one of the family."

That explained why he was in attendance at Flora's engagement ball. He was Admiral Edwards's trusted advisor. But family member? An attachment to one of his daughters would make it official. Flora was already spoken for, and Hyacinth had her eyes set on higher pursuits. But Rose was young and innocent. Her head might be easily turned with William's charm and good looks.

Amelia handed him his tea. "How well do you know his youngest daughter?"

His hand wavered but only for a second. He sipped his tea, studying her movements as she returned to the chair. His eyes were amused and full of tricks. "Not as well as you might have heard."

Despite her best efforts at nonchalance, she blushed, and it seemed to give William a thrill. A smile spread across his face.

He set down his teacup, leaning in over the table. "Miss Rose is a kind girl, but a foolish girl. I prefer women of above-average intelligence, such as yourself." His right eye closed briefly.

Did he just wink at me? She sipped her tea to avoid his gaze.

He crossed one leg over the other. "Of course, I've never been one to let down a friend. If I can help with Rose's . . . situation, I will. Admiral Edwards has been very good to me. But things—and people—do come up."

He knew rumors were flying about his and Rose's private encounter; he'd caused them. And here he was flirting with Amelia, in case she could make him a better offer. She would disabuse him of that notion right now. "You are right, Mr. Donahue. Things do come up, like my appointment with Lord Bainbridge. I hate to rush, but I have a lot to do before he arrives." She stood. "Thank you for returning the scarves."

With a plunk, William's walking stick fell out of his hand, landing on the floor, and he scrambled to retrieve it. "You're welcome. If I can be of any other service—"

"I can't imagine how." Amelia walked to the door. "Mr. Jones will show you out."

"Tell the marquis hello, will you?" William tipped his hat. "Good day."

"Good day." Which it would be, when the cad was out of her house. After hearing the door shut, she walked into the entry to watch him leave.

And good riddance, she added silently.

On the hall table, a missive sat atop a small stack of correspondence. Something familiar drew her near, and she reached for it, running her fingers over the ivory envelope addressed to The Right Honorable Countess of Amesbury. *It was the handwriting.* What was it doing in the middle of her entryway? She ripped the envelope open.

DEAR LADY AGONY,
YESTERDAY YOUR FRIEND LOST A HAT. WHO
KNOWS WHAT YOU MIGHT LOSE TODAY. THIS IS
YOUR LAST WARNING. STOP ASKING QUESTIONS.

It hadn't been sent to the magazine. It had come directly to her door. There was no question now. The person knew who she was and where she lived. And where her family lived.

A shudder traveled the length of her spine. What if the person threatened dear Winifred or Aunt Tabitha? If anything happened to either one of them . . . She shook off the possibility. She wasn't going to allow that to happen. If she had to search all day and night, she would locate the letter writer and bring the killer to justice. She had to. Her family's safety depended on it.

She reread the note. Although short, it told her something new: the writer had witnessed yesterday's fiasco on the docks.

Her mind flew to William, who was not only there but in her house this morning. Could he be the murderer? He and Flora had exchanged words the night of her engagement party. If his attempt at bribery failed, he might have grown desperate. But would he have done something so desperate as to push her off the balcony?

If William didn't leave the letter, her footman Bailey might know who did. She flung open the door and rushed to stop him. He was on his way to the baker. "Bailey, a moment, please. I need to ask you about this letter." She waved the envelope in the air. "Do you remember who delivered it?"

It was as if the question yanked him from another world, a world of baked goods, recital flowers, and dress alterations. Bailey paused and changed directions. "A letter?"

"Yes," said Amelia. "It doesn't have a return address."

The young man squinted at the envelope. "It's been a hectic day, my lady. I've been in and out of the house all morning. I don't recall."

"I understand." Amelia clasped her hands behind her back. "Take your time."

They both stared at the missive as if the sender's name would appear by magical ink.

Bailey rubbed his forehead. "I'm sorry. I just can't remember."

"I understand." Amelia tried to keep the disappointment out of her voice. "It's fine. Nothing to worry about."

"What's nothing to worry about?" asked Simon.

Speaking of magical ink. Simon appeared as if from thin air. She hadn't noticed his carriage arrive, which said something about where her mind was. It was a handsome traveling carriage, complete with the Bainbridge crest and four striking black horses.

Amelia slipped the letter behind her back, and Bailey hurried off toward the baker's, glad to be finished with the conversation. "I'm sorry. I didn't see you pull up. I, for one, am looking forward to our trip. It's a nice day for travel, is it not?"

Simon scanned the darkening sky. "It is not. What's behind your back?"

"My back?" Amelia stalled for time. *If only dresses had pockets.* There was enough material for one. Yet the convenience was never afforded.

"Yes, the paper you and your footman were ogling when I arrived."

"'Ogling' is such an unfortunate word and hardly the right choice here." Amelia tried a chuckle. It fell flat.

Simon held out his hand. "What is it?"

She didn't *have* to give him the letter. After all, it was *her* correspondence. But he was her confidant in this crime, her partner of sorts. She had to inform him. He deserved to know what they were up against. He also had the right to know he might be in danger as well. If the sender had seen her, he had probably seen him. She handed Simon the envelope.

He opened it and read the note. His green eyes flashed to hers. "Who sent this?"

"That's what I was trying to find out, but Bailey doesn't recall," she answered. "He's been busy with the details of Winifred's recital."

"The writer knows who you are and where you live. He addressed it directly." Simon returned the envelope to her. "I must find him immediately."

"We can't postpone our trip to the admiral's," Amelia insisted. "It's late enough as it is. Besides, finding the murderer means finding the letter writer. They're the same person. We both know it's true, and we have no other leads. Unless you have new information?"

"No . . ." Simon checked the sky. "I've been to the estate many times. It's not far, as long as the weather holds out."

"Let's depart right away, then." Amelia turned toward the door. "We'll resume our discussion in the carriage. I might have an idea on the writer's identity. I just need to fetch my parasol."

"You don't go anywhere without it, do you?"

She threw a look over her shoulder. "In this climate, never."

Fifteen minutes and many goodbyes later, Amelia and Simon were on their way to Dartford, headed to the admiral's family estate just outside of London. Simon had written ahead, informing the admiral of their visit. Simon had land in the area, and it wasn't unusual for him to stop if he was nearby. They visited each other's estates quite frequently.

"And what of my presence?" Amelia adjusted her hat, which had gone askew when she ascended the carriage. "What reason did you give for my coming along?" Since the Bainbridges and Amesburys were longtime family friends, they didn't need a reason for traveling together, but it wouldn't hurt, either.

"I didn't mention it." Simon helped her straighten the brim, the scent of sea salt filling her space as he did. "I assumed you would think of something. You have the time and are inventive. Make something up."

It was true. Storytelling was in her family's blood. They told tales and acted out plays to entertain themselves and their guests. Spinning yarns was a great way to pass the dismal winter months in the English countryside. Inventing a story came as easily as breathing. She took a deep breath. Nothing yet.

"What of this idea you mentioned?" Simon prodded. "Who do you think wrote the letter?"

Amelia relayed her suspicions about William. He'd conveniently dropped by her house just before the letter arrived. And he'd been at the docks and most likely witnessed the trouble with Kitty's hat.

Simon's eyes flickered emerald at the information. Perhaps it was the overcast day, the rain clouds the color of steel, or the dip of his jet-black hair over his eyebrows.

The look gave her pause. He was a man of the sea, a man who was used to navigating dangerous waters. He was not only capable of violence but used to it. If he thought William had threatened her, he would act, and act decisively. She wished she'd considered the claim more carefully before opening her mouth. Quickly, she added a caveat. "It's just a theory, mind you. I have no evidence it was he."

He tapped his fingertips, shifting his gaze to them instead of her. "It's a plausible one. He knew about the business at the docks, and he was in your house this morning."

"Right," agreed Amelia. "It might be the reason he didn't send it to the journal, like the first missive."

His eyes flew to hers. "What *first missive*?"

She slapped a hand over her mouth. Of all the ways she wanted the discussion to go, that was not one of them. It wasn't as if she were hiding the information, but now it would seem so. The last few days had been incredibly busy. If not for her trip to the docks and Kitty's fall into the river, she would have gotten around to telling him. Eventually.

"Amelia," he prompted. His voice was insistent.

She took a breath. "I received a similar note yesterday, but it arrived with my regular post from the magazine. It's one reason I was so desperate for answers." She gave him an apologetic smile. "The only recompense is we're getting closer. We must be, because the murderer feels threatened. Today will bring us even closer. It has to."

Simon shook his head, unable to answer right away. Instead, he looked out the window. "If someone would have told me two weeks ago that I'd be in this carriage, with Edgar's widow, chasing down a killer, I would have told them they were mad. Yet here we are. I am starting to think *I'm* the one who's mad." He returned his gaze to her face. "I shouldn't have agreed to your proposition. It was foolish and put you in harm's way. I don't know what I was thinking."

"You were thinking it was the right thing to do, and it is." Amelia touched his hand. "Two women are dead, and only *we* can solve their murders. We're the only ones who have all the information. We must follow this through. It's our duty."

He glanced at her hand, still covering his. "I feel responsible for your safety."

"Don't. It's a bad habit of yours." She squeezed his hand and released it. "First Edgar, now me? Is this something we should discuss?"

A brief smile touched his lips. "No."

"I imagine it comes from your time in the navy."

A second passed before he answered. "Perhaps. I'm used to being responsible for the lives of my men." His chin dipped. "But it is nothing compared to the responsibility I feel toward you."

Her brow wrinkled. "Because I am a woman?"

"Because you're Edgar's widow."

Amelia's gaze fell, watching the city streets turn to green hills. In her heart, she knew the answer. Still, it stung to hear him say it out loud. For the first time, she felt something new for a man. Maybe it was her youth coming back to her after years of mourning. Or maybe, as he said, it was physical desire. An attraction that had more to do with natural appeal than the man himself. But he didn't reciprocate the feeling. He was here for one reason—or person—only. Edgar.

Pushing aside the hurt feelings, she told herself it didn't matter why he was here. Finding justice for Charlotte was the goal, and he was helping her accomplish that. She needed him, and he needed to relieve his guilt. It wasn't ideal but it could work. The admiral's sister-in-law held a clue to Flora's death, which, in turn, might hold the answer to Charlotte's death. If they followed the clues, they would lead to justice. They had to.

Chapter 26

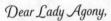

Dear Lady Agony,

What do you make of country house visits? With the
necessary tips et cetera, they're becoming costly affairs. Do
you think they are worth it? I would like to go very much, but
my husband dreads the additional expenditure. How might I
convince him?

Devotedly,
Trip Taker

. . . .

Dear Trip Taker,

There is nothing better than a country house visit if you
wish for a change of scenery. It will cost you, certainly,
but nothing in this life is free. I say it is better to invest in
memories, not merchandise. Inform your husband the former

*will outlast the latter. The logic will surely appeal to his
wallet.*

*Yours in Secret,
Lady Agony*

The admiral's country estate was on the outskirts of Dartford, tucked behind a green thicket of trees and an apple orchard, where Amelia imagined she could still smell fragrant blossoms despite the lateness of the season. If she inhaled deeply, she could almost taste the sweet heady scent that must have filled the air a month ago. A rickety wooden bridge gave way to the large, square home that itself was a statement among so much rolling green. A rustic gem, it had the advantage of size and privacy, two benefits the admiral's London residence didn't afford, while still being close to the city. Amelia assumed he needed to remain in contact with the navy, as well as his shipbuilding business, which made the location ideal, not to mention beautiful.

As they drew closer to the house, Amelia noted an impressive garden, lush with flowers and foliage. Like the house itself, it was square, bordered by a perfectly cut hedge. A double fountain stood in the center, making music with its spilling waters. On a bench sat an old woman, her face hidden by her hat. Her age was revealed by the hunch of her back and the twist of her fingers that worked a knitting needle. Could she be the admiral's sister-in-law? She was certainly the right age. Amelia made the suggestion to Simon.

He leaned past her. "It might explain why his gardens are considered some of the nicest in the area. I never understood why he would invest so much care in them, being a water lover himself."

Amelia snapped her fingers. "I'll ask him for a tour of his gardens. I'll tell him I'm looking for ideas to redo my own. It not only gives me an excuse for coming, but also a reason to get close to that woman. We'll be able to ask her about Flora's engagement party."

The carriage stopped, and the footman opened the door. Simon lowered his voice. "*You* will ask her. I'll keep the admiral distracted. Just be careful. If she's as unhinged as Henry says she is, she might do something untoward. Promise me."

"I promise."

Simon descended the carriage steps and helped her do the same. A moment later, the admiral was greeting them. Despite the relaxed country atmosphere, the admiral was crisply dressed in a white shirt and an old-fashioned cravat. His expectations didn't relax because he was outside of London. His beard was as straight as Aunt Tabitha's stitches and his hair perfectly trimmed over his ears. Only his barrel-shaped belly betrayed his indulgences.

"Hello, Bainbridge." Admiral Edwards gave her a short bow. "Lady Amesbury, it's an unexpected pleasure to see you again."

"The pleasure is mine." Amelia indicated the gardens. "I've heard about your impressive gardens, but seeing them for myself is a treat. I hope you don't mind my coming along. I need ideas for reorganizing my garden."

The admiral's ears perked up at the word *reorganizing*. "Not at all. Glad you could come. Restructuring a garden is no small task. It takes planning, patience, and logic."

Not the three words I would have associated with gardening, but no matter. Amelia smiled. "My thoughts exactly."

The admiral tilted his chin toward the sky. "I recommend we start with a short tour first. Rain is headed in our direction."

"Excellent idea," agreed Simon. "Lead the way, Admiral."

Up close, the gardens were even more striking than they were from a distance, and Amelia didn't have to pretend to be interested. She would love a garden such as this one. It reminded her of Kitty's, except Kitty's was smaller and stood below the balcony of her tall London home. Here, the lushness sprawled into a copse of English oak, giving one the impression of endless time and space. English roses as lovely and as round as tea saucers spoke to time-honored traditions yet were no match for the white magnolia blooms, which were as fragrant as they were full. Hydrangeas splashed lavender and pink into a border that led to the garden like a riotous band. In the shade of the house, and closest to the windows, a fernery gave one pause from the explosion of color, a menagerie of soft green, blue-green, and the palest mint.

"What size is your garden?" asked Admiral Edwards as they passed the gate.

Amelia gave him an approximation.

The admiral stopped, appearing to do a quick calculation in his head. "Your property is in Mayfair?"

"Correct," she said. He continued walking, his strides short but brisk, and she had to hurry to keep pace.

"The purpose is to impress, then," he continued.

"Not at all," answered Amelia. "I would like something simple yet beautiful, like this."

"Ah, but it should impress. The worst thing a garden can be is out of place. You must consider the setting first and foremost." He paused at the fountain, the sound of tinkling water filling the void of his boisterous voice. "In London, this garden would be very much out of place. Its size would be garish and overwhelming. What you need is something upright and refined. Something that fits with the elegant homes in the area." He put a stubby finger to his temple. "Keep that in mind."

"Excellent advice." Simon nodded. "I see your expertise expands beyond the sea."

Admiral Edwards smiled. "When you consider it, the sea and the land are not so different. They both require firm control. It's a matter of organization."

"Which reminds me," added Simon, "I have a question regarding a ship. A situation off the African coast."

"Do you mind if I wander around while you gentlemen discuss?" asked Amelia. "I'd like to cover as much ground as possible before the rain arrives."

"Not at all." The admiral gestured ahead. "Take your time."

Amelia walked in the direction of the bench where she'd originally seen the old woman. It took several turns to get there, and she understood what the admiral meant about organization. The garden reminded her of small rooms, each connected to the next. It was quite impressive, when she thought about it. As the admiral had said, beautiful gardens took a good deal of planning for the separate areas to flow together so seamlessly.

Unfortunately, when she reached her destination, the bench was empty. She scanned the surrounding area, stopping to examine a copious vine of purple wisteria. The flowers were a brilliant shade of violet under the day's cloud cover. She reached out to touch the velvety bloom.

"I wouldn't do that if I was you," came a voice from behind. Amelia spun around. "Why not?"

The old woman stood before her. Barely five feet tall, she was short and stout, wearing a shapeless black dress. Her face, too, was cloaked in a scarf that disguised her features.

The woman lifted her chin, revealing blank eyes that were vaguely frightening. "They don't like it."

"The Edwardses?"

"The flowers." The woman clicked her teeth. "They don't like to be touched."

"I understand." Amelia swallowed, determined not to let her first impressions get the best of her. She stuck out her hand. "I'm Amelia Amesbury. I'm here with Lord Bainbridge."

The old woman wiped her palm on her dress before taking Amelia's. "I'm the queen of England."

Though gnarled, the woman's hand was surprisingly soft. Perhaps it was the plumpness of it. "You must be the admiral's sister-in-law. I've heard so much about you."

"I doubt that, deary. My brother-in-law pretends I don't exist."

"Families can be challenging." Amelia sat on a nearby bench, hoping the woman would join her. "I have three sisters, and they might say the same thing. I haven't been in contact with them much since my husband passed away."

The old woman turned an ear toward her. "What's that, you say? Your husband died?"

"Two years ago," Amelia confirmed. "He suffered from a debilitating condition. He had been sick for a while."

"You must be cursed, like me." She shuffled toward the bench but didn't sit down. "My husband died, too."

Henry had said her husband had died on their wedding day. He hadn't said how. Maybe Amelia could find out. "I'm sorry to hear that. Was he ill?"

"No. It had nothing to do with him."

Amelia's brow furrowed in question.

"I said I was cursed, didn't I?" The woman's voice rose sharply. "All the Engelthorpe women are cursed."

Amelia saw her chance to bring up Flora and took it. "You mean Flora."

The old woman's eyes flashed. "Yes, Flora. She's dead now, too."

"I heard it was an accident, not a curse." A raindrop fell on Amelia's dress, and she brushed at it. "She had a habit of sleep-walking, I'm told."

The woman scooted next to Amelia. "My husband died the day of our wedding. He was bucked from his horse and broke his neck. I warned Flora of the curse, but she wouldn't believe me. That one was stubborn." She grinned, revealing a missing tooth. "I bet she believes me now."

Despite the cool day, a prickle of sweat formed on the back of Amelia's neck. "Were you there? Did you see her fall?"

"Of course not. I was in bed, asleep." She tilted her head. "But I heard her scream, and I knew. You never forget a sound like that." She took a haggard breath. "Sometimes I hear it in my dreams."

The scream haunted the old woman's dreams. Maybe it was because she was the one who had pushed her. The old woman was stout enough. Still, it didn't add up. She lived here, in Dartford. Yet the trouble continued in London, first with Flora, then Charlotte, and finally the threatening letters. "Have you been back to London since then?"

"No." She pressed her lips together. "I never want to go back. I like it here, in my garden."

Several raindrops fell in succession. "We should find the admiral." Amelia put a hand on the woman's arm. "The rain has started, and you'll catch a chill."

The woman leapt up as if bitten by a snake. "I told you, they don't like to be touched!"

"I apologize. I won't touch the flowers again."

"I am the flowers! I am the flowers!" She stumbled in the direction of the house, uttering the sentence over and over.

Amelia stared after her, popping up her parasol. The old woman was daft. Maybe even dangerous. Amelia couldn't trust what she said. Still, she needed to consider the possibility that Flora's and Charlotte's deaths were unconnected. The old woman could have killed Flora but not Charlotte. Even as she contemplated the idea, her brain rejected it. They had to be connected. What other explanation could there be? Two separate killers?

"There you are," called Simon. "The rain is here. Good. You're protected." He peeked under her parasol, lowering his voice. "The admiral's waiting inside with tea. Did you talk to her?"

Amelia slowly nodded.

"And?"

"She is stark raving mad."

Chapter 27

Dear Lady Agony,

I wonder if you know anything about weather? Not the weather, specifically, but its effects on the human condition. What is one to do when it rains like this? How is one to overcome the longing to be outside and away from people?

Devotedly,
Soaking Wet

. . . .

Dear Soaking Wet,

Never underestimate the power of rain. Someone famous said that, or if they didn't, they should have. Bad weather has the ability to shred our patience. But one burst of sunshine is all it takes for optimism to break through. Until that sunny day, dear

reader, stick to your dry corner and take a good book. It is the
cure for the rainy-day doldrums.

Yours in Secret,
Lady Agony

Simon and Amelia enjoyed the rainy afternoon with Admiral Edwards by a cozy fire and a delightful assortment of sandwiches and cakes. The rain, soft droplets at first, was coming down in slanted sheets now. The road was becoming a real concern, as it quickly turned to mud in the country. Rain was as certain as sherry before dinner, but not downpours like this. Even Simon looked worried. Despite the admiral's engaging story, he kept checking the window. A deep rumble rattled the glass in the windows, and Amelia jumped.

"Terrible weather." The admiral picked up a hand telescope from the table and aimed it out the window. He closed one eye as he peered into the instrument. "I don't think you'll be leaving anytime soon, Bainbridge."

"We cannot be delayed," Amelia insisted. "Winifred's recital is the day after tomorrow. There's much left to attend to."

The admiral laid down the scope. "No changing the weather, as much as we'd like to. Just be glad you're next to a warm fire and not out at sea. You wouldn't believe what it can do to a grown man's fortitude."

"We're grateful to be here, inside." Simon turned to Amelia. "The admiral is right. There's no changing the weather. We will have to wait it out."

Amelia knew it was true, but she also knew she had to get home to Winifred, who was anxious about her first performance.

Amelia would move fire and mountains if it got to that point. She squinted at the window, streaked with rain. Hopefully the storm would pass as quickly as it had arrived.

Admiral Edwards picked up his teacup. "Was your walk in the garden inspirational?"

"Very much," answered Amelia. "The fernery in particular is striking. How do you manage it all? Does it require a large staff?"

"You might be surprised." Admiral Edwards paused to sip his tea. "With the right help and consistent care, you can do very much with very little, and my sister-in-law, Dahlia, tends to it regularly. She might not be good with people, mind you, but she is very good with plants. The key is consistency. If a day goes by without attention, you'll find yourself behind." He frowned. "That's my problem in London. Being down one maid has set the entire house off course. I haven't been successful at finding a replacement."

His lament sparked an idea in Amelia. "Tabitha Amesbury is an expert on household management. You would appreciate her attention to detail." She paused for a moment as she considered the pair. Actually, they would make a nice couple, romantically. A lightning bolt flashed, returning her thoughts to the present. "She could suggest someone."

Like the sky, the admiral's face lit up. "Would she? It'd take a considerable load off my mind. I'm hesitant to move staff from this house, because they prefer it here, in the country, but I need someone for Rose straightaway. Her first season has already had its hurdles."

"Flora's passing?" asked Simon.

Admiral Edwards bristled. "That, among other things." He returned his teacup and crossed one leg over the other. "You know young men, Bainbridge. They can be very convincing when they want to be, but Rose is young and ignorant. Her mother has been gone many years, bless her soul, and Flora was her trusted mentor. Without her, I'm afraid Rose will be lost."

"What about Hyacinth?" asked Amelia. "She's older than Rose."

Admiral Edwards swatted away the thought. "Hyacinth doesn't have the same constitution Flora had. Flora was like me. Hyacinth is like a seed in the wind. She travels whichever way the wind blows."

Now it made sense why the admiral rejected a memorial garden. Flora had been *his* daughter, good with ships and numbers. He wouldn't want a memorial garden for her any more than he would want one for himself. Simon was right. He wasn't being callous. He was just being himself.

"Hyacinth flung herself at her sister's own fiancé," continued the admiral, shaking his head in disgust. "He, of course, wants nothing to do with her. He was crushed by Flora's passing, which makes it worse for everyone. In fact, it would be better for everyone if he just disappeared. His moping about helps no one."

Simon's eyebrows rose at the comment.

The admiral noted the change. "I'm sorry, Lady Amesbury. That was insensitive of me to say out loud. Flora's death has hit me harder than I care to admit."

Amelia held up her hand. "No need to apologize. I understand what it means to grieve."

"Yes, you do. Your husband was a fine man. You can take comfort in that."

A new sheet of rain pelted the window, and the admiral stood. "I'm going to inform the cook you'll be staying for dinner. Not a chance you'll be leaving tonight."

After he left, Amelia twisted to face Simon. "What are we going to do? I cannot be stuck here all evening."

"Nothing can be done about the weather." Simon lifted his eyes to the window. "We have to wait it out."

"Winifred needs me," Amelia pressed. "I need to get home to her."

"Winifred needs you home alive. Leaving in this storm would be foolish. It would put your life in jeopardy."

That was an overstatement. She'd ridden in storms worse than this one. A thunder crack vibrated the walls. Perhaps not worse than this one, but at least similar. "What did you think of the admiral's comments about Hyacinth? Do you think she might have killed Flora to have Henry Cosgrove for herself?"

"The idea has crossed my mind." Simon paused for a moment. "But I've known Hyacinth as long as I've known the admiral. She was always a flighty little girl and hasn't changed. I can see her pushing her sister off the balcony in a fit of hysteria, but killing Charlotte?" He shook his head. "I don't believe she has it in her to plan something."

She ran the idea past him that struck her in the garden. "Do you think we have two murderers?"

"I don't," Simon quickly dismissed. "Too many similarities exist. Plus your letters."

Amelia leaned back in her chair. "I thought the same thing about the admiral's sister-in-law. She might have hurt Flora but not Charlotte. It's impossible."

"We have to follow where the clues lead us." Simon shrugged. "It's all we can do."

They had no other choice but to eliminate possibilities one at a time. Amelia scratched her head. It felt as if she was missing something.

The admiral returned, asking if they'd like to see his maritime memorabilia, and they followed him into the library. It was musty and damp, and the pages of a book on Robert Heriot Barclay stuck together as Amelia turned them. The admiral had had a long, illustrious career and talked about missions, crews, and men of distinction. Simon seemed fascinated, but Amelia was distracted. Her mind kept straying to Winifred and how to get back home. When the admiral mentioned a particular ship, however, she saw a way to introduce Fair Winds. She seized the opportunity to discuss his clerk William Donahue.

"You know what it takes to make a seaworthy vessel," Amelia interceded. "Is that why you went into business?"

The admiral's barrel chest swelled. "That and my years at sea. Of course, the navy can't have us old men hanging around forever." He and Simon shared a look. "It's up to young captains to lead their crews. But I missed being on a ship, which is why I turned to building them. It satisfies me a good deal."

Amelia set down the book she was thumbing. "I've met your clerk William Donahue. He seems very dedicated to the business."

"Donahue is a good man," he said. "His uncle is an earl, you know, and his father owns land around here. I've thought of him often for Rose. He'd be a worthy suitor . . . and solve this business of a season." He rubbed his forehead. "The sooner it comes to a conclusion, the better."

"What do your daughters think of him?" asked Simon.

"Flora didn't care for him. She considered his bookkeeping deficient, but that's because she was better at it than he was." He smiled a lopsided smile. "Don't share that with Donahue, though."

"We won't." Amelia returned his smile.

"But Rose enjoys his company," the admiral continued. "Maybe a little too much, if you get my meaning. Hyacinth has higher aspirations, which is to be expected since she is now my eldest daughter and Flora was engaged to a duke."

"Did Flora find fault with William's bookkeeping?" asked Simon. "Was that the trouble between them?"

The admiral picked up the compass on the table, watching the needle as it moved. Earlier, he'd said it had been passed down from his great-grandfather, who had also been an admiral. The gold, while dull, still glimmered in the spark of the firelight. "Now that you mention it, yes. She did say something about an error in the books. What that error was, I couldn't say. We never had a chance to discuss it, and it does not matter now." He put the compass down and smiled a sad smile. "It's funny how what seemed important then is not so important now." He clapped his hands on his thighs. "But enough of the past. How about a drink before dinner?"

Amelia knew he didn't mean for her to join them. "I would like to freshen up if I could."

He stood, walked to the door, and shouted for a maid. "Of course, Lady Amesbury. Mrs. Rutgers will be happy to assist you."

Newly arrived in a starched apron, Mrs. Rutgers wasn't pleased with the admiral's unconventional summons. Her narrow eyes, aimed in the direction of Admiral Edwards, relayed her displeasure. She refocused on Amelia and bobbed a curtsy. Amelia stood and followed her.

She took in the house on the way to powder her nose. She passed through a large hallway that showcased the admiral's maritime lineage. Men of great distinction—and great beards—stared down at her from gilded frames. All wore the British naval uniform, navy blue and white with broad hats.

Having three daughters, Admiral Edwards was the last of a great line of officers. A son's portrait wouldn't be placed after his.

Did it bother him? If the world were a different place, maybe Flora would have followed in his footsteps. She had had an aptitude for mathematics; maybe she had also had an aptitude for command. As it was, however, the line stopped with him.

The officers' wives took up a smaller space on the wall but were regal in their own right. Pride shone in their eyes—and determination, too. With their husbands at sea, perseverance was key. Their chins were set in a way that told their own stories of persistence. The women had endured hardships, but the collective narrative was one of victory.

Amelia paused at the last portrait. It must be the admiral's wife, long deceased. Like the other women, she was beautifully dressed in a low-cut gown that revealed a snow-white décolletage. There was something familiar about her, and Amelia decided it was her similarity to her daughter Hyacinth. They had the same blue eyes, deep-set and somewhat unsettling. They also had the same lips, where a smile seemed to play. "Is this the admiral's wife?"

Mrs. Rutgers gave a brief nod. "Yes, it is. God rest her soul."

"She's been gone a long time?"

"Over sixteen years," answered Mrs. Rutgers.

"She wasn't very old when she passed." Amelia waited a moment for Mrs. Rutgers to explain. When she didn't, Amelia pressed, "Was she ill?"

Mrs. Rutgers studied the portrait. "On the outside, she was the picture of health. A beautiful woman, as you can see. Porcelain skin, a stunning figure, and those beautiful eyes. But inside . . ." She cleared her throat. "She'd only just had Rose, her third baby in five years. Childbirth takes its toll on some women, emotionally."

Amelia pondered the statement. Her mother had told her

stories of some women growing despondent after childbirth. While most people brushed off the condition as temporary, Amelia knew it could be serious. She remembered hearing about a young mother taking her own life in Mells. Was that the case here, too? It sounded like it, but it was hard to determine for certain without asking. Yet there was no way to ask the question without being indelicate.

Mrs. Rutgers motioned around the corner. "You may wash your hands at the first door on your left. Do you need anything else?"

"Nothing, thank you." Amelia smiled. "You've been very helpful." When Mrs. Rutgers was gone, Amelia gazed at the portrait a minute longer. The resemblance between the mother and her daughters was striking. They definitely took after her, not their father.

"I see you found my sister, Iris."

Amelia's neck prickled with realization. She forced herself to turn around even though she knew whose voice it was. Dahlia stood before her without a scarf, and Amelia better understood the resemblance. The pale skin, the thick brown hair, parted severely in the middle, and the deep-set eyes. These traits were visible not only in Mrs. Edwards and her girls but Dahlia, too.

Amelia took a breath. She was accustomed to uncomfortable conversations. She'd had plenty with guests at the Feathered Nest and wouldn't let Dahlia rattle her. "She was quite beautiful."

Dahlia lowered her lids. "Yes, she was."

"Mrs. Rutgers said she passed away after Rose was born." Amelia forced herself to keep her voice even. "What happened?"

She didn't answer. Instead, she stared at the portrait, her lips moving wordlessly.

Was she saying a prayer? Reciting a curse? Indeed, she looked like a witch. Her brown hair was streaked with iron gray, and her profile revealed a bump on her nose. Amelia stared, waiting for her to answer the question. When it became clear she wasn't going to, she sidestepped her to go wash her hands.

Dahlia gripped her arm as she passed. Her hand felt like a claw. "Sister says I should tell you the story. She says you're trying to help."

Amelia jerked it loose. "Let go of me."

Dahlia spoke to the portrait. "I heard you the first time!" She turned to Amelia. "You asked me what happened. I'll tell you." She held up a hand and said to the painting, "Hush, Iris. I'm telling it. I'll do it my own way." She returned to Amelia. "The admiral had taken her to Devon, for holiday. She wasn't well, and he thought the waters would help. They bring some visitors peace of mind, but not Iris. Restless, she wandered off. They found her three days later—washed ashore on the rocky coastline." Her dark eyes flicked to the portrait for approval. Satisfied, she nodded.

Amelia was speechless. First, Dahlia had been speaking to the portrait as if it were speaking back. Second, she had divulged Iris committed suicide. After a few seconds, Amelia expressed her condolences. "I'm so sorry."

The creases in Dahlia's forehead deepened. "Don't be sorry. She's still here with me. Didn't you notice? In the garden?"

Amelia had no idea what she was talking about.

Dahlia tilted her head, revealing a mole on her cheek. "They're all flowers."

It clicked, and Amelia understood. Iris, Flora, Hyacinth, Rose. They were all named after flowers. Perhaps that was the reason Dahlia spent all her time in the garden. The thought endeared her to the old woman. Maybe she wasn't daft after all. Maybe she was just lonely. "Of course. I see it now."

Mrs. Rutgers's voice interrupted the companionable moment of silence. "Mrs. Engelthorpe, please step aside so that Lady Amesbury can move past. It's time for your tonic. You must take it before dinner."

All animation left Dahlia's face. The deep-set eyes became vacant and the lips drooped into a frown. She didn't move.

Mrs. Rutgers touched her arm, and, as she had done in the garden, Dahlia recoiled with force. Mrs. Rutgers stood firm, gesturing to the staircase. Dahlia took a step, then turned back to Amelia. "Remember what I said. It's important."

Mrs. Rutgers followed Dahlia up the stairs, and Amelia used the washstand. When she was finished, Mrs. Rutgers was waiting in the hallway. A patient smile was plastered on her lips. "I apologize for Mrs. Engelthorpe. She's an old woman. She is easily confused."

"No need to apologize," said Amelia. "I understand. Has she always been this way, or just since Mrs. Edwards passed?"

Mrs. Rutgers dismissed her concern. "She came here when her sister was married. She had nowhere else to turn, and despite his tough talk, Admiral Edwards is kindhearted. Too kindhearted, perhaps. The woman becomes more of a challenge each day."

They walked toward the dining room, and Amelia paused outside the door. "Is what she said true? Did Mrs. Edwards . . . drown in Devon?"

Mrs. Rutgers lowered her shoulders in silent protest of the question. "What Mrs. Edwards did is between her and God. It's no one's business."

"I didn't mean to imply—" started Amelia, but Mrs. Rutgers

turned on her heel and left. Suicide was not discussed in any company, especially polite company. The church shunned people who committed the dastardly deed, which was one of the many reasons the subject was off-limits. But how else was she supposed to gain confirmation of Dahlia's admission? She certainly couldn't ask Admiral Edwards. If the cold shoulder of Mrs. Rutgers was the consequence, so be it. She'd taken the same from others in higher positions. She would be lying, however, if she said the rebuff hadn't stung.

Simon waited for her in the dining room and led her to their seats. A half smile touched his lips as he adjusted the napkin on his lap. "Is something the matter, Lady Amesbury?"

She cracked open her napkin. "What makes you ask?"

"You look annoyed."

She gave him a side glance. "I've been scolded, rather handily, and for nothing more than asking a valid question. It's incorrigible that I should have to watch what I say everywhere I go."

"Who scolded you?"

"The maid," answered Amelia. "Mrs. Rutgers."

"How humbling."

"Polite conversation drives me mad. If I have a question, I should be able to ask it to queen, countrymen, or maid without fear of offense." She pointed her fork at him. "Don't you agree?"

Simon lowered her hand with the fork in it. "I suppose it depends on the question."

She let it drop. "How can you say that? You do not bend to convention. You wouldn't be here otherwise."

"Partly true. But I also have the utmost respect for rules." He waited for the footman to set down a dish before continuing. "They're put in place to protect people."

She knew he was being honest. He wouldn't have been promoted to captain in the Royal Navy without adhering to rules. (Actually, being a marquis, he might have.) But he'd also told Edgar to hang the rules when it came to finding a wife. Was it because of his own history with Felicity or perhaps a deeper history within his own family? Like so many things, his past was an enigma. One she'd like to get to the bottom of.

"I do not need protection," answered Amelia.

He shot her a look. "Two letters in your possession say otherwise."

"Assistance is not protection," she quipped.

"It is in my book."

Amelia opened her mouth and then closed it. Far be it from her to challenge Simon Bainbridge's rule book.

Chapter 28

Dear Lady Agony,

I cannot sleep. The moment my head hits the pillow, my mind begins to race. I fell asleep above my soup bowl yesterday. Tomorrow it might be my teacup. Do you know of a remedy for sleeplessness?

Devotedly,
Sleepy Sarah

. . . .

Dear Sleepy Sarah,

If I had the remedy for sleeplessness, I would use it to cure myself, for I, too, suffer from it. So, I do not have a solution, but I do have empathy, and will tell you what has worked for me. Brisk daily exercise. I walk two miles every day, regardless of the weather, and I read until my book falls into my lap. These habits, practiced regularly, help moderately. When they do not,

*a snifter of brandy doesn't hurt. Anyone who tells you it will has
not suffered from a poor night's rest.*

Yours in Secret,
Lady Agony

Amelia knew it was going to be one of *those* nights, the kind
where she tossed and turned and eventually rose from bed out of
sheer frustration. Sleeping in a strange place, she expected it.
When the storm didn't abate after dinner, Admiral Edwards
insisted she and Simon stay the night, and they had no choice
but to take him up on his offer. The roads were all mud and could
not be traversed even with Simon's first-rate carriage. Still now,
after midnight, the thunder rattled the windows of the old country estate, and the blowing trees made terrifying shadows on the
walls. It was not just damp but cold, extra cold because Amelia
was sleeping in her drawers and chemise. But it was better than
putting on a dead woman's clothes.

Mrs. Rutgers had lent her some of Flora's old sleeping gar-
ments, and, although suitable, Amelia couldn't bring herself to
don them. Freezing cold, she needed to do something to encourage sleep—and warmth. Her mind was on Winifred and the
recital and how to get home in time for it. What if the storm
raged on another day? What if she missed the performance?

No. If she had to ride through driving wind and rain, she
would. She wouldn't miss Winifred's big day. She'd rather face
a tempest than let that little girl down. Even so, Winifred would
be worried. Although Tabitha would surely console and reassure
her, Amelia wouldn't feel right until she was back in Mayfair.

Amelia hopped out of bed to fetch a book from the library,
and when her feet hit the cold floor, she almost got back in. She

quickly slipped on Flora's pale blue dressing gown, hastily tying a bow at the waist. The extra layer felt good and warmed her slightly. Now, if she could just get down to the library and select one of those dull maritime tomes, she would surely be able to lull herself to sleep, if only for a few precious hours.

Taking her bedside lantern, she opened the door slowly. The hinge made a terrible creak, and she paused in midstep. When no one awoke from the sound, she continued tiptoeing into the hallway and down the stairs. A draft caught her dressing gown. Shivering, she looked left and right, not remembering exactly where the library was. She turned a corner, hoping she'd chosen the right direction.

Noting the familiar portraits, she knew she was on the right path. In the flicker of candlelight, the portraits took on a menacing feel. Now the admirals appeared like ghosts in the frames, with hoary beards and white heads. Their wives were no better, and Iris, Admiral Edwards's wife, was perhaps the scariest of all. Her deep-set eyes were vapid, vacant of meaning.

Iris's portrait was crooked. Amelia reached for it and stopped, remembering Dahlia's sensitivity to touch. Had Iris had the same sensitivity? Would the picture come alive if she straightened it? And why was the portrait crooked in the first place?

"Can't sleep, deary?"

Amelia had her answer. Dahlia stared back at her in the flesh. The old woman must have been downstairs. Dressed in a white sleeping cap, she was like one of the portraits, ghostlike and silent. "Goodness, you startled me," answered Amelia. "No, I couldn't sleep."

"I could never sleep, even when I was a young woman like you."

That doesn't bode well for my future, thought Amelia, but gave her a sympathetic smile. "It's hard sleeping in a strange place. I was on my way to the library to borrow a book. Reading always helps me sleep."

Dahlia's eyes were as empty as a newly tilled garden. "What do you mean? You're not in a strange place."

Amelia took a step back. There was something unsettling about the old woman's words. "I just meant it feels strange, being away from home."

Dahlia stepped forward, touching Amelia's dressing gown. "This is your home, Flora."

The statement was disconcerting at best, hair-raising at worst. How could Dahlia believe she was Flora Edwards? Even if they were similar in age, they looked nothing like each other. The woman was delusional. Amelia needed to get out of there—now.

"Come back upstairs. I'll tuck you in."

"No, thank you." Amelia ducked her touch. "I'm going to the library. Have a good night."

"Listen to your auntie, Flora." Her voice was harsher. "Go to bed. Before something bad happens to you."

"I will," Amelia lied, turning in the other direction. Her candle blew out with the rush of her footsteps, and she cursed her bad luck. Not only was she alone in a strange house with a madwoman following her, now she was plunged into complete darkness. She scurried left and then backtracked right. A light was visible a room away. She changed directions, hoping someone was awake who might help her.

Without warning, she hit something solid. A yelp escaped her lips.

"Amelia! What's the matter?"

Amelia released a breath. It was Simon. She fell against his chest, not caring if it was appropriate. She needed a moment to collect herself.

Simon didn't care, either. He stroked her head, his fingers following the long tendrils down her back.

His steady heartbeat quieted her own, and she started to feel like herself again. She pulled back, missing the warmness of his body. "It's Dahlia. I think she's following me."

He kept an arm around her. "Let's go to the library. I left my light in there."

"That's where I was headed before she stopped me."

"Shh," he whispered. "Wait until we're alone."

The light grew brighter as they entered the small but respectable library. Simon's candle was on a table in the center of the room. The fireplace was out, and the candlelight was the only flicker in the room, except for the occasional burst of moonlight when it escaped the cloud cover. Amelia noted the open book on the couch near the table. Simon must have been reading when he heard her footsteps and left the book behind. She sat down, and he joined her.

"Tell me what happened."

Amelia explained her conversation with Dahlia. Recalling her blank eyes, she shivered. "It was as if she wasn't fully present. I can't explain it."

"Was she sleepwalking?"

That was an idea. Flora had been a sleepwalker. Sleepwalking might run in the family, and Amelia had heard stories about sleepwalkers holding entire conversations they didn't recollect the next day. Still, something didn't add up. "Maybe, but she mistook me for Flora. She called herself 'auntie.' It was the oddest thing."

"Perhaps not as odd as you think."

Amelia's forehead wrinkled in question. "What do you mean?"

Simon touched the lacy cuff of her sleeve. "You're wearing one of Flora's dressing gowns, aren't you?"

How could she have been so dense? "Yes, of course." She touched her gown. "This is Flora's. No wonder Dahlia thought I was Flora. Why didn't I think of that?"

"Because you were too busy retreating from a madwoman." Simon smiled lightly. "Besides, you look nothing like her. Your hair is richer, your skin is warmer, and your eyes . . ." The comment trailed into silence.

She blinked. Her eyes were what? *His* eyes were as green as the thickest blades of grass. In the candlelight, they reminded her of galloping down the steep hill that led to Mells. Her horse, Marmalade, could run like the wind, making it seem as if she were flying. The rush of feeling was like no other.

Until now.

Simon cleared his throat. "The point is, the dress doesn't explain the exchange entirely. It might have been momentarily confusing, certainly. But if she were thinking clearly, she would have realized it was you when you began speaking."

"Do you think she is mad?"

"I do," Simon affirmed. "Her mental soundness has always been in question, and this exchange answers it, in my opinion. What I want to know is if her senility is due to age or something else."

A thought niggled at the back of Amelia's mind, and she tried to place it. Like a puzzle, she was arranging the information to make sense of it. Simon's comment connected a missing piece.

"You said she became angry. Why? Was it something you said?"

Amelia tried to recall the conversation exactly. "She wanted me to go back upstairs. She said she would tuck me in. I declined."

"Interesting . . ." Simon leaned closer, his voice a murmur. "Remember that Flora died in the middle of the night, also after going to bed."

Amelia checked the door. They were still alone, so she continued. "Dahlia told me she suffered from insomnia. Obviously, she's telling the truth. She was up tonight, and I assume she was up the night of Flora's death, too. Yet she claimed she was in bed, sleeping, when she heard Flora's scream. Do you think she saw something?"

"She might not have only seen something but *done* something."

Amelia wasn't as sure. Yet, in light of this new information, maybe Simon was correct. Maybe Dahlia had done something to Flora. Honestly, she had no idea what to believe anymore. She folded her hands in defeat. "I'm the mad one to think I could solve Charlotte's murder. You must think I'm an imbecile."

Simon unfolded her hands. "No, I don't. I think you are one of the most remarkable women I've ever met." He lifted his eyes from their hands. "You're not only smart but courageous. Edgar was a lucky man."

The compliment was so unexpected that Amelia felt the heat rise in her face. Caught up in the moment, she hadn't realized the intimacy of their position. She tried to convince herself it was their shared secret that created the familiarity, nothing more. But with him this close, it was hard. Why did he hold back? Didn't he feel it, too? Did the memory of Edgar get in the way?

He might be a paragon of self-control, but she was not. She

hadn't been raised to be. From the time she was little, her parents had encouraged her curiosity and free spirit, and if anyone aroused her curiosity now, it was Simon. He was so different from the men she'd met in Mells or London. He was complex, unpredictable, and maybe even haunted by his past. If he would just stop worrying about what he should do for a moment and do what he wanted to do . . . what would that be?

It wasn't a question she was able to ask, for a look of surprise changed his face, and the color drained from his skin. He was staring at a spot behind her, studying it as if he was afraid to look away. She didn't have to follow his eyes but did anyway. Seeing Dahlia in the doorway was confirmation: the old lady was there in the library, watching them.

Chapter 29

Dear Lady Agony,

Have you ever been caught in the act? I just have. My neighbor caught me and her son having a private moment under the willow tree. She came upon us without warning, so you can imagine our unpreparedness. She promised to tell my father, but it's been a fortnight, and he's said nothing. Do you think he knows? Should I tell him?

Devotedly,
Longing for Another Kiss

. . . .

Dear Longing for Another Kiss,

Have I been caught in the act? A lady never tells. If you make the unfortunate choice to be indiscreet, don't make another one by talking about it. Should you tell your father? That's a difficult question, and one that only you can answer. Does he know?

That's an easier question. No, he doesn't. If he did, he would
have reprimanded you and the neighbor boy as well. Next time
you choose to be indiscreet (and if you are longing for another
kiss, there will be a next time), make certain no one is
watching—and select a bigger willow tree.

Yours in Secret,
Lady Agony

Dahlia closed one eye. "What do you think you're doing in here? Alone, without a chaperone?"

Amelia nearly jumped off the bench. "I told you. I'm here to borrow a book. Why are you following me?"

"It's my job to watch after you." Dahlia leveled a look at Simon. "Which is more than I can say for this *gentleman*." She uttered the word with disgust.

"I, too, was here for a book." Simon gestured to the open tome on the table. "I was reading Lady Amesbury an interesting passage on . . . naval strategies when you arrived."

"That's not what it looked like to me." Dahlia's eyes grew wider, as if to emphasize their capabilities, the amber flecks cat-like. "It looked like you were trying to seduce my niece."

Amelia flung up her hands. "I'm not your niece! I'm Amelia Amesbury."

But Dahlia's eyes didn't register the comment. They flicked by it without recognition or response.

Simon stood with his lantern. "May I escort you back to your room? I wouldn't want you tripping in the dark, and there's a chill in the air." He shrugged off his night jacket.

Dahlia crooked a finger at him. "You're not getting off the

hook that easily, sir. You'll promise to marry my niece right now, or I'll wake the admiral!"

A gasp escaped Amelia's lips. She couldn't wake the admiral. She just couldn't.

Simon attempted to place the jacket over her shoulders, but she quickly shrugged it off, and he picked it up off the floor. "Come, now. Let's be reasonable. This is Lady Amesbury, and we were doing nothing wrong. Reading is a noble pursuit. What books do you enjoy?"

Amelia admired his cool head and ability to switch topics.

Dahlia faced him, her shoulders square. She looked little like the bent-over elder from the garden now. She was a passionate aunt with feelings and pride. She wasn't going to allow one of her nieces to be compromised without a fight. "Say it. Say it or I'll scream."

Amelia looked between Dahlia and Simon. What would he say? What *could* he say?

He nodded curtly. "Very well. I promise."

Amelia bit her lip to prevent her mouth from dropping open. Dahlia was confused. Perhaps even touched. The main thing was to get her back to her room—quietly. Simon had no choice but to lie.

But what a lie.

Amelia thought about it all the way down the hall, around the corner, and up the stairs. Being married to a man like Simon? She couldn't even imagine what that might look like.

Actually, she could.

It would be challenging, and Amelia liked nothing better than a good challenge. They would argue—a lot—about topics big and small. Exasperating each other was becoming too easy—

and, if she admitted it, a little too fun. Sparring with Simon was exciting, and she hadn't been excited by another person in a very long time.

But neither of them would be marrying anyone anytime soon. They both enjoyed their independence too much. They would say whatever they needed to get out of this sticky situation. But in the morning all bets would be off.

Dahlia stopped in front of the first door on the left and turned to Simon. "Mind your promise, deary. If you think I'm upset now, see what happens if you leave her at the altar." And with that, she shut the door, deserting them in the hallway.

Simon smiled. "I thought she'd never leave."

Amelia returned the smile despite her fears.

"I'm sorry she scared you. She's—"

Amelia put a finger to her lips. The last thing they needed was someone overhearing the conversation. "I'm fine. We'll talk in the morning."

But she wasn't fine. She tossed and turned all night, replaying the night's events. Dahlia loomed large in her dreams, chasing her down hallways, through rooms, and eventually off a balcony. She remembered falling and falling, not ceasing until she hit the cold, hard ground. When she awoke the next morning, the memory of the dream physically stung, and she cringed as she recalled Dahlia's crooked grin.

She shook off the memory and climbed out of bed. The exchange was eerie and left her off-kilter. All she wanted to do was go home.

She wasted no time getting dressed in yesterday's clothes. The sooner they left, the better. The sun ducked in and out of the thick clouds, as if it couldn't make up its mind, and she was determined to start before it faltered and the rain returned. Spending two nights under the same roof as Dahlia would be too many. Plus, Winifred's recital was tomorrow. Amelia needed to be ready.

Sticking a pin in her hair, she gulped a shaky breath. Aunt Tabitha would be furious. Winifred would be confused. And the whole house would wonder what had become of her. She jabbed another pin in her auburn locks. As Simon proclaimed, the weather couldn't be helped. It was no fault of hers they had to stay the night. Would Tabitha rather they had taken off in a rainstorm? One thought of Tabitha's face told her yes. Tabitha would have said she shouldn't have gone in the first place, and perhaps she'd be right.

Amelia was a mother now. She had to put Winifred before herself. But that didn't change who she was. Edgar sought her out for her difference. He admired her adventurousness, determination, and honesty. Once when a children's home came calling for money, and he was upset by the intrusion and sent them away, she'd told him he was stingy. He'd laughed, saying he was used to being told what he wanted to hear. Then he retrieved his pocketbook for a donation.

Gathering her parasol, Amelia descended the stairs. She was more determined than ever to find Charlotte's killer. Meeting Dahlia had filled a large blank in her mind. Armed with new information, she could move forward.

The dining room was laid with the traditional breakfast fixings, and Amelia hurried to select a bowl of porridge and a plate of fruit and cheese. She had just taken her first sip of coffee when Simon entered the room. His black hair was damp enough to tell her he'd come down immediately after washing, and the intimate detail brought a rush of warmth with it. She gave him a quick hello and focused on her food. It was uncanny how young she felt when he was around.

"Did you sleep well?" Simon asked as he gathered his breakfast at the sideboard.

"Not very, but I did sleep. You?"

"No." He selected a chair across from her. "I kept thinking about last night."

She concentrated on the shape of the slice of cheese on her plate.

"Let me rephrase that. I kept running the conversation with Dahlia over in my mind."

Amelia glanced up. His lips hinted at a smile, but she was determined not to let the reminder of their exchange get the best of her. She was a widow, for goodness' sake, not a schoolgirl. She couldn't lose her head every time the conversation turned friendly. "It was troublesome, for certain. But I think I understand." Amelia leaned over her plate and lowered her voice to a whisper. "If she believed I was Flora, perhaps she believed you were Henry Cosgrove."

Simon leaned back in his chair. "Of course. Why didn't I think of that?"

"Because you were too busy making a hasty departure," she said.

"Trust me, departing was the last thing on my mind."

Determined not to let the comment poke a hole in her composure, she nibbled her fruit, but it was hard not to imagine what might have happened had Dahlia not walked in. She took a sip of coffee, washing down the thought.

"I know it doesn't fit, but we cannot rule her out—not yet," he continued.

Amelia agreed. "Something tells me she holds the key to these crimes."

Footsteps sounded on the stairs, and they ate their breakfasts without further comment. A moment later, Admiral Edwards entered the room, filling the void with his boisterous greeting.

"I've always been an earlier riser myself, and I knew you'd want to leave before the next rainstorm." The admiral walked to the window and pulled back the drape. His beard was snow-white in the daylight. "The roads will be muddy. But I'm sure your driver has considered that." He allowed the curtain to fall.

"He has," said Simon. "Thank you, Admiral. I don't know what we would have done without your hospitality."

"Yes, thank you," Amelia added.

"You're welcome." After loading his plate with eggs and kippers, Admiral Edwards joined them at the table.

The next thirty minutes were a mixture of conversation and impatience, at least for Amelia. Feeling very much like a child, she wanted to *go*. She tapped her toes silently under the table—or perhaps not so silently—as Simon pushed away from the table, making their excuses. Luckily, the admiral was a practical man and had no reason for ceremony. He gave them a quick goodbye and went back to his newspaper.

Although the road was muddy and the drive was slow, they returned to London in time for tea. Winifred was the first one to greet them, bursting out the door and down the steps, her pink dress flouncing in the wind. She had a parcel in her hand, and when Amelia hugged her, she felt the bulk of it press between them.

"It's wonderful to see you, Winifred. I've missed you." Amelia took in the scent of the girl, a mixture of soap and lemons. If heaven had a smell, this was it. Clean and bright, it was the essence of innocence and promise.

Winifred talked into Amelia's chest. "Aunt Tabitha said you must've taken shelter from the rainstorm, but I knew you were with Lord Bainbridge and was not worried." She pulled back to show Amelia a parcel. "I kept your correspondence safe. I knew you'd want me to."

"You know me well." Amelia took the package. "Thank you."

Simon edged closer to the pair. "May I have a look?"

Winifred shook her head. "Sorry, my lord. It's Amelia's *private* affair."

Amelia bit back a smile. *That's my girl!*

"I understand." Simon accepted Winifred's proclamation at face value. "Perhaps a cup of tea, then?"

Winifred flashed him a wide smile, motioning to the front door. "Cook has everything ready. Wait until you see it. It's a regular feast!"

Amelia agreed with the description. A hearty meal was awaiting them in the drawing room. Cook knew they would be famished from their travels, and she was right. Although the admiral's house wasn't far, the terrain was difficult to traverse after the rainstorm. Amelia enjoyed a second scone, slathered with Devonshire cream and jam, as Winifred told them all about Tabitha and a missing corsage. That was where Tabitha was now, picking out a replacement.

Winifred brushed a stray crumb from her dress. "I thought it matched my dress fine. But Aunt Tabitha said it was an . . . a-bom-i-na-tion." She pronounced each syllable distinctly. "Do not tell her I told you, though. She was upset I'd overheard the word."

Amelia chuckled. "Which explains why you've repeated it so carefully."

"You're always telling me to increase my vocabulary." Winifred shrugged. "If I want to be a writer like you someday, I need practice."

Simon covered his smile with a napkin.

"Goodness, no," Amelia was quick to answer. "I am not a writer."

Winifred's brow furrowed. "But you like to write. You're always doing it in the library."

"True," admitted Amelia. "But it's not the same thing."

Winifred scooted down from the chair. "It kind of is, in my opinion. Excuse me. Too much tea."

"I love this age." Amelia smiled as she watched the girl walk away. "She is too old for dolls but not too old to announce when she needs to use the lavatory."

"You've done a good job raising her," Simon complimented. "She has your spirit and fortitude."

Amelia was pleased with the comment. "Thank you. I appreciate that."

He checked the door, and his green eyes flicked with intensity. "Now let's see those letters."

Amelia touched the package. It was there, like a gun waiting to be fired. "I'm sure they contain the regular problems: debutantes, dates, and other disasters." She turned it over, noting a single envelope. Winifred must have collected it with the parcel. Like the second letter, it was addressed to her full title. But when she opened it, the missive used her pen name, Lady Agony.

"It is he?" asked Simon.

Her hand paused on the familiar stationery. The handwriting was recognizable. Yet something was different. She'd need her reading glasses to figure out what. "I believe so."

"What does it say?"

They read the missive together.

> DEAR LADY AGONY,
> YOU'VE HAD AMPLE WARNINGS, BUT LIKE
> A FOOL, YOU'VE PERSISTED. THIS IS MY
> FINAL LETTER. IF YOU DO NOT HEED MY
> WARNING, I WILL BE FORCED TO RID THE
> WORLD OF ANOTHER DERANGED FEMALE.
> TRUST ME. THE WORLD WILL THANK ME.

Like the other letters, this one was unsigned. Amelia turned it over in her hands.

"May I see it?" asked Simon.

Amelia gave him the letter. She'd already committed the lines to memory. The killer was coming for her; it was as plain as the nose on her face. But she would not surrender without a fight. And without getting justice for Charlotte.

Chapter 30

Dear Lady Agony,

Everyone wonders about your identity, but do you ever wonder about ours?

Devotedly,
Any Reader, Any Place

....

Dear Any Reader, Any Place

I wonder all the time. Are you a baroness, a vicar's wife, or a shopgirl? Would I recognize you if we passed on the street? What if I dropped by your store? Would I know you by your complaint? I hope, given the opportunity, I would. Until that day, dear reader, I will keep my eye out for you. However, I ask that you not do the same of me.

Yours in Secret,
Lady Agony

Simon looked up from the letter, his eyes betraying his fear. "This is worse than the others, far more threatening—desperate, almost. Something must be done straightaway."

Amelia nodded in agreement.

He rubbed the paper with his thumb. "I know this stock." He held it up to the light. "It's expensive. My father orders it."

"May I see it again?" She realized that was the difference she first noted: the weight of the paper. The other notes had been scratched on small billets, such as a woman might use to dash off a quick response. This was traditional, five by eight inches, the size used for men's longer correspondence. It betrayed the writer's identity. He or she was wealthy, and from the letter's wording Amelia presumed it was a *he*.

"We have to assume the writer is a person of distinction," said Simon.

"Or that the person wants us to *believe* he is a person of distinction." She stuffed the letter into the envelope. "The other missives were on small notepaper. The writer might be trying to divert us with the change."

"Or, in a hurry, he forgot himself." Simon drank the remainder of his tea. "The penmanship is better than the last note, which tells me he might be trying to write badly. Writing neatly might come easily to him."

"Perhaps you're correct," Amelia agreed. "One thing we know for certain is that we have a single killer. He admits as much."

Simon put his teacup down with a plunk. "It's brazen to put the admission in writing. I'm afraid for you, Amelia. I won't feel good about your safety until the person is caught."

"Nor I." She leaned in conspiratorially. "Which is why we must catch him."

"How do you suppose we do that? We've been searching for days."

"We're closer. I can feel it." Amelia recalled the last twenty-four hours. The more she learned about the Edwards family, the more motives she found. Both victims were members of the family, Charlotte by employment. "Do you think it might be someone in the admiral's family? They have some wealth and have been acutely aware of my movements."

Leaning in also, Simon's head was almost touching hers. If she strained, she could smell cedarwood. "It's as good a guess as any, but who?"

"Amelia Amesbury."

Amelia jumped at the sound of her own name. "Aunt Tabitha!" She stood to greet her. Simon followed suit.

Dressed in a dark purple frock with black lace trim, Tabitha's words were as foreboding as her dress. Her Amesbury eyes landed on Amelia with cool blue certainty. "I wish I could say I'm surprised by your absence last night, but I am not. I assume you have a good reason."

"Lady Tabitha." Simon bowed gallantly. "I will give you two a private moment."

Amelia silently willed him to stay. Tabitha couldn't kill her in the presence of a gentleman.

"You will do nothing of the sort," declared Tabitha. She jerked her cane at an empty seat. "Sit down."

Simon blinked and returned to his chair. Amelia did the same.

"My deepest apologies," said Simon. "The storm prevented our return last night. We spent the night at the admiral's estate. I brought Amelia home as soon as I was safely able."

Tabitha wasn't mollified. Her lips pressed into a thin line. "I have known you since you were in knickers, Simon Bainbridge. Your good looks and smooth tongue do not comfort me. And you." Tabitha pointed her cane at Amelia. "You can bewitch even people with the best intentions."

"I resent that, Aunt. Would you have me risk my health?"

Tabitha tapped her cane on the ground. "I would have you act like an Amesbury! The butler asked after you. I didn't know what to say."

Amelia held her head high. "This is what an Amesbury looks like now."

Simon peeked at the pair from beneath a dark shock of hair that crossed his brow, surprised and perhaps proud of Amelia's declaration. He'd wanted her to assert herself, and she had.

As if coming to a decision, Tabitha dipped her chin slightly. "So it is. But do not dismiss me so easily. Tell me what's going on—and not the tepid version. I know something took you to the Edwardses' country estate. Let's have it."

Amelia stood and linked her arm in Tabitha's and led her to the settee. "I could never dismiss you. You are our rock and foundation, and I love you." Even as she said the words, Amelia felt their truth. Tabitha was difficult, but she was also loyal and resolute. The type of person one wanted in her corner during a crisis. Amelia admired her a great deal.

Tabitha was moved slightly by the admission. She relaxed her shoulders, anyway.

Amelia proceeded to tell her about the admiral's sister-in-law. When she was finished, Tabitha's lips twitched with a smile.

"You didn't have to travel to Dartford to find out about Dahlia Engelthorpe," Tabitha said smugly. "I could have told you about her."

Painfully, Amelia waited for Tabitha's tea to be brought, the sugar cubes to be placed, and the first sip to be taken. As soon as the cup hit the saucer, she prompted Tabitha to continue. "How well do you know her?"

"Not well, but well enough. How do you think I knew about the curse?" Squinting at the tea, Tabitha added another lump of sugar and stirred. It must not have been up to her standards. "Dahlia told me of it at Iris's funeral. It caused quite a commotion at the time, and afterward the admiral sent her to Dartford, and rightfully so. Can you imagine his daughters growing up around her?" She shook her head. "No one ever saw her after that."

"Until Flora Edwards's engagement party," Amelia added.

Tabitha paused in midstir. "She was in attendance?"

"She was," confirmed Simon. "Henry Cosgrove met her. She told him about the curse."

"How unfortunate." Tabitha set down her spoon. "I suppose the admiral felt obligated to invite her. She *is* the girls' aunt, and Flora was the first to be married."

"The admiral lost *two* women he loved, first his wife and then his daughter. Two tragedies in one family seems unlucky." The change on Tabitha's face told her the misfortune of Amelia's words. The Amesburys had lost an entire family at sea and then Edgar. How could have she been so thoughtless as to utter the idea aloud? "I'm so sorry. I was thinking out loud again."

"But Lady Amesbury has a point." Simon scratched his head. "Something does not add up. Is the family really cursed, or is Dahlia the one doing the cursing?"

"You met her, Aunt Tabitha. Do you think she could have done something to Flora the night of the engagement party?"

Tabitha dabbed her lips with a napkin. "That was many years ago, of course, but at the time she made a striking impression on me, and not in a good way." She smoothed the napkin on her lap. "I remember thinking, *I do not want to be alone with that woman. Something about her was very unsettling.*"

"It's her eyes," suggested Amelia. "They're deep-set, eerie almost."

"Yes, her eyes." A shudder crept up Tabitha's shoulders. "To answer your question, I don't know if she hurt her niece, but I do think she was capable of it."

The words hung in the air, unchallenged. Dahlia was not well, mentally. This point was irrefutable and important. Yet, in her heart, Amelia did not believe she had harmed Flora. She might be threatening, but she wasn't violent. When she mistook Amelia for Flora, she was protective. Why would she harm someone she wanted to shelter? It didn't make sense; then again, madness never did. Even so, her mental state was important to the mystery. Amelia knew if she could figure out why, she'd solve Charlotte's murder.

"Lady Amesbury?" Winifred's maid, Clara, interrupted. "May I have a moment?"

Tabitha fisted her napkin into a ball. "If this is about Winifred's hair, I told her already that she is to wear the ribbon. The peach roses were a dismal match."

Clara's hazel eyes sent Amelia a silent plea, and Amelia quickly bid Simon goodbye, excusing herself to see what the matter was.

The matter was not the flowers or the ribbon but a small tear in the lace on Winifred's dress. "How the devil did this happen?" asked Amelia.

Winifred stared at the floor.

Amelia turned to Clara for an answer.

"Winifred's friend Miss Cassandra popped by, and I didn't see the harm of letting Winifred try on her dress. Cassandra won't be at tomorrow's concert, and Winifred was desperate for her to see it."

"Cassandra leaves for Brighton today," added Winifred. "She'll be gone three weeks."

"I didn't notice the tear until I returned the tissue paper to the sleeves a few moments ago." Clara clasped her hands in front of her apron. "I'm so sorry, my lady. I didn't know where to turn."

She knows where to turn, all right. She just doesn't want to, and I don't blame her. Patty Addington was an excellent seamstress and could have mended the delicate lace straightaway. She did not, however, tolerate last-minute alterations, especially when the reason was folly. There was only one person to repair the trim, and it was Amelia herself.

Amelia put on a smile. "It's no tragedy. Give it to me and I will fix it."

Clara released a breath. Her face looked young again with the pinched expression gone. "Oh, thank you, my lady!"

"See, Clara?" Winifred said. "I told you she could do it. Mrs. Addington says she's the best stitch in three counties."

Best in three counties might be overstating it, but Amelia took up the dress immediately and went to work. When it came to sewing, she was known for her accuracy. She didn't have the patience for longer projects, as her sisters did, but small details and delicate fabrics delighted her. If one of her family members needed a steady hand, they came to her, and she was always ready to provide it.

She focused on the material. Her father said the skill came from her penchant for reading. She pored over newspapers, devoting details to memory as quickly as she could before guests woke for the day and took the papers for themselves. With practice, she could recount a story within a word or two. Reading material was hard to come by, and although she and her sisters wrote plenty of stories and skits, to read someone else's was no effort, just pure joy.

She glanced up at Winifred and Clara, who were watching her from the corner of the room. The same feeling of joy washed over her now. It was no effort to mend the lace. She was happy to do it for Winifred. It felt wonderful to be needed—and loved. Winifred was her family now, and all that word entailed.

Chapter 31

Dear Lady Agony,

There's a thief in my midst. I can't prove it, but I'm hoping you can. A fortnight ago, I heard a noise outside my door. I walked the entire perimeter of my townhome but saw nothing. The next day, however, my favorite brooch was missing. Yesterday I heard the noise again, and again repeated the search. Today, my matching ear bobbles are gone! I asked my niece, who is staying with me, if she noted anything suspicious, but she did not. She was in her bed asleep the entire time, and, to be honest, I'm glad she's leaving the day after tomorrow. Who dares have a young woman around with the increasing crime in London?

By the way, I've included my full address in case you are equipped to help catch the culprit as you did in the case of the Dreadful Dressmaker. You have my permission to make a full inquiry.

Devotedly,
A Victim of London's Ill Morals and Thievery

· · · · · · · · · · · · · · · · · ·

Dear A Victim of London's Ill Morals and Thievery,

It occurs to me that you might not be the victim of London's increasing crime rate but of your own ignorance and good heart. As I peruse your letter, one detail looms large: the departure of your niece. Did she arrive, may I ask, at the same time as the theft of the brooch? If so, turn to her satchel before you turn to the constable. It might provide the answers you are seeking.

Yours in Secret,
Lady Agony

Later that night, Amelia was enjoying a meal in her room when she heard a plunk at the window. Exhausted by last-minute arrangements for tomorrow's recital, as well as the long day of travel, she was eating mincemeat pie and sipping a glass of claret when the noise sounded at the glass. Startled, she dropped her fork on the plate, wondering what else could possibly happen before Winifred's big day. Murder, storms, missing corsages, torn lace—what was next?

It's probably my imagination. It did have a tendency to run amok. She retied her dressing gown and went to the curtain, pushing it back at the corner. Squinting into the darkness, she was surprised to see a woman in a maid's uniform. *Who in the world?*

"I s-s-see you up there, Lady Amesbury," the woman hollered. "You can't hide from me."

Amelia recognized the voice. It was Lena, the woman who had been demoted to scullery maid. By the slur of her words, she had been drinking. A lot. What was she doing outside?

Amelia slid open the window and leaned out. "I'm not hiding. This is my home. What are you doing here?"

"Everything was going fine for me until your little visit the other day. After that, the master tells me he don't need me anymore." She fisted her hands on her hips. "You got s-s-something to do with that, Countess?"

"You were let go?" Amelia asked.

"Don't act s-s-surprised. I know you were behind it. You told the Van Ackers to let me go. That I wasn't good enough. Now where am I to work?" Lena flung up her hands, losing her balance and stumbling backward. "Your house?"

"I did no such thing," Amelia insisted. "You have my word."

"That don't mean nothing."

"Please come in," encouraged Amelia. "I'll meet you downstairs and we'll talk about it. I didn't say a word to your employer. I promise."

She crossed her short arms. "Your butler wouldn't let me inside, and I don't believe you anyways."

"I'll speak to Mr. Jones. He'll allow you in with a word from me."

"No, thank you." Lena stuck out her chin. "I just wanted you to know that I know. We serving classes aren't as dumb as you think. And we got feelings, too."

"Of course you do," Amelia empathized. "Let me help you."

Lena let out a guffaw. "I think I've had about enough of your *help*."

"Wait there. I'm coming down."

That was all Lena needed to make a tipsy bow and stomp away.

Shaking her head, Amelia closed the window and returned to her pie. Suddenly she wasn't hungry. She covered the dish with her napkin and took a sip of wine. Why had Lena been fired? The black list was the obvious answer, but her employer must have known about the black list. It was the reason she'd been demoted to scullery maid. Why fire her now? Were they worried Lena might start a new list about them? The timing didn't make sense. If she were Lena, she would have suspected her visit, too. It was the only change in her routine.

Amelia put down her glass. She had to figure it out, and catching up with Lena was the only way to do that. She twirled her hair into a bun, threw on a cloak, and hurried down the stairs.

"Lady Amesbury."

The voice of Patty Addington put a skid to her steps. Amelia spun around to see Tabitha's maid, who took on the unnecessary role of a general housekeeper, with her hands placed on her wide hips. Unlike her daughter's, her face held no playfulness, only deep frown lines of censure. If not for the severe look, she would have been a beautiful woman, with dark brown hair, wide almond-shaped eyes, and feathery eyebrows. But now those eyebrows were knitted in an angry glare.

"Are you leaving?" asked Mrs. Addington.

Amelia swallowed. Obviously, she *was* leaving. Her cloak was evidence of that. So was her rush of footsteps toward the door. But how to explain her departure was a different question, one she couldn't come up with a good answer for. "Ah . . . yes, I am."

"Whyever for?" The disbelief in Mrs. Addington's voice was palpable. "Whatever it is, I'm sure Mr. Jones can fetch it for you."

Mr. Jones would not be fetching Lena Crane. She was the last person he would be fetching. In fact, he was the one who had sent her packing in the first place. "Thank you, Mrs. Addington, but I have to do this myself."

Patty Addington tilted her head. "Do what?"

Amelia should have known she wouldn't get off that easily. The cool look in the woman's eyes demanded an explanation. *Fine.* She would give it to her. She wasn't a child anymore. She was the mistress of the house. If she wanted to dash out, no matter the hour, it was her business.

Amelia squared her shoulders and answered the question. "To talk to Lena Crane. She was here a moment ago, and I have some questions for her."

Mrs. Addington's almond eyes grew even wider. "That serving girl who came to the door, the one who was inebriated?"

"We don't know she was inebriated," Amelia declared. "Something was wrong, however, and I'm going to find out what."

Mrs. Addington took a step toward the door.

Amelia held firm. "I won't let a woman leave my house in distress. It's my prerogative—my duty—to understand the problem. If I can help her, I will."

Mrs. Addington didn't budge. In her full black skirt, she stood like an immovable boulder near the door.

Immovable, perhaps, but not impassable.

Amelia stepped around her. "Excuse me."

She waited for a hand to reach out and grab her or a voice to argue with her. Neither came, and as she reached the front landing, she made a silent cheer. Facing one's fears was hard, but the feeling of accomplishment that came with it was worth it. Confronting Mrs. Addington was like confronting Tabitha herself. Except for the age gap, the women could have been twins. They were of one mind when it came to what one did and did not do. Following angry scullery maids into the darkening night was definitely in the did-not-do category.

Lena had turned south, so Amelia followed in the same direction, walking as quickly as her tired feet would take her. But the girl was several minutes ahead of her, and Amelia saw nothing.

The streets were dark but quiet, and if she listened closely, she could hear what she thought were clumsy footsteps. They were coming from Hyde Park. Trying not to run, she half skipped toward the green. She must remain as inconspicuous as possible. Winifred's recital was tomorrow. She couldn't chance someone seeing her argue with a drunk woman before Winifred's big day. Although she declared it was her prerogative to follow the girl, Mrs. Addington was right to caution her. It might mean a scandal if the wrong person took in the scene.

Her breath caught as she saw a brown coat disappear through the gate of Hyde Park. Could that be Lena? The shape was large and nondescript. It might not have been her, but Amelia had to try.

A rush of horses' hooves and then a holler came from behind her. "Lady Amesbury, I must ask you to stop at once."

She spun around. Jones was behind her in the Amesbury carriage, sitting next to the coachman, looking very unlike the placid butler she knew him to be. His hair was flung forward, revealing a patch of balding scalp, and he was out of breath. *Blasted Patty Addington!* She'd told on her.

"The woman you're chasing was drinking and perhaps even dangerous," Jones continued. "She took a swing at me, and I sent her away from the house."

"I appreciate your concern, but I must speak to her at once." Amelia turned back toward the park. "It's important."

Jones cleared his throat. "I'm afraid I must insist. Lord Bainbridge told me your life may depend on it."

"Simon Bainbridge?" Amelia heard the crack in her own

voice. "Did I hear you correctly? What has anything got to do with him?"

Jones sat up taller in the seat. With the light streaming on his pale face, he might have been a statue. "I promised him I would look after you in case of trouble. Running into Hyde Park after a drunkard seems like one of those times."

Amelia looked from Jones to the park. He wasn't going anywhere, but Lena was getting away. "Come along, then, quick. Leave the carriage with the driver and let's go."

Mr. Jones carefully climbed down from the seat. He was not accustomed to the job of a footman, and it took him a few minutes to descend the steps.

Amelia clapped her hands. "Quickly! A woman's life is at stake."

"Yes, my lady." Jones brushed off his trousers. "I'm afraid it may be yours."

By the time they passed the park entrance, Amelia, who was used to brisk walking, was jogging. Jones was struggling to keep up. She kept stopping every few seconds so as not to outpace him completely. But she had a terrible feeling in the pit of her stomach, and it wasn't the mincemeat pie.

She was afraid for the girl.

A moment later, her fear was realized. A dull brown coat was floating on the top of the Serpentine. She knew without looking that Lena was beneath it. Jones caught her arm, but she jerked away and rushed toward the edge of the water. She flung off the hood of her cloak. Maybe she could save her.

One look at the dead eyes staring back at her told her she couldn't. Lena, like Flora and Charlotte, had been murdered.

Again, Amelia had been too late.

Chapter 32

Dear Lady Agony,

I host an annual ball, and although everyone looks forward to it, I do not. The planning, the cleaning, the food—the seating charts! It takes the joy out of the day. Not to mention the guests, who are less mannered and more ravenous each season. Is it my age? Or is it the nature of the event? What do you suggest for a remedy?

Devotedly,
Humdrum Hostess

....

Dear Humdrum Hostess,

I understand the condition perfectly, for I, myself, suffered with it before I knew I was the cause and therefore also the remedy. Fretting days, weeks—even months—before the party, you wear yourself out. By the time the event arrives, you are exhausted.

Everything appears less attractive when they are a chore to complete instead of an opportunity to reconnect. The good news is the solution is simple but hard: Do less and enjoy more. Trust me. Your friends will thank you for it.

Yours in Secret,
Lady Agony

The next morning, Amelia awoke with one thought in her head: time had run out. While she and Simon searched for clues, trying to identify the killer, the killer had acted again. Last night, Lena had died in much the same way as Charlotte, with a blow to the head. But this time Amelia had gone to the constable. Mr. Jones had taken her, and she'd explained the girl's erratic behavior at the house to the police.

The constable wasn't moved, or at least not motivated. He took in the scene with resignation, saying the city lost a lot of young girls to alcohol and poor working conditions. Amelia insisted Lena hadn't killed herself, but the officer stuck to the facts: Lena was inebriated, out of work, and angry. He thought her death a suicide, plain and simple.

Amelia threw back the bedcovers and wrapped herself in her warmest dressing gown. If these tragedies had taught her anything, it was that nothing was plain and simple. Another woman had died, proving to Amelia that the killer would act again without hesitation. If he wasn't caught, Amelia or one of her family members could be next. Or Simon. Would the killer go after him? So far, the killer had focused on women.

Sitting at her dressing table, Amelia considered the reason. Women often knew details that escaped men's notice. Lena, for instance, had known intimate details about the Edwardses' household. Had she known what happened the night of Flora's death? Could that be it? Could she have known the identity of the killer, too?

The idea was so incredible that it took her breath away.

"I see you're up early." Lettie brought in a tray of coffee. "As well you should be. Lady Winifred has been up since six this morning. She's played that song fifteen times if she's played it once."

Amelia stood to take the tray. "The one that—"

"Yes, that one." Lettie fussed with the napkin.

"For goodness' sake, Lettie. I can get my own napkin. You must remember I'm used to doing things for myself."

Lettie let the napkin go. "Mum says we need to do our best to ignore that."

"Does she, now?" Amelia poured the coffee from the silver pot into the dainty cup and inhaled deeply. Nothing was so delicious as the first taste of coffee in the morning.

"It's a pleasure to go to the wardrobe again, isn't it?" Lettie opened the double doors. "Especially on an occasion such as this." She ran her hand over the choices. "So many options . . ."

"Edgar bought me many clothes I've never worn."

"Which will you choose?" asked Lettie.

"The dark green," Amelia answered.

Lettie pulled the emerald dress from the closet. "Good choice. It will match Lord Bainbridge's eyes."

Amelia fumbled the coffee cup, rattling the saucer as she put it back on the tray. "That's not the reason. I've always been, ah, um, fond of green."

Lettie's smile widened. "But it's true, isn't it?"

"It is." Amelia gazed at the gown, the skirt gored to provide a fashionably small waist and wide hem. The tight bodice and beautiful neckline would create a nice silhouette of even the dullest figure. *And the material.* Amelia reached for the fabric. It was the softest satin she'd ever felt. It would pair wonderfully with her olive skin tone and warm auburn hair.

"Let's give it a go." Lettie's voice was tinged with her customary enthusiasm. She'd waited years to play dress-up. Now was her chance.

Amelia gave her coffee a parting sip. "Why not?" She stood. "There's lots to be done, and not much time. Best to be ready early."

An hour later, Amelia floated down the staircase feeling, perhaps for the first time, like the Countess of Amesbury. It wasn't just the dress; it was the feeling inside her. Winifred was her charge, her own dear daughter. She was giving her first performance, and soon the whole world would know what a wonderful girl and musician she was. They would also know how proud Amelia was to be her mother.

If only she were as proud of her progress in solving Charlotte's murder.

While she hadn't figured it out, she *had* concluded several points. One, the killer was wealthy, or had access to wealth. The linen paper was evidence of this. Two, he was respected. How else could Lena's employer be so handily influenced? Three, he was deceitful. Lena, and perhaps Charlotte (she had also gone to bed early), had been lured into drinking the night of their deaths. Combined, these conclusions narrowed the field of suspects, and Amelia had a certain man on her mind when another one met her at the bottom of the stairs.

"Simon?" said Amelia, forgetting herself. "What are you doing here? It isn't time for the concert yet."

"Lady Amesbury." Simon greeted her with a gallant bow. Dressed in a black coat with an exquisite collar that emphasized the ruggedness of his jawline, he kept his hands behind his back. "I'm not here to see you, although you are a vision."

Amelia smiled at the compliment.

He cleared his throat, all business. "I'm here to see Lady Winifred."

Winifred heard her name and came rushing from the morning room. "Lord Bainbridge!"

He pulled a bright bouquet of peach roses from behind his back. Their delicious scent filled the area. "Good morning, my lady. These are for you."

"For me?" She stared openmouthed at the large arrangement.

"Yes, you. I know what it means to put on one of these performances." Simon lowered his voice, bending at the waist. "My mother made me give one once. Nerve-racking, to be sure. But I know you will perform splendidly."

"Thank you, my lord." She twirled in a circle. "They match my dress."

Simon smiled. "I know it's your favorite color."

"I'll put them on the pianoforte." Winifred inhaled deeply. "That way I can smell them when I play."

"Good idea," Amelia agreed. "I will find a vase."

Behind her, Lettie interjected. "*I'll* get the vase, my lady."

Winifred bobbed a curtsy and followed Lettie.

Alone in the entryway, Amelia nodded toward the morning room. "A moment, if you please. I need to talk to you."

He joined her in the empty space.

She turned to face him. "First of all, I don't need your protection. You cannot set my own butler against me. You have no authority here. I make the rules, and I won't have the staff watching my every move."

"Jones caught you at something, didn't he?"

"That's not the point. The point is you cannot tell a member of my household what to do. Is that clear?"

Simon tilted his head. "Clear, yes. Obeyed, I'm not sure. I cannot make any promises."

"I mean it, Simon."

"Fine, but tell me what happened."

Amelia relayed the details of her conversation with Lena, the subsequent jog to the park, and the discovery of the woman's body in the Serpentine. By the time she finished relaying her conversation with the constable, Simon's eyes were a storm of sea green.

"You're certain she was murdered?"

"As certain as the day of the week."

"Then there's no time to waste." He turned to the door. "We must find the killer, and we must do it today."

She touched his elbow. "But the recital. I won't miss it."

"*After* the recital."

"Agreed." After the recital, they would figure out who killed Flora, Charlotte, and Lena. They had no other choice.

Two hours later, Simon rejoined her for the concert in the drawing room. Everyone was there. *Everyone who is important, anyway*, thought Amelia. Aunt Tabitha had made certain of it, for the concert wasn't just about Winifred's performance but her future. Tabitha wanted to secure her place as a virtuosa among the *ton*. Amelia, on the other hand, just wanted to keep her breakfast in her stomach.

She couldn't believe how nervous she was for the girl. It was as if she herself were at the instrument, plunking away at the keys, which would have been a disaster. Her sister Sarah was the pianist in the family. Amelia was the singer and actress—admittedly, more of an actress—but she did love to sing.

Crossing her feet beneath the small white chair, Amelia refocused on the music. It was the second-to-last song Winifred would perform. Mozart was last, and that was the cause of Amelia's anxiety. She willed Winifred to go slowly, take her time, and enjoy her performance. The end would be what guests remembered most. But willpower had little to do with the future. Winifred would perform how she performed. Amelia couldn't wish away her concern.

As long as Winifred didn't fumble the keys, what did it matter? She was a wonderful pianist. Anyone could see that. Staring at Winifred's straight back, a sign of strength and determination, Amelia understood the concert meant a great deal to her. Situated at the pianoforte with the peach bouquet of roses above her head, the girl looked much older than her ten years. And in some ways she was. She'd lost her parents and beloved uncle, but she hadn't lost herself, which was a testament to her strength and skill. If anyone could finish strong, it was Winifred.

Aunt Tabitha grasped Amelia's hand and squeezed briefly. Maybe she could feel the tension rolling over Amelia like carriage wheels. One look at Tabitha told Amelia the older woman suffered from no such problem. Tabitha was pleased with the performance and the event as well, and why not? Her preparations had paid off.

The furniture had been removed for adequate seating, and the tiny bouquets of flowers fastened to the end chairs were so perfect that they looked as if they were part of the ensemble. Furthermore, they matched the flowers on Winifred's corsage, as well as the three-tiered cake, which Amelia was looking forward to tasting. Indeed, Tabitha was a master at understated elegance. It never looked as if she was trying. Things just turned out as they were supposed to when she was around.

The song finished, and the audience clapped briefly. Winifred started her final piece. Amelia shared a glance with Simon, who sat behind her to the right. He gave her an almost imperceptible nod. Winifred would be fine. Amelia laced her fingers together in silent prayer. No matter what happened, she wanted Winifred to know it would be all right.

Winifred started strong. She was as sure of the notes as the color of the sky. And it wasn't just the notes; it was the feeling behind the music. It was the mark of a true musician. Anyone could tell stories, but to convey feeling without saying a word? That was a gift, and Winifred had it.

The final measures came without Amelia realizing it. That was how well Winifred performed. As Winifred took a bow, Amelia blinked back tears, but when they hugged, the floodgates opened, and the tears left her eyes. They truly felt like mother and daughter, and Amelia couldn't have been prouder if Winifred were her own flesh and blood.

"Congratulations," Amelia whispered. "You did it."

"With your help," said Winifred. "Thank you for being a mother."

Enjoying the moment, Amelia embraced her tighter. "Thank you for allowing me to be."

"Well done," interrupted Tabitha. "Mozart himself would be envious of that performance."

It was strong praise coming from Tabitha, and Winifred basked in the compliment.

"Thanks, Auntie." Winifred spun left and right. "Everything looks beautiful." She lowered her voice. "And so many people are here, too."

"Of course." Tabitha surveyed the room. "They wanted to see if I was fibbing about your talent. I'm glad you didn't make a fibber of me."

Winifred giggled. "Can we have cake now?"

"Indeed," said Tabitha. "You deserve it."

On the way to the luncheon table, they met Simon, who gave Winifred his heartiest congratulations. He said he'd never heard anyone play better.

"And I was fairly good, mind you." Simon gave her a sly wink in jest.

Winifred tilted her head, her blonde curls falling to one side. "Maybe you could play for me sometime?"

"I wouldn't want to embarrass myself," he admitted. "Your skills far surpass mine."

Winifred laughed, but Amelia could see she was pleased with the compliment.

For the next several minutes, Winifred accepted felicitations from well-wishers. Many attendees commented on her musical gift, including Henry Cosgrove, who carried with him two fine boxes of chocolates and the eyes of many surprised onlookers. Not that the attention of a duke mattered to Amelia. She was just happy to see he'd brought Winifred her favorite bonbons.

After giving Winifred a box, which she promptly whisked off to show Simon, Henry handed her one. "I couldn't forget the hostess, especially when I saw her pilfering the shelves of my favorite chocolate shop."

"I was not pilfering—well, perhaps I was." Amelia smiled.

"The day was growing late, and I was hungry. I might have been a little overzealous."

"No judgment here. You know my affinity for chocolate." Henry pointed to the box. "I think you'll like these. I had the chocolate maker whip up something special."

"You can do that?" she asked.

"As I said, I *am* his best customer." He winked. "Take a look."

She untied the box, lingering over the blue satin ribbon. Perhaps Tabitha was right. Details really did make the difference, for she stared at the trimming a full ten seconds before opening the box. Inside, each bonbon was frosted with a white musical note. Amelia gasped in delight. "This is remarkable. What a wonderful idea."

"And you haven't even discovered the best part. Taste it."

"You don't have to twist my arm, Your Grace." Amelia picked up the dainty confection. "Other ladies, perhaps, but not me. As you know, I have a terrible sweet tooth."

He chuckled. "Me, too. But don't tell anyone."

She lowered her voice. "Your secret is safe with me." Taking a bite of the chocolate, she let her cares drift away. The concert had been a triumph. The luncheon was going well. If she could just find Charlotte's killer, the day would be a success.

The sweetness hit her with surprise. Her nerves being what they were, chocolate might have not been the best option for her stomach. She put the box down on a nearby table.

"Lady Winifred did very well today," continued Henry. "You must be proud."

Her chest puffed with pride. "I couldn't be prouder if she were my own daughter."

"You and Edgar never had children."

It wasn't a question but a statement. Still, she felt compelled to explain. "Edgar had a degenerative disease. He didn't want to risk spreading it to a child."

Henry nodded in understanding. "A wise decision. A condition like that can ruin a family's legacy. It's best not to take a chance."

Amelia felt the sting of his words. Edgar had had a good life, and they had had a solid friendship. Perhaps Edgar felt the same way, but who was Henry to say a child would ruin his legacy? Anger swelled inside of her, and she tamped it down with another bite of chocolate. It hit her stomach like a fist.

"At any rate, Winifred was brilliant and will enjoy much success as a musician." Henry looked around but, not seeing her, continued. "Please give her my regards again. I wish I could stay, but I have another engagement."

Amelia swallowed, unable to rid herself of the chocolate's sweetness. She needed a drink of water. "Of course. Thank you for coming."

"You don't mind my early departure?"

"Not at all. I'll walk you out." The words sounded odd in Amelia's mouth, and she laughed lightly. No one noticed but Henry.

"Share the joke?" Henry asked.

Out of habit, Amelia grabbed her parasol. She felt as if she were in a dream. "I haven't been sleeping well. When that happens, everything is very funny—or very sad. Laughter or tears are my only option."

"Anything I can do?" Henry descended the front steps.

Her head was beginning to spin, and she steadied herself with her parasol. "There does seem to be something, now that I think about it . . ."

"Whoa." Henry took her elbow. "Are you ill?"

"I'm sorry," Amelia apologized. "I'm afraid I need to sit down."

Henry opened his carriage door and helped her in. She watched the motion like a spectator at a play. Why was she getting into his carriage? Why was he shutting the door? She couldn't remember. All she knew for certain was that Winifred was in the house and they were driving away from her. She reached for the latch.

"Oh no, Lady Agony." Henry's smile turned into a deep crease. The shadows around his eyes were no longer a sign of grief. They were hollow and sinister. "You're not going anywhere."

Chapter 33

Dear Lady Agony,

You seem like the type of woman who's been in a bind. How does one get herself out without damaging her reputation?

Devotedly,
Stuck Like Jam

. . . .

Dear Stuck Like Jam,

I have been in my fair share of sticky situations, thank you very much. They can be difficult, but one untangles herself with as much grace as possible. The fear of damaging your reputation must not deter you from righting a wrong. If one isn't making mistakes, one isn't living. Do not allow silly etiquette handbooks to tell you otherwise.

Yours in Secret,
Lady Agony

"I knew it was you." Amelia tried to spit out the words, but her tongue kept getting in the way. It was heavy and thick. "You killed Flora and the serving girls, too."

He slipped on tanned gloves. "It would appear we're *both* in the know. I knew you were Lady Agony the moment I spotted you at St. James's Park. Even with your disguise, I recognized you from the recent gathering at the Turner house. How can you write that drivel?"

"It's not drivel. It's advice!" The *c* in *advice* caught on her lips. "What's happening to my s-s-speech?" She touched her mouth. "It's the chocolate, isn't it? I recognized the ribbon from Charlotte's pocket. You poisoned her, didn't you? What did you use?"

"Not poison, a drug. Laudanum. It will help you relax. First your brain, then your muscles. The feeling is quite enjoyable, actually. A treat, just like the chocolate, which disguised its taste perfectly." He clasped his hands as if to contain his enthusiasm. "The chit ate quite a few, not knowing the sympathy gift was from me." He chuckled. "Nerves, I suppose."

Amelia took comfort in not having eaten the entire chocolate. A few crumbs still lay in its wrapper. She would fight her way through this. She had to. The main thing was to keep him talking so she would have time to escape. If only her mind wasn't like quicksand! Every idea she had sank as quickly as it came to the surface. As soon as she had one in her grasp, it slipped through her fingers. "That's how you were able to catch Charlotte and Lena off guard. With the drug."

"Who?" He squinted out the window. "Oh, the second one. Yes. She went rather handily. She inhaled the chocolates, thinking they were a gift from an admirer. All women enjoy chocolate, you see. They can't resist a tiny box with a pretty bow. When the laudanum took effect, the Van Ackers mistook her odd behavior for intoxication, and she was fired. An unforeseen benefit but still not a complete solution if she knew details of the engagement party. The slightest rap on the head was all she needed to secure the secret."

The carriage turned, and Amelia slid across the seat. She gripped the cushion to stop herself, calling out to the driver.

Henry shook his head and chuckled. "It's no use, Lady Amesbury. I pay my driver very well for his services. He will not be assisting you, so you might as well enjoy the ride."

How could anyone enjoy this feeling? The sense of euphoria was offset by dizziness and numbness. Focusing on his eyes, Amelia understood he took the drug himself. His pupils were abnormally small, and he admitted to being the chocolate maker's best customer. It would explain how he knew the effects and incorporated them so effortlessly into the sweets. "But why kill Flora? Sh-sh-she was your fiancée. *You* proposed to *her.*" Amelia said each word carefully. "You had to care for her."

For the first time, he waffled. "I . . . Of course I cared for her. She had nothing else to recommend herself. Her father was not titled, and I had no need for her dowry."

Amelia believed him. "Then why?"

"I had my suspicions, but the night of the party I knew for certain." Henry rubbed his palms nervously. "That old woman with her talk of curses." He blinked, and his face cleared. "She was mad, mad like Hyacinth. Perhaps Flora would go mad, too. I could not take a chance. Yet I couldn't break the engagement without associating myself with a scandal. So I did what I had to do to save my good name. When Flora wasn't looking, I dosed her champagne with laudanum. Luckily, I always carry the drug with me." He winked. "I can't resist its charms, either, and I knew the opportunity wouldn't come again. Flora did not partake in spirits."

When Henry met Dahlia, he understood the truth of Flora's history. Her mother had drowned to death, and her aunt was touched. He'd met Hyacinth, a scatterbrain. It didn't take much imagination to guess Flora was predisposed, too. Madwomen! How they filled the books and the duke's head with fears. He couldn't risk spreading the condition to the Cosgrove line. He admitted as much when he concluded Edgar had made the right decision. Amelia understood the entire truth now, but it didn't make it any more palatable. "No one could accuse you of the crime because you didn't stay overnight at the house. How did you get back in?"

His pinpoint pupils darted back and forth. "That was easy. Crawling up the trellis to the balcony was the only difficulty. Once I got there, I called Flora's name, and she came, albeit unsteadily." His mind seemed to flick back to the night. "Little did I know her righteous maid was watching and followed her. I had no idea she'd witnessed me push Flora off the balcony until I saw a letter addressed to Lady Agony. Too bad I couldn't have killed her before she posted it."

So he *had* spotted the missive. Charlotte had been right; she was being followed. "I understand about Flora and Charlotte, but what did Lena have to do with them? Sh-sh-she didn't live with the Edwards family any longer."

He breathed a chuckle. "I have you to thank for that little bit of information. I didn't know she'd created a black list until you mentioned it at the chocolate maker's. I couldn't risk her knowing any details that would lead to my involvement."

A wave of guilt washed over her. She held her head in her

hands. The killer had found out about the black list, all right. *She* had told him.

"Don't let it concern you. She was a scullery maid. Nothing to bother yourself with."

Her head snapped up. "How can you s-s-say that? She was a person, just like you and me."

He looked out the window, not bothering to meet her gaze. "How incredibly charitable—and common."

"How dare you insult me. S-s-stop the carriage this instant! Help—"

Henry put a large hand over her nose and mouth, smothering her. "One more word and I will kill you right here."

With her air lodged in her throat, she understood he was serious. She nodded, and he released his hand. She gasped a breath. "Where are you taking me?"

More poised, Henry crossed his gloved hands over his knee. "On one of your famous walks. The recital gave you a case of the nerves. You needed some air. So you went for a stroll. Too bad you're going to take a tumble."

"That will not work." Amelia gripped the parasol in her hand. "They are sh-sh-sure to connect you to the crime. Everyone saw me leave in your carriage." At least she hoped they did. Truth be told, everyone had been inside. She hadn't seen a single person when she left, but then again, she wasn't exactly clear-headed.

"You think you're so clever, don't you? You think you can tell me what to do, like the little women who write you letters? Think again, *Lady Agony*."

He could criticize her all he wanted, but criticizing her readers went too far. "My readers are far smarter than you. I can tell you that."

He checked the window. They were just outside Green Park. "I didn't want to kill a countess. I knew it would draw more attention, which is why I tried scaring you off with the letters. But I have to say, I'm going to enjoy this so much more than the others."

She regretted leaving the busy London street, but here they were, turning into the forty-acre park. With a swift turn, they entered the greenway. Filled with towering plane and lime trees and not much else, she regretted the location. But she supposed here was as good a place as any for a brawl, for she was determined to fight him with everything she had. He himself was on laudanum, which might make him an easier match. Hopefully, someone would hear them scuffle. She didn't see a single person.

"There's no water in this park, I'm afraid," said Amelia in a last-ditch effort to divert Henry from his plan. "No chance of drowning here. We'd better get back to the street, where s-s-someone might run me over. You know what traffic's like this time of day. A much better idea."

The carriage rocked to a stop behind a thicket of trees. "Get out." Henry gripped one of her arms as he led her down the steps.

Amelia stumbled when her foot touched the grass. "S-S-Simon Bainbridge will come looking for me. What are you going to do about him? Kill him, too?"

"That's none of your concern." Henry gave her a shove in the direction he wanted her to walk.

She held firm, trying not to budge. It was difficult at best. A foot slipped forward. "And my editor knows, also."

He stopped. "What did you say?"

"My editor at the magazine. He knows the entire s-s-story and will print it if anything happens to me." Amelia hated to involve Grady, in case she was killed and Henry sought him out, but it was the only thing she could think of to keep Henry from pushing her farther into the park. So far it had worked.

He crossed his arms. "Why hasn't he printed it before now?"

"He . . . I . . . Well, you see." The drug had put her brain in a fog. She had a hard time forming words.

"You have nothing. He knows nothing."

"He does," she insisted. "It's me. It's the laudanum you gave me. I cannot think straight."

Done listening to her, he scanned the area. "Quit your complaining. It contains the purest opium in all of London."

"Why not an overdose, then?" Amelia was thinking out loud. "Wouldn't it have been just as effective?"

"And waste my expensive drug?" He chuckled. "Medicine is not an exact science. I had to make sure. I had to know for myself they were dead. I couldn't leave it to chance."

He bent down to pick up a large rock, and she knew this was her only option. She considered herself an athletic woman, but her limbs felt heavy. Still in her hand, the parasol had a blunt point. If she could connect it with his head, she could make a run for it.

She brought it up as far as she could and hit him smack on the skull. He fell to his knees, and she whacked him again. She hit him a third time before she realized she'd forgotten to run. She spun on her heel, and the world spun with her. The trees tilted in a dizzying array of greens. She stumbled toward the path. A man on a horse was coming, and she screamed for help. "You there, on the horse! Help me!"

But there was no need for yelling. He was galloping in her direction already, and for a second she thought he might run her over. Maybe he was an assassin sent to kill her. But he whizzed past her in a blur. She turned around, surprised that she'd traveled only a couple of yards from Henry. The man leapt off his horse, and she realized it was Simon. He crushed Henry's wrist with his boot.

"Do not try it, Cosgrove," warned Simon. "I'll kill you, and you know it." He turned to Amelia. "Are you all right?"

She held up her umbrella. "My para-s-s-sol came in handy."

Henry grabbed for Simon's leg with his free hand, and Simon kicked him in the face. Henry lost consciousness, and Simon met her on the path. "What did he give you?"

"Laudanum." The word was complicated in her mouth. "He dosed Flora's champagne the night of her death."

"Are you certain you're all right?" He gently clasped her shoulders. "You don't look well."

She indicated Henry. "I look better than he does."

"True."

"I'm fine. I promise." She swallowed, willing away the numbness of her tongue. "He put the laudanum in my chocolates, just as he did Charlotte's. Remember the ribbon in her pocket?"

He gave her a once-over before answering, making certain she was physically unharmed. "It makes sense why there were no signs of a struggle. She was too drugged to fight back. And the same goes for Flora. Pushing her off the balcony would have been easy with the drug in her system."

"And we s-s-saw him at the chocolate maker's that day," added Amelia. "I mistook his dull appearance for grief, but he himself is a user of the drug. I cannot believe I didn't make the connection earlier."

"Nor I." Simon glanced back at Henry, who was still not moving. "But why?"

"For the sake of the precious Cosgrove line," she explained.

"He met Dahlia the night of the ball. He surmised her condition at once and would not risk passing it on to his kin. Rather than break off the engagement with Flora, which would have been nearly impossible at that point, he did the next thing that came to mind. Kill her—and Charlotte and Lena. To him, they were s-s-simply loose ends that needed tying up."

"We need to get you to the doctor." His eyes were full of concern.

"I'm okay," promised Amelia. "The laudanum was just enough to put his victims at ease. He enjoyed finishing the deed himself. Besides, we cannot leave him here."

Simon's coachman wheeled into the park, thundering toward them. Next to him, the constable hung on to his hat. The coachman halted the carriage with a quick tug of the reins, and dust rolled up in front of them.

"Don't worry," said Simon. "This madman isn't going anywhere."

Madman. After Henry accused the Engelthorpe women of being insane, Amelia thought the title was just deserts.

Epilogue

That evening, Amelia sat with Winifred in the girl's room. It was a relaxing way to end an otherwise fraught day. Henry had been hauled off to jail a half hour after Amelia had beat him with her parasol, and Simon had brought her back to the recital, loading her up with several cups of sobering coffee. It was difficult playing the part of hostess with laudanum coursing through her veins, but with Simon's help she'd done it, and now she was exhausted.

Winifred was also exhausted from her performance and her party. Dressed in a floor-length nightgown, she still wore her cameo necklace, and when Amelia noted its sparkle, she smiled. The present had been a success. Winifred claimed she was never taking it off.

"It's been a long day." Amelia pulled back the bed covers. "You should try to get some sleep."

"I can't believe it's over." Winifred yawned loudly. "It wasn't nearly as bad as I thought it would be."

"It was perfect."

Winifred's yawn turned to a grin. "Are you going to tell me where you and Lord Bainbridge disappeared to? I know you did."

Amelia fluffed Winifred's pillow. "No, not today—but some-day."

"Like your letters?" She climbed into bed.

"Yes," said Amelia. "Like my letters."

"Good night, Amelia."

"Good night, sweetheart. Congratulations again on your su-perb performance."

Amelia had just shut the door when Jones met her in the hallway.

"I apologize, my lady, but Lord Bainbridge is in the drawing room." Jones sniffed. "He insists on seeing you."

"I understand, Jones." She smiled a tired smile. "Thank you."

A visit from Simon was unexpected but welcomed, especially if he had more information about Henry Cosgrove's arrest. However, it was late, and she was beyond tired. All she wanted to do was slip into her bedclothes and fall fast asleep. Instead she smoothed her windswept locks, straightened her wrinkled dress, and proceeded to the drawing room.

"Lord Bainbridge, you must miss me already to pay a call at such a late—" Amelia stopped her jest in midsentence. Simon's face conveyed dread and panic. Something was very wrong. "What's the matter? What's in your hand?"

He unfolded a piece of paper. She noticed his hand shook. "It's a letter from my sister, Marielle, to you."

Amelia frowned. She didn't know his sister.

"Not you—Lady Agony."

"What are you doing opening her correspondence?" Amelia

was incensed. Even if he was her older brother, he had no right to go through her mail.

Simon swallowed. "I was walking past the salver when I spotted the address. It was a chaotic day, and our butler is not as young as he once was. He must have missed the post. After this business with Charlotte, I was concerned. And rightly so. Look for yourself."

Warily, Amelia took the letter. What she and her readers shared was private. A certain amount of trust was necessary between writer and reader, and Simon had broken that trust. What choice did he leave her, however, but to read it? She glanced at the missive, aware of his watchful eyes.

Dear Lady Agony,

I'm very much in love with a man my father will never consent to. His opinions on marriage are quite strict, for ours is an important family. But my heart is mine alone to give. I will not marry a man I do not love. Therefore, we must depart for Gretna Green at once. I see no other alternative. Do you?

Devotedly,
Going to Gretna Green

Amelia understood Simon's panic. Gretna Green was just across the border, in Scotland, and while it now required a twenty-one-day residence for marriage, the requirement was easily circumvented. Even if it wasn't, his sister's reputation would be tarnished by the trip alone. It would change her circumstances forever.

She met his eyes. They were studying her with the intensity

that might be applied to a perplexing math equation. "This is a problem."

"A problem?" He ran a hand nervously through his hair. "It's a catastrophe. You need to write her back at once. Tell her absolutely not. She is not to elope to Gretna Green. And that is final."

Amelia blinked. "The process doesn't work that way, I'm afraid. I do not write people back directly. I answer them in the magazine. And I cannot tell her what to do. I can only offer her my advice."

"Which she will follow."

"Hopefully." Amelia gave him a weak smile. She wasn't as confident as he was.

He stuck his hands in his trouser pockets. Still nervous, he couldn't seem to quit fidgeting. "But you *will* help me, won't you, Amelia?"

For a brief moment, Amelia relished the request. How good it felt to have the shoe on the other foot. Then she answered in the affirmative. "Of course I will help you. What are friends for?"

Author's Note

Readers have turned to magazines, newspapers, and books for help with their problems since the invention of print, but it wasn't until the late seventeenth century that they could submit actual questions. The *Athenian Mercury* was the first periodical to encourage reader participation, asking subscribers to write in with life's difficulties. Early *problem pages*, however, little resembled later advice columns. The subjects covered were often scholarly or obtuse, and problems of a personal nature were seldom mentioned. In 1693, the *Ladies' Mercury*, the first-ever women's magazine, was one of the earliest publications to focus on ordinary issues, and it certainly wouldn't be the last.

Founded in 1785, the *London Times* newspaper would also tackle readers' daily woes. The *Times* featured a front-page column listing correspondents' problems, or *agonies*, and it was in reference to this section that I first encountered the phrase *agony column*. Readers submitted problems, signing their letters with first names, with initials, or anonymously. In turn, the column printed their wide variety of issues, including lost banknotes, lost puppies, chance meetings, hopeful reunions, and other concerns. Newspaper subscribers were privy to the mysteries that made up other people's lives, and those mysteries sparked my initial interest in the topic.

The agony column evolved with publishing, and in the 1830s penny weeklies, which were weekly magazines printed on inexpensive paper, devoted entire sections to correspondents' problems. Unlike the notices in the *Times*, however, the letters would not enter a void. They would be answered by columnists, later called *agony aunts*. Columnists championed a new format different from their seventeenth-century predecessors. They summarized the correspondent's problem, to save room, and replied with a solution. As the Victorian age progressed, new printing technology, cheap postage, and better education allowed for mass production, distribution, and readership. The *London Journal*, a popular penny magazine with a regular agony column, had an outreach of over 500,000 subscribers by the mid-1850s.

Consequently, advice columnists were in high demand. They used pseudonyms, and often an illustration of an idealized woman, not them, graced the tops of their agony columns. They gave advice on health, beauty, courtship, and even parenting. Most columnists spouted societal norms, touting morals and manners, but not the fictional Lady Agony in *Murder in Postscript*. She realizes that her correspondents, like society itself, are undergoing vast changes, and she isn't afraid to give unconventional advice.

Which brings me to my mother, whom I would be remiss not to mention. My mom suffered from COPD, a debilitating lung condition, and in the last years of her life she and I considered the two dozen steps it took to get from her apartment to the small sitting area a success. There, I would pick up the daily newspaper and read aloud Annie's Mailbox. She and I would discuss the advice given and amend it drastically according to our own experiences. I didn't realize it at the time, but those daily walks were an inspiration. Lady Agony would also amend her advice, relying not on rules and mores but on her own practical know-how.

If you're interested in reading further on the topic, I would recommend perusing the *London Times* archives, where you can still read the original correspondence on page one, column two. The *London Journal*, though harder to find, is also fascinating reading. Two books on the subject that were helpful in my research include *Never Kiss a Man in a Canoe: Words of Wisdom from the Golden Age of Agony Aunts* by Tanith Carey and *Aunt Agony Advises: Problem Pages through the Ages* by Robin Kent. The first is readily available; the second can be purchased used.

ACKNOWLEDGMENTS

I've loved historical fiction since I was a teen. Instead of homework, I pored over Victorian novels, allowing them to whisk me away from the often-harsh realities of high school. It was a world I loved spending time in, a world where I belonged, a world I still cherish today. So to say writing *Murder in Postscript* has been a dream come true isn't an exaggeration. It truly describes my passion for the project. But this longtime love wouldn't have come to fruition without the help and encouragement of many individuals, and I'd like to take a moment to thank them here.

Thank you to my super supportive agent, Amanda Jain, for her encouragement, advice, and steady resolve. Thank you to my incredibly kind editor, Michelle Vega, for her enthusiasm, grace, and expertise. Thank you to all the people at Berkley who dedicated their time to this work, including production editor Megan Elmore, copy editor Randie Lipkin, and editorial assistants Candice Coote and Annie Odders. Thank you to first readers and editors Amy Cecil Holm, who answers my odd questions day or night without fail, and Elena Hartwell Taylor, whose sensible advice I've come to rely upon. Thank you to my husband, Quintin, and our daughters, Madeline and Maisie, for championing my writing, even in its earliest days. Finally, thank you to my extended family, especially my dear mother and father, who are gone but never forgotten. Their best advice was to follow my dream of writing. I'm so glad I took it.

Author photo by Julie Prairie

Mary Winters is the author of the Lady Agony mystery series. A longtime reader of historical fiction and an author of two other mystery series, Mary set her latest work in Victorian England after being inspired by a trip to London. Since then, she's been busily planning her next mystery—and another trip!

CONNECT ONLINE

MaryWintersAuthor.com

Ready to find
your next great read?

Let us help.

Visit prh.com/nextread